BENEFICENCE

Beneficence

A Novel

MEREDITH HALL

DAVID R. GODINE, *Publisher*
BOSTON

Published in 2020 by
DAVID R. GODINE, *Publisher*
Boston, Massachusetts
www.godine.com

LIBRARY OF CONGRESS CATALOGING-IN-PUBLICATION DATA

Names: Hall, Meredith, 1949- author.
Title: Beneficence : a novel / Meredith Hall.
Description: 1st. | Boston : David R. Godine, Publisher, [2020] |
Identifiers: LCCN 2020019029 |
ISBN 9781567926699 (hardcover) |
ISBN 9781567926750 (ebook)
Classification: LCC PS3608.A5474 B46 2020 | DDC 813/.6--dc23
LC record available at https://lccn.loc.gov/2020019029

FIRST PRINTING, 2020
Printed in the United States of America

To my children

Alstead, Maine

PART ONE

····························

BEFORE

I have loved, O Lord, the beauty of thy house
and the place where dwelleth thy glory.

Psalm 26:8

[1947]

Doris

EVERY MORNING, EARLY, when Tup and I get up to start our chores, the whole house still quiet and the children asleep, I turn and pull the bed together, tugging at the sheets to make them tight and smooth. They are warm with our heat. I slide my hand across the place my husband slept, drawing the blankets up and closing in the warmth, like a memory of us, until night comes when we will lie down together again.

Our room has big windows on the back of the house, looking out on the near pasture and the creek running through it. It is very nice to stand first thing every morning looking out over the land. The trees along the hayfields look like ghosts some summer mornings when the ground fog hugs the warm earth. And then the mist slowly drifts up and away, so that, by the time I am doing breakfast dishes, the sun makes sharp shadows of the fence wire, like long neat stitches binding us to this place. Tup and I have enough sense to know that we are blessed people.

You cannot know what will come. Once, when Sonny and Dodie were just toddlers, both of them locked themselves in the milk room by mistake. Tup was busy in the north pasture. I could hear the tractor in the distance working—that must have been the year he bought the new tractor, 1938—and I was the one who was supposed to keep an eye on the children. I always did. I learned as soon as Sonny was born that when you have a child your own life diminishes to just about nothing, and willingly so. Growing up, you are so full of dreams of what your life will be and how you will use all those years that sit like a promise, and always it is you at the center. And then you get married and those dreams change, but still you have big ideas about it all—maybe the farm will extend or you will have enough money to take the train to Sarasota one winter or you will be paid by folks to cut and sew dresses and skirts you've learned how to copy from the magazines.

We can't ever know what will come. You meet a man and marry him and find out whether you made a good choice or not. If you did, you love each other and work hard, and then you have your first baby and whatever it was you ever dreamed about changes the first time you hold him and feed him and watch him study your face. Sonny came when I was nineteen years old and I forgot forever any of those things I had ever thought I wanted. I felt as if I were God, making such a good world for our children. When Sonny came, and then Dodie, and later Beston, I was willing to leave the life Tup and I had and let my children take that place. I am more than willing.

So that morning the children were out back with me while I hung out the clothes. This was before Beston was born, and about the last year before we got the washer. I heated water on the wood-stove in the kitchen and lugged it out to the back dooryard and did the washing on the pump platform. The kids liked laundry day. It was all play for them, dipping little cups into the water and pouring it out on the dry gravel. On a warm morning, you could watch the water disappear like a stain from cloth. I pumped cold water for rinsing and poured it into the tub, and Sonny and Dodie would beg me to dump some over their heads, with them shrieking and running away. It was a game we played every laundry day all summer. The kids would get soaked and muddy, so it was all a good morning for them.

Well, that day they got bored, I guess, and wandered off without my realizing. I never even noticed they were gone. I had carried the basket of wrung clothes over to the lines and was pinning them up when I suddenly heard nothing but the breeze rustling the wet cloth, and the soft sound of the distant tractor. Like a terrible dream, your worst dream—that moment of inattention when you had forgotten for one minute that you were the mother, the one whose single purpose it was to keep your children safe, and that awful silence that jolted you back. I remember feeling so helpless, as if I couldn't fix this no matter what I might do. I ran to the kitchen door and then back to the pump and then turned toward the noise of the tractor so far off in the field, as if Tup could pluck my children out of the air. I needed Tup to give me a shake and tell me to think. And then I was back inside myself again and I could say, *They can't have gotten to the creek yet so wherever they are they are all right.* After that it was just a story like all mothers have, that cold fear when your child takes off from your sight for just long enough to scare you into thinking you have lost him forever, and you know you are a terrible mother who cannot keep your children safe.

I called and called, "*Sonny! Dodie!*" turning slowly in place so my voice would carry across the whole yard, and then I heard Sonny's little yell from the milk room, "*Mumma! Mumma!*" As scared as I was, I heard the panic children feel when they have moved beyond the reach of their mother's protection.

"I'm coming. I'm coming!" I called, running to the barn. "You silly ducks! Where are you?" I called in a false and cheerful voice to reassure them and to dispel the terror that had caught me, to assert that this was just an incident, a small event Tup and I would laugh over with relief when we shared supper.

I could hear the door to the milk room rattle, and when I lifted the latch and pushed the door open, my children pressed their tearful faces into my apron, their arms clasped around my legs, the sweet animal smell of fresh milk tumbling out the door around us. "My silly ducks," I said, stroking their tight little shoulders and hair wet from our laundry-day game. "It's all right." But I still remember the sound of my cries out into that sudden silence, and of Tup's tractor off in the north pasture, so far away.

Tup is very smart. He keeps a beautiful dairy farm. He works harder than any man I know and can still come to the table at night ready to tease his children with his jokes and listen to their chatter. It's a magic he has, this energy to love the land and love his family, this intelligence, this big personality that makes people notice him. He creates something around himself I can't describe, something that draws people to him, makes them want him, want to be with him, want his attention and his affection. Tup has a fire that burns in him that I have never known in any other person.

He is a tall man, with long legs and arms and fingers and toes. He is so thin I am sure people in town think I don't feed him enough. It's that fire, I think, burning so hot that nothing will ever feed it enough to let a little flesh stick to his bones. He is a graceful man, for all the hard work he does. He tells me not to say that about him, that a man doesn't want to be graceful. But I think he likes it, and likes that I watch him move. That is the first thing I ever noticed about him the day I met him, the way his body hangs together so loose and easy. He was twenty years old, and I was only eighteen, just graduating that spring from school. My parents and I lived in town in Colebrook, in the hills west of Portland, in the neat little house on Clay Street. Tup was a student at the state college in Claremont studying engineering. My cousin, Fred Canton, kept telling me he knew a fellow at school I should meet, so Fred and I concocted a plan for them to stop by my father's store one day after school when I would be working. Nothing about it felt like a coincidence, though, and we all stood around looking at our feet.

Then my father called me to help a customer and I turned to Tup and said, "Well, it was very nice to meet you."

And he blurted out, "I'd like to stop by again on Saturday."

After he left I kept trying to bring Tup into my mind. The one thing I kept seeing was his grace. His hair was jet black. Sometimes it would slip over his eyes and he would reach up and push it out of the way, the tendons in his wrist and arm tight against the skin. His eyes were blue, clear and shining. Sonny got those eyes. And Tup's big mind that keeps everyone wanting to be near him.

We knew right away that it was just right and we got married on a hot sunny day in August at the Methodist church. That was in 1933, a hard time for anyone to start a life. We rented an apartment on Benton Hill in Claremont that fall. Tup was a good student, and a very quick study. His father paid for Tup's schooling, the oldest son. The farm was a dying enterprise by then, after thriving in the hands of five generations of Senters. The Depression hit the farms in Maine very hard. No one could get any kind of money for milk or meat or vegetables. Everything was barter, and barter didn't pay the taxes or put a new roof on the house. Tup's father had saved all his life to send his first son to college. The younger boys would stay on the place when they grew up if they wanted to, but it was a real gift Dad Senter wanted to give to Tup—freedom from the farm.

Dad Senter was a good man, but he was not a happy or satisfied man, nothing like Tup. He was gruff and short-tempered. I think he was just tired. His wife died when Tup was only eleven, just the age Dodie is now. Dad was left with four children and two hundred thirty-six acres of land he couldn't get to produce a cent. It was too much work, too much worry with no one to take up part of the load. Tup insists his father wasn't always so grim. He remembers his mother and father laughing at the kitchen table. He has no memory of what their pleasure was, but carries still a sense of that real joy children feel when their parents are joined in a separate happiness. That would have been right here in this kitchen, at this same old table. Hard for me to realize that. All the generations that have lived in this house. All the words said that should never have been uttered, all the laughter, the births and the deaths.

After Dad was left alone, he came to hate the farm. All he wanted was for Tup to get away from it. Tup may have been the only boy in all of Alstead who went off to school at that time. He was going to be an engineer for the state, planning all the new bridges and roads the government was building. Tup, I think, loved the farm, but maybe only in the way children love home, every detail sweet and nostalgic just because it belonged to childhood. He certainly knew what it meant to work like a man, even when he was little. Dad asked a lot of all four children after his wife died. It was unhappy work, real drudgery, with nothing working right, everything breaking with age and overuse. Not enough hours in the day. Dad wanted one thing: for Tup, at least one of his sons, to have work that didn't break him.

Tup knew what that cost his father in cash and in lost labor, and he took his studies very seriously. He read until late every night, taking notes in his big, bold, up and down handwriting. We had a plan. When Tup was finished in two more years, I'd go to school myself and prepare to teach. It was a happy time for us, in spite of the Depression and Tup's long hours and both of us living away from home. I worked doing filing for the Chipman Agency. We had our first home, and it was enough for me to fix it up and cook good food for my skinny husband at the end of the day. And then Dad Senter died that first winter we were married. Tup's brothers told him there was no more money for school. They weren't willing. He had nearly two more years to go and couldn't figure out any way to pay for it. So he went back to the farm. He made his claim as the oldest son and took over the whole place. His brothers didn't complain. They split between them the money Dad had intended for Tup's education, giving nothing to their sister, May, and they left. So Tup and I suddenly owned a dairy farm with no hands to help out. And we had a big surprise that spring—Sonny was on his way.

Those first few years were hard, there's no question about it. It was a big change for me, after growing up in town. I think I speak for both of us when I say that we have been very happy here. That we have come to love this place. Of course, Tup has brought the place back to life so it's easy to be happy here.

I was talking about Tup's grace. We've been here for thirteen years now. Tup works hard every day of the week. And still he walks like a boy, all loose and easy. Still I love to watch him. When he sits, he crosses his long legs at the knee and sits back, his arm across his lap, his fingers working together at the tips. He is a beautiful man. And for all that work, his smile flashes like a light. Like a spark from that fire inside he stokes so hot.

Our children all like to read books. Tup has been determined about that. And I can see that somehow each of them has that fire inside that their father has. I don't know if it was inherited or they just somehow were ignited by Tup, like sparks jumping across gaps in a wildfire. But it is lovely to see, for Tup and for me. I live with people who seem bigger than the world. I hope that a little bit of that fire has found its tinder in me.

GOOD WORK HAS drawn this place from the battered, has-been place it was during those hard years to the place it is now. It is a handsome farm, but simple. The house is quite big, with four bedrooms upstairs and the big kitchen downstairs, and in the front, the dining room we never use and the front room where we sit in the evening. It's a lived-in house. You can tell that a lot of generations have made their lives here. The wood floors are dented and scratched, and so smooth and dark from a hundred years of feet and scrubbing they look like soft old shoes. When I moved here in 1933, the place was clean but so dreary. Everything needed paint, the wallpaper was yellowed and peeling, the ceilings were smudged with soot from the woodstoves. I was pretty discouraged at first. I taught myself fast how to scrape and paint the wood trim and hang wallpaper. Tup did the ceilings. By the time Sonny came, we had a good room waiting for him, and our room was done, and all the rooms downstairs. I got to Dodie's room just in time for her to come, and Beston went in with Sonny.

Those were busy years. My arms and legs shook with the wobbles at the end of each day, a nursing baby and all the farm chores and the house and cooking and not enough sleep for Tup or me. You forget between babies how hard it is. But we felt good about the farm. The house was a home again. Tup says to me once in a while, "You make a nice house, Miss Doris." It makes me proud and satisfied. He's right. I make a very nice house. I am a good wife.

The big round table and chairs in the middle of the front room are scratched and worn with such long use, but the children and Tup do their projects there in the evening and are comfortable. I reupholstered the sofa and chairs, and I get Tup to help me lay the rug out in a good snowstorm once every winter so the snow can work it clean. The furniture is what we inherited when we moved in, so it's old, but Tup is attached to it and I don't care as long it's polished and dusted.

Somehow Tup finds the time to keep white paint on the clapboards and green on the doors and window trim, house and barn. The house is nice from the front. There are two big elms Tup's great-great-grandfather planted when he settled the farm in 1834, one on each side of the walkway that comes in off the road. That was tradition, planting two trees, and you see it still at all the old farms. It was to welcome the bride and the groom, two people, as they walked to the door of their new home. The trees tower over the house now and keep it shaded from the sun in the summer. I've always told the children that the elms are like guardians, protecting us from harm. Although there are a lot of farms with old elms sheltering them that have sons and husbands who never came home from the war, so maybe there's nothing that can keep us from that kind of trouble. My mind can't approach such thoughts.

On the north side is the porch, screened in against the mosquitoes and midges that can make you crazy on a spring morning or evening. It's cool and dark there on a hot day. Once the warm nights come, we move from the front room to the porch and watch the fireflies over the fields, tiny green lights that blink on and off.

Beston likes to walk through the grass with a coffee can and catch them. He brings them onto the porch and lets them go. They fly straight to the screens, trying to get back out to the open land. They seem a bit forlorn to me as they blink on and off, like a distress signal to the ones still outside, but the children only see the magic of it. Tup doesn't explain to them how everything in the world works. He lets them just look and dream. The truth is never as interesting as what we imagine.

And running back off the kitchen is the shed, and beyond that, the outhouse. We have electric now and plumbing in the kitchen, but we have never built a real bathroom in the house. It just hasn't seemed necessary. Tup plumbed water to a good bathtub in the shed by the kitchen door and that's where we take our baths. The hot water comes from the copper tank behind the cookstove, so there's always plenty. And Tup and I keep the outhouse sparkling clean and fresh, dug out and limed and painted shiny white, not smelly and frightening like the old outhouse that was here. We never even think of it. The school in town, in fact, still has boys' and girls' outhouses. Lots of schools do. Dodie has learned that people feel good in a pleasant house, and sometimes, all on her own, she picks flowers and puts them in the house, maybe on the kitchen table or my little sewing table in the front room. And sometimes she picks a few little sprigs of violets or forget-me-nots and puts them on the bench in the outhouse.

The road to our farm is still dirt, and will be forever, I think, because it doesn't go anywhere. It comes from Four Corners, over Crockett's Hill, past our house, and moves down across the creek and wanders on to the backside of Arnie Sherman's hayfields. There are only three other farms the whole length, all before ours. When I first moved here, I felt scared. What if something happened to Tup while he was working, he cut himself or caught his hand in the baler? Or the children, if they had a high fever?

But I have learned that nothing terrible is going to happen here. You have to be careful, to pay attention, and then you just trust that everything is going to be all right. It's a price you pay for the quiet and beauty of the land. Sometimes I think, *We're a little family on an island here, protected from all the world's problems.* There's been a terrible war since we moved here, and another war is brewing now on the other side of the world, but we just keep milking the cows and birthing the calves and planting the seeds in the garden. The children go to school and do their chores and then go off to play in this wide open space, or they sit and read in the front room by the stove or in the hammock on the porch on a nice day. We are apart from the world here and make our lives the way we want them to be.

When the night comes, Tup and I lie down in our bed, where the deep and private love we share waits for us. Sometimes all we do is hold hands, the night keeping us, the owls calling out, back and forth, in their soft, reassuring *o's.*

Sometimes Tup rolls on his side and draws me toward him, his large warm hands cupping my face. "I love you, Doris," he whispers. "We love each other. Thank you for loving me."

We let ourselves slip into the depth of skin and weight and breath.

DODIE IS LEARNING to put up the garden with me this summer. She's eleven and wants to be a big help, and she is. "She is your daughter," Tup says. She does take after me, I can see that. She has friends at school—Marion and Flora, especially—but she likes to just come home and help out with whatever it is I am up to for the afternoon.

This summer, Dodie became interested in the details of canning and freezing. We have been canning tomatoes every day for two weeks as they come ripe. We'll put up eighty quarts by the time we're done. I picked all the ripe Brandywines this morning, and I waited until Dodie got home from school so she could help. I love these afternoons with my daughter, with the kitchen windows open and the September breeze lifting the curtains and the clear sky and everything in order around us. We could hear Sonny and Beston out back, stacking wood in the shed with Tup, laughter rising now and then and the solid heavy *tonk* of the logs as they landed in place. Each day is a gift.

While we blanched and peeled the tomatoes and stuffed them into the steaming jars, Dodie chattered away to me about the small doings of her day at school. She is the most forthcoming child I have ever known. There are no secrets for Dodie. She believes in the world, and trusts it. Nothing bad has ever happened to my daughter. In fact, I see now that nothing very bad has ever happened to me. I have lost both my mother and my father, but that is the course of a life, I know that. I hope I have taught my children to trust the world. Dodie is like a little singing bird, her voice high and clear, with that eagerness to be part of everything, to jump in and do it all.

We put up a dozen quarts. Before she went to bed, Dodie proudly carried the cooled jars, two at a time, down to the shelves in the cellar, calling out at each trip to her father and brothers in the front room, "Two!...Six!...Ten!" until all twelve jars were put away. Tup called back for each jar, "Oh, I can already taste the tomato soup your mother is going to make this winter! Oh! I can taste right now the stew she is going to make!" I was dead tired when I lay down beside Tup, and I knew each of us was thinking of all the jars lined up and all the wood stacked, ready for this coming winter.

This has always been Tup's family's farm. Now it is ours. Sonny and Beston will marry someday, and maybe they will stay on this land. Dodie will marry, and if her husband is willing, she will stay and keep the garden we work in together now. There is plenty of land for them all. Tup sometimes sketches out a plan he has to build a house for each of his children, the big barn still the center of it all. Sometimes he holds me and says, "Doris, we will get a chance to rest as soon as these children grow up and take over the farm." I know he is joking. Neither one of us wants to rest, or to be done with the work of raising our family. When we wake in the night, our fingers and feet touching, we sense the grace of this time. The children sleep, the cows rest in the barn, the grass in the hayfields moves in the wind like waves rolling across a vast and familiar ocean.

ONCE, A YEAR or so before I ever met Tup, my father and I closed the store as usual and walked home together for supper.

But instead of turning in at our gate, he nudged my elbow and said, "Let's stay out a while longer. It's a nice night."

It was nice, a cool late spring night still lit pink in all the darkness. No stars were out yet, although it was clear. Colebrook was once a busy town, with the mills working two shifts and men and women going to or from work at all hours, but then the Depression ended all that. Those were hard years for everyone. I remember that night as a time of quiet with the mills closed down or on reduced shifts, an absence of the old noise and hellos and good evenings on the sidewalks. The town was out of work, and men and women sat on their doorsteps smoking cigarettes, nodding seriously as we passed, while their children played in the side streets.

My father was a silent man, a kind but formal man. We worked together every day in his store, Canton's Grocery, which he had built up enough that he was able to stay open through those hard times. He sold groceries and meat, and was known as a good butcher. Women in the neighborhood came every day to buy their food from Jack Canton. He never said more to his customers than he did to me or my mother. But people liked and trusted him, you could see that.

I spent my whole childhood in that store. If I wasn't at school, I was there helping out. Sometimes my mother let me go off with a friend who stopped by, and my father always nodded his yes. But I enjoyed being at the store and seldom asked to be allowed to go out. It was an old building my father owned outright, long and narrow with a counter running almost the length. The meat counter was in the back. It was dark inside the store, warm in the winter and cool in the summer. The floors sloped to the back, as if you were walking down a slight hill and then back up, and they creaked in a comforting way. By the time I was in high school, I could have run the whole place myself. I knew the business end to end, the ordering and the stocking and how to display the produce and weigh and bag the dry goods, how to tally the receipts and put the cash in the safe for deposit at Gardiner Savings each Friday night. I used to say to my father, "I'd like to run the store after you get tired of it," but he would sort of shrug and say, "I don't imagine the man you marry would agree to that." I felt a pang of fear when he said that, unable to picture my future or any of the mysteries it held for me.

I must have been about fifteen that night he asked me to walk with him. I remember feeling scared. I had never known my father to deviate from his routine, and I felt off-balance. Even then I did not like surprises. We walked elbow to elbow in silence up Jackson Street and across to Governor. Every house had its lights on by then, and the families had all gone indoors for supper, whatever it might be in those times. My father was a generous man and did what he could to help his neighbors, extending credit for basic necessities that might never get paid for. But we were beyond our own little world by then, walking streets I had no reason to be on. My father seemed to have no purpose, no intention in where we walked. And although I was young, and although he said almost nothing, I felt a deep sense of dread, as if he were opening a door onto possibilities that I must resist.

And then I sensed that he was crying. Silently, the way he did everything. I felt his grief—whatever it was—draw me to him like a gentle but insistent arm. He did not raise his hand to wipe his tears. They flowed down his narrow, tired face, dripping off his jaw and his chin. We walked from pool of light to pool of pale light, away from home. I had a great need to know what this terrible sadness was my father carried, and a great need to never know its name, a sort of superstitious belief that if we did not speak its name out loud it would never come to find me. I could not imagine what could cause my father such sorrow. Was it simply a loneliness from all that gentle silence? Did he wake up that morning unable to justify the path his small life had taken? But isn't every life small, I wondered, and a gift in its everyday inconsequence? Was this about love? I felt a stab. Did my father long for something more than my mother's steady and practical love? Had he glimpsed something in the store that day, a look or a laugh or a sigh, a small comment about how lovely the springtime air feels on your face, something that reminded him of another life he had once imagined, of something lost forever? Each possibility frightened me. Why did he need me to walk beside him while he let this swelling current pass? Would I ever feel such an awful loneliness in my own life?

He never changed his pace. When we got to the bottom of High Street, we turned together back toward home, where my mother waited for her husband and her daughter. The porch light was on, an inquiry into where we had been. My father took out his handkerchief and blew his nose, folded it carefully, and nodded for me to go ahead of him through the door to our family supper.

THE SCHOOL PLAY was coming up and Dodie and Beston had parts. Sonny was growing up and wouldn't participate, which I was sorry about, his unwillingness to pretend for one hour that he was someone or something other than thirteen-year-old Sonny Senter. But Best and Dodie were still just children and believed in that kind of play and so that Saturday was a day of excitement around the house. Dodie let the chickens out of the coop and fed them without any reminders, and swept the door yard and shed, running from task to task. Beston filled the crock in the outhouse with lime, lugging the heavy bag between his legs, and ran to me to ask what he was supposed to do next. They were both going to be poor villagers in a play the students wrote called *Tomorrow*, and I told them we would choose their costumes and wash their hair after noon dinner. We dug around in the closet in the upstairs hall. It's a place that gathers boxes of outgrown clothes and wool coats that are too frayed to be worn. Tup says I shouldn't collect things we don't use. I tell him that we can't be certain that we will always have the shoes and clothes we need, and at least we will be warm, no matter what comes. He snorts and tells me that his wife and children will never need to wear rags.

But today those rags were handy. The children were very pleased with themselves. They ran out together to show Sonny their get-ups, and then refused to take them off until I called them in for hair washing. I cleared the counter by the kitchen sink and laid down a big towel.

"Who goes first?" I asked, and Dodie said she would.

They pulled off their jerseys and my daughter climbed from a chair and lay down, her soft dark hair trailing in the sink and her skinny legs stretched out along the counter. I told her to close her eyes and ran the water until it was warm. As I lathered her hair, I watched her beautiful little face, somehow so like mine and Tup's all at the same time, her hands, clasped on her chest, so familiar. How can I love such a simple chore, one among hundreds in a week? I rinsed the soap down the drain and wrapped her head in a towel, and she let me hold her to me while I rubbed the water out of her hair. I combed it out and lifted her down, and we were done.

And then I lifted Best up and he laid his little boy's body out on the counter so earnestly, another job to be done in his day, and I offered him a washcloth for his eyes because he is frightened of the soap, but he said no because, I knew, Dodie had not used one, and he closed his eyes tightly and let me scoop the warm water over his short dark hair. Here was a face I knew less fully, my youngest and most mysterious child. Beston asks so little of me. Of Tup and his brother and sister. He watches and smiles and knows how to be by himself. While Dodie chatters to me and Sonny makes his way to his father's side to work, Best is always on the edge of things, it seems. I often have the urge to gather him up and tell him that he is as important as the noisier, older children, that Tup and I love him and admire him just as much, but he doesn't seem to need to hear that, and the days go on with all of that just a thought. This child's face is open, guileless, and I was flooded with a feeling that I had unwittingly withheld something from him that a mother owes her children.

"You're a very good boy, Best," I said.

"Yes," he said, his eyes still closed, his arms relaxed at his sides, trusting me.

I don't remember the play now, only those minutes in the old closet and Dodie and Best prancing around in their costumes and their little bodies stretched out on the counter for their hair washing. I remember pulling Best to me as I had Dodie, his willing lean into me as I rubbed his hair dry.

LAST SATURDAY, DODIE asked Marion to come for the day. They would clean out the henhouse as Tup had asked, and then have the rest of the day free to play. Marion arrived as Dodie helped me wash the breakfast dishes. Dodie was very excited to have her town friend visiting. Marion is a nice girl, very polite with Tup and me but not a goody-two-shoes. She is an even match for Dodie's strong sense of herself here at home. When the dishes were done, I found chore clothes for Marion to wear, and the girls headed to the henhouse. They were little girls, happy to start their day of play together with this unpleasant task.

Dodie had already put the hens out before breakfast but left the eggs for Marion to collect in the wire basket. They shoveled the litter into the wheelbarrow and swept, cleaning the nesting boxes and then laying clean shavings. I could hear their chatter as I worked in the garden. When they were done, I praised their work and told Dodie they could go play for the rest of the day. The girls changed in the shed, dropping their dirty clothes into the basket. Marion worried that the boys might see them in their underwear, something that doesn't worry Dodie one bit. I made them a bag with sandwiches and cookies, and Dodie and Marion rode their bicycles along the tractor road to the creek. I felt a flow of quiet apprehension watching them ride away together.

When Tup and the boys came in for noon dinner, I said what I knew I should, that I was very pleased that Dodie had a best friend.

"May I have Daniel over next Saturday?" Sonny asked.

"And Hovey?" asked Beston.

I felt a pang, resisting the expansion, the opening of what had been, for all these years, solely mine and Tup's.

"If you do your chores and don't leave them to Daddy," I said vaguely.

"I'll save something you can all do together," Tup said. "It's good to have friends around."

I thought of my days at my father's store, rushing home from school, preferring the store to being with friends. I hadn't felt lonely. But Tup was right. There was no reason to hold so jealously to my children. They need to know how to make their way among people. But these invitations felt somehow like a threat, like a crack under a door letting in an unwelcome chill. I pushed away the sudden creep of dread. Our children love us, and they love our home. I need to share them, I know that. I had felt such pride watching my young daughter teaching her friend how to work in the henhouse. Watching her carefree enthusiasm and kindness. Her unguardedness. Dodie was so ready to love. It was time to start sharing that around.

The girls came back late in the afternoon with muddy feet and legs. They washed off at the hose, giggling in pure silliness. I listened from the well cover where I was sitting in the warm sun, snapping string beans.

"Can Marion spend the night, Mum?" Dodie asked.

"May," I answered.

"May she," Dodie said. "We want to make my room into a theater with a stage and pretend we are singers."

Dodie was brimming with excitement, I could see that, but I felt something else, too, something about the long afternoon off with Marion, plans now for an evening, a night over, the intrusion into the family's quiet that settles in after our day of work.

"What kind of singing?" I asked, and regretted it as soon as I said it. I added quickly, "Yes, of course, but you need to do your chores and ask Daddy if he will drive you to ask Marion's mother."

Dodie and Marion were silly during supper. They offered to wash all the dishes themselves, and Beston said he'd help. I stayed in the kitchen watching, aware that I was looking for trouble. I kept busy sorting the odds and ends that had collected on the shelf by the door, listening to the children laugh and tell small stories on each other. Tup and Sonny were in the front room, working at the table on a model plane Sonny had ordered in the mail. I wanted us all to be in our places in that room. Wasn't there enough companionship here without prematurely bringing in the world? The children finished with the dishes and I thanked them.

Marion said, "Thank you for a very nice supper," and I smiled, a kindly smile, I am sure, and told her she was very welcome. "I like it here," Marion said.

I could see Dodie and Beston felt very pleased. They know they are farm children, different from the children in town, and sometimes, I think, they wonder if their differences will cost them anything.

The girls went up to Dodie's room, Beston tagging along, and I went to my chair in the front room. I took up my mending and watched Tup and Sonny with their heads close together, the smell of the airplane glue sharp and comforting. Several times I got up to stand at the foot of the stairs and listen. Dodie's singing stood out, a voice unusually low and smooth for a child, Marion's and Beston's wavering and thin above it.

I recognized some of the songs from the radio station Tup plays in the barn. Then he came to me and said quietly, "Leave them alone, Doris. They're having fun."

I felt embarrassed. What was I resisting here? Somehow the presence of someone else's child in my daughter's room, the muffled sound of songs I did not know the words to, pressed at me with a feeling of real sadness, as if something was being lost even as I listened. Their shrieks of laughter tumbled along the hall and down the stairs, and I felt myself stiffen with helplessness.

I finally said to Tup and Sonny at seven o'clock that I was going to get the girls and Beston off to bed.

But Tup said, "Let them be for a while, Doris. It's a special night for them."

I allowed them another hour and then called up that it was time to get washed and turn the light out. When I went up to kiss Beston good night, I could hear my daughter whispering to her friend in the dark, a conversation that was far outside me.

I opened the door and said quietly, "Good night, you silly things. Be quiet now and go to sleep. No more talking."

Dodie said, "We won't, Mum. We promise." But I could hear their whispers even after Tup and Sonny came up to bed.

I lay awake after Tup fell asleep. The girls had given themselves to the night, and the house was quiet. I thought of Daniel and Hovey coming in a week, and what I would say when Dodie asked if Marion could come again. Why was there a sudden interest in these outside friends? This is all just new for us, I thought. That's all. I have to get used to it. I let my thoughts go to the animals in the barn, the grass in the hayfields growing tall and green, the water in the creek sliding in its old and familiar course through our land. I turned to Tup's steady back and said my prayers, thanking God for my husband and our children, so contented and undisturbed.

The morning came, Sunday, and before church we dropped Marion at home. After church, we spent the day at our routines of

Sunday dinner and chores and rest. I found my children and Tup several times during the day, wanting to be near them. They did not seem to notice, for which I was relieved. At dinner that afternoon, we all laughed with Beston and Dodie as the children replayed their music show from the night before. I felt the watchfulness lift. It was as if we had managed to relock a door we needed to guard. I understood that my hope was not reasonable, but the release from vigilance was a great relief. We've been too much a family, I know. Whatever is beyond us must come. I'll get better at this.

Dodie

MUM SAID SONNY and Beston and I could walk home from school today instead of taking the bus. It's nearly four miles but it's a very pretty walk home if you cut through the Munfords' pasture and down to the creek. It's cooler down by the water and sometimes we take off our shoes and socks and sit on the rocks in the stream and watch the striders and minnows while Mr. Munford's cows watch us. I like this time with my brothers because Sonny is usually off in his own world these days. Mum says be patient, he's thirteen, he'll be back eventually, but I don't see him coming around for a while. He's a good brother, but he doesn't talk to Beston or me at home much anymore. He sits with Daniel and Jordan Chester on the bus now. I know he's embarrassed to be with his little sister. I don't even look at him when he's with his friends. I believe he is grateful for that. I keep promising myself that one of these days I'm going to stand up in the bus and shout, "Sonny Senter plays house with me and Beston," but that would be a lie, a sad lie, too, because it's been a long time since he's played house with me, so I keep my mouth shut and let him have this other world Mum says he's visiting and will return from.

When we walked down by the creek after school, we came back to our world for a while and I was very happy.

"Did you see that huge water bug?" Sonny yelled, and he leapt out of the water laughing and Beston and I leapt, too, and we yelled, too.

All the noise felt good. The water bug had slipped into the eddy of our rock. A close call with his huge pincers.

"*Lethocerus americanus*," Sonny said.

"I don't think so," said Beston. "I think it's a *Hydrophilus triangularis*."

[25]

Beston wasn't arguing. He was adding in. He's a very nice little boy, very serious, and Sonny likes him. Beston likes Sonny. On days like this by the creek, we all like each other and don't want to go home to the chores and everyday.

"No, this is the bigger one, Best, so it's *Lethocerus*," said Sonny, not showing off, and Beston was satisfied.

We all moved back onto our own rocks and watched for caddis-fly larvae and hellgrammites, but who cared if one of them really came by? The sun was warm on our backs. The Munford's cows weren't our responsibility, and they knew it, so they watched without telling us what to do.

The creek cast a spell over us. Water running fast downhill to somewhere else, with enough rocks to make the trip noisy and interesting. The sun on the water. In the water. You couldn't hear anything except that ride to the sea, no weaned calves bawling all day for their mothers in the far pasture, a sound I just can't stand, no truck left running in the yard by the barn while it's getting filled up with yearling steers going to slaughter at Chevie's, no radio on after supper telling us about the children in Japan who are being born with too many hands at the ends of their arms or no legs at all.

Sonny said, "Sounds nice, doesn't it?"

Best and I didn't say anything.

This same creek, Senter Creek, runs straight on through our fields and pastures and curls around under the road beyond our house. Senter Creek, as if it's ours even though it runs for miles and miles beyond our farm. This same creek sounds just like this every single day in our fields and woods, even if we aren't there listening.

EVERY SPRING DADDY brings us all the way down to the mouth of Senter Creek where it opens to the sea at Carry Cove. We go down at night when the moon is full but it's very cloudy, so everything looks like it's glowing from inside, trees and fences and even barns, silver and lit up by a light you can't see. This is the time to dip for smelt, which we love to get and love to eat. Daddy doesn't tell us ahead of time and then he's by our beds in the middle of the night whispering, "Want to get some smelt?" and we know we have about five minutes to wake up enough to get into our chore clothes and our boots and our hats and mittens, because it's very cold on smelt night, and climb into the warm truck.

This year it was the end of March when Daddy believed the time was right. He put the radio up high in the truck and sang "Till the End of Time" as if he was the happiest man in the world. He reached over and squeezed the funny spot above Sonny's knee so hard it made Sonny laugh out loud and then Daddy told him, "Wake up, wake up! We have smelt waiting for us!" and he held Sonny's hand.

Sonny's grown big for that, but still, whenever Daddy is in the truck with one of us, even Sonny, he holds our hand.

We drove on the dark roads all the way to Chase Mills and turned down a tote road Daddy's grandfather showed him a long time ago, and we parked the truck. The wide cove spread silent beyond us. We carried the buckets and dip nets on the path through the black woods and then we could hear our creek, all the way down there near the ocean, roaring down the hillside and running out to the bay while all the smelt tried to run upstream five miles to lay their eggs. Daddy said we were there to put them in our buckets and give them a lift.

By now we were awake and cold before we even got into the water. Daddy put the big metal buckets on the rocks along the stream and told Sonny to take the net and move into the tumbling current. Daddy clicked on the flashlight and there they were, pushing desperately upstream. He chose the night just right, so many little silver fish packed side to side they made their own river of light in the stream. Sonny braced himself against the hard run of water and swept the net into the current and it was full in a flash. Daddy held the bucket out over the creek to receive the shimmering fish, and again, and again, and then Sonny and my father had filled the first bucket and it was my turn, always in order with everything, Sonny-Dodie-Beston, and I waded out to just below the tops of my boots. I could feel the fish slither and thump against my shins, wanting so much to go home to make their babies.

"It's not something you have to think about, Dodie," my father always says. "Everything is part of the good world, a perfect system, and us eating these fish is part of that order. You can't be making every little fish something you need to save."

My father is right. It felt like the most natural thing in the world to be standing in the icy water with fish bumping against me trying to get past, and me reaching in among them and hauling them up, the water dripping in the silver light, the fish slapping silver, the trees glowing silver, my father and my brothers dark shadows with silver in their hair, their hands silver reaching to help me, the fish sliding into my bucket so I could place the net again. Beston's turn, then Daddy's, and then we each carried our bucket along the rocky path up to the truck, Daddy helping Beston but letting him feel that he was doing it himself, and we didn't speak along that path or at the truck or on the long ride home. Daddy had the radio low now and the heater high, and we settled in close to each other for warmth and because we were happy and sleepy and satisfied. Daddy held Beston's hand, letting go to shift, and drove slowly so we could watch the woods and the farms in all their dark quiet and peace.

Mum was up when we got home, nodding and smiling as we lugged our buckets to the sink. No one talked. We washed our hands in warm water and threw our clothes in the basket in the shed, and Sonny and Beston went to their room and I went to mine, climbing back into our cold beds that were soon warm. No one would wake us for school in the morning.

The sun was up and the kitchen was warm and the fish were slit and gutted and in the chest freezer when we came down.

"Why don't the fish come to our farm?" I asked my father once. "Why do we have to go so far to find them?"

He said, "Everything we will ever need or want is close enough, Dodie. Are you telling me you don't like my singing in the truck?"

On cloudy full moon nights I will remember all my life that soft silver light and the four of us standing in our creek, so far from home but Senter Creek still, no matter what, the fish rushing into our net and my welcoming mother waiting for us at home.

ONCE, WHEN BEST was too little, and while I was Sonny's only friend, or at least his best friend, he called to me from the upper hayloft. He was allowed up there by then but I still wasn't. A few times I snuck up, when Mum and Daddy were busy and thought we were just working or playing in the old horse stall, so I knew how nice it was up there, especially in the spring when the hay was gone from that loft and mostly gone from the lower one so we could move around in the soft chaff and sit in the beam of dust light that came through the big window at the top of the barn wall, as if God was shining on us and everything we were doing or ever would do.

"Come see what I found," Sonny called down to me in his quiet, serious voice.

The loft ladders were very steep and it was hard for me to swing up onto the floor from the last rung because you had no place to hold on to, and it felt like the ladder was going to pull away and lean through the air all the way to the barn floor below. Sonny knew that and came down to the first loft and held my hand when I got off and then he went ahead up the top loft ladder and held my hand again and then he led me all the way to the very back under the sloping roof.

"Look," he whispered.

We knelt in the soft hay leavings. There was a small indentation in the hay, a rough circle packed down with strands of hay laid up like a make-believe roof that you could look right through, like a playhouse, and inside were four tiny pink kittens. We watched them, but all they could do so far was lift their heads from the nest a little way and then rest.

"Let's take them into the kitchen and feed them," I whispered, but Sonny held my hand back.

"No, they aren't kittens, Dodie," he whispered. "They're baby rats."

I could see now that they weren't kittens. I touched them anyway. Their skin wrinkled when I drew my finger along. It was as soft as anything I had ever touched. Their eyes were still closed. They had pointy tails, not even as long as my finger, and pointy faces like a cartoon of mice. They laid close by each other.

"Where's the mother?" I whispered to my brother.

"Getting food so she can make milk to feed them," he said. "Here."

He picked one up and put it in my hand. He took one, and we sat down next to each other, stroking the warm, tiny bodies.

"Daddy will drown them if he finds them," he said.

I had pulled lots of dead rats out of my father's traps and thrown their stiff, creased bodies in the incinerator barrel. I had never thought about their bodies burning along with the trash. I had never thought about their babies. I knew that Daddy wouldn't be up in this loft again until June when he cut the new hay. He'd never find them.

We sat for a long time, our hands hot, the loft glowing with the yellow light that came in the high windows and filled the place under the roof every day. We couldn't see down, only up into the rafters, whole trees cut from this land by someone connected to us from a long, long time ago.

Sonny brought his closed hand close to his mouth and breathed in, smelling the warm air. "It's okay," he whispered. "It's okay." His short blond hair was the color of the hay around us, the color of the light that came to us, like light through a tunnel in the floating dust.

"What will we do?" I asked my brother. He was quiet. We put the baby rats back in the nest and sat back watching. "I wonder where the mother is," I said.

[30]

"Watching us," Sonny said. "She's waiting to come back to her babies. They must be hungry."

Sonny held the ladder and helped me swing my leg out into space to catch the first rung.

From here we could see down past the lower loft and all the way to the barn floor below. It was swept neat. Nothing blocked the center aisle between the rows of stanchions and pens. Sonny had laid loose hay in the racks that morning, ready for the cows to come home at night to be milked and to rest before moving out again in the morning to the orderly green pastures that fed them. The water buckets were filled with fresh water, and the hose was coiled by the spigot. The huge old bins were full of sweet grain, the scoops hung on nails next to my father's careful charts of feeding measures for every calf and cow. We climbed back down to the floor of our barn.

That night at supper, while I kept our secret, Sonny was quiet, and then he told our father we had found a nest of baby rats in the upper loft.

"Well," my father finally said. He didn't ask us what I was doing up there. "Well," he said. "I'm very sorry to hear that. That's a very sad piece of news. I appreciate your telling me, Sonny. You're a good boy."

When the sun goes down, I knew, the barn lofts go darker than the darkest woods. I knew the mother would get away, and I knew she would make more babies that would look to me just like these. But in the night I could feel still the softness of their skin. I could feel Sonny lying in his bed across the hall, and I knew my father was right about him. I knew that I would not have told. I would have let the babies be safe, and they would have grown to be the rats that eat and soil our grain, the rats we have to kill in our traps. I wondered about me, then, having kept this from my father. Was I a bad girl? The next morning we never even looked up to the high space inside the barn. We had a lot of chores to do, sweeping and dragging the hose from bucket to bucket and carrying kindling wood from my father's pile to the kitchen. The sun was out, a good spring day, and it filled the place under the roof with its golden, dusty light.

ONE NIGHT I got up and walked down the hall to my mother and father's room. Mum and Daddy sleep with their door open, we all do, and I stopped and peered in from the edge of the doorway. Daddy was sitting up, his book open beside him, and Mum was lying with her head in Daddy's lap. His hand was in her hair, moving up and then slipping the long golden strands through his fingers, slowly, over and over, her thick hair falling heavy onto her shoulder. They didn't say a word. The light from their lamp fell short of the door, leaving me outside in the half-dark of the hallway. My mother's housedress and slip hung over the chair, my father's pants and shirt from the drawer knob on their bureau. I waited, wanting something to happen, a laugh or a rearranging of the blankets or a hand reaching to turn off the light, a movement to relieve me of the ache that was settling inside my chest. My mother and father were mine, and Sonny's and Beston's, mother and father and children, but while we slept, each in our faraway rooms, my mother and father belonged to each other. I knew this. We all knew this. I had seen them like this, separate from us, joined in ways that had nothing to do with their children. But a new day would start, the morning light filling the house, my father in the barn and my mother in the kitchen, and I would forget those reminders. On that night, it frightened me, my mother's shoulder in the circle of light as my father stroked her. They love each other, I said to myself. They love you. There is enough love here.

SONNY AND DADDY built shelves out of boards Daddy had milled from the pine logs he cut off the hill by the graves. I was allowed to watch, but Daddy said these were Sonny's shelves to hold the specimens he collects. Sonny isn't like Daddy in that way. He doesn't like to build things and isn't patient with the tools. I am, and I would have liked to do that building, but I watched as I was told. Daddy showed Sonny how to sand and varnish the shelves, and when they were dry they carried them up the front stairs into Sonny and Best's room and put them under the windows. It took Sonny about one day to fill them up with the things he had laid out in boxes under his bed.

"Don't you come in here anymore," he told me. "This is my room and these are my things you can't touch."

Sonny and I had always sat on the floor going through the boxes and making little piles of things to organize them. It felt as if my brother had slammed his door on me. I went into my room and sat on my bed, then went downstairs and sat on the glider on the porch. It was warm and all the windows in the house were open.

I started to sneak into Sonny and Best's room when they were outside. At first I just looked at my brother's things laid out like a museum case of treasures collected in Egypt. Then I started to touch things. I already knew them by heart: plates from a wood turtle's shell and a whitetail dragonfly with her shiny jet-black wings, and pink quartz and seedpods from the honey locust by the tractor shed. I'd start at the top shelf, putting my finger on each piece, pushing just a little bit to say I can be here, moving from one end to the other, and then down to the lower shelf and back along, each thing mine as much as Sonny's while my finger lay on it.

Sometimes there was something new, a mantis egg case or owl pellet, or something I had never seen and didn't know the name of, but Sonny started making little cards with his tiny, neat printing just like a museum, and I read each one as I touched them down the line, making my voice speak out loud—skin of a ribbon snake, *Thamnophis sauritus*, sycamore spur, *Platanus occidentalis*, mummified newt, *Lissotriton vulgaris*, assassin bug, *Pselliopus barberi*—and sometimes I pressed harder until I heard a little snap of bone or a soft crackle. I made my way to the end of his shelves and went downstairs, still feeling the giving way in my finger. At supper

[33]

when Sonny sat next to me I believed he could feel the little breaking of bones in his own finger and knew I had trespassed. He never
told my mother or father that something had been broken.

Then Mum and Daddy moved Sonny into the bedroom re-
served for visitors, who almost never came, the bedroom next to
mine, with his bureau and his new shelves with each object just
where it had been before, his church shoes in the bottom of the
closet and his pants and shirts and sweaters in the same drawers
in the bureau and his new dictionary upright on the desk they
got for him.

Then Sonny's old bed was left in Best's room, and Best would
ask me if I wanted to play in there with him. He was just a little
boy, though, and we couldn't come up with the right things to do.
After that, even when the house was cold and the stove downstairs
was roaring trying to keep each room warm, Sonny closed his door
when he wasn't in his room, and I didn't dare open it and touch
his objects anymore. Sometimes he brought me a cicada husk or
a small sheet of black mica, and he would make a neat little card
and tell me to put it on my bureau. Sometimes he called to Beston
and me to ride our bikes with him on the tractor road through the
fields to the pond to look for snipe eggs. We'd always say yes, and
we'd rest in the grass on our bellies beside Sonny, watching the
universe in the pond while the light filled the depths and became
sustenance for all the living beings we could see and all the ones
we could not.

The days of summer slipped one to the next. Best and I played
in the dark barn and by the creek, adapting to each other's age.
We waited for Sonny to come back to us. The light in my mother
and father's bedroom illuminated a soft shoulder, the stroking of
hands, fingers intertwined. Like little planets in a solar system, our
bedrooms encircled theirs, the haylofts full of summer hay, our
creek running miles and miles down to the sea.

I SAT ON the grain bin with Best, out of the way. It was a very hot, still day and the barn was sweltering. Sometimes a spin of breeze would lift and swirl down the center aisle, picking up hay chaff in little eddies along the clean floor. And then the air would settle again, heavy and full. All the two-month bull calves milled loose in the tie-up area, bawling incessantly for their mothers, who bellowed back to them from the pasture beyond the barn, the heifer calves pressed safe and hard to their mothers against the noise and frightened movement inside the barn. The bull calves were just babies, with soft eyes and long gangly legs. My father walked in among them and slipped a rope noose over the neck of one, sweet and dark-faced with long eyelashes and wild rolling eyes. The calf bolted, swinging his head against my father's chest. My father laughed and teased him, calling him a naughty little boy. Sonny stood among the calves, his hands on their backs, quieting them with soft words I couldn't hear. He had taken off his jersey and I could see that he was not a skinny child anymore. He was as tall as my mother, his feet and hands too big, his chest suddenly lining into muscle. His pants hung loose on his hips, his belly white and smooth. I felt lonely for my brother that day. He followed my father through the stanchion line to the central aisle and took the rope, stroking the calf's neck and sweet-talking him.

My father pulled the castrating pliers from his pocket, slid a small elastic band over the plier heads and opened them wide. The calf bawled, and his mother responded from outside with a deep, sad bellow. Beston slid his arm over mine and touched my fingers. Daddy moved behind the calf, saying, "Hold him, Sonny!" when the calf twitched away. Sonny didn't answer. He just pulled the calf's head into his bare chest, his arm over the calf's neck. He looked at the floor as Daddy grabbed the calf's little sack and slipped the elastic off. His hands were quick. The calf leaped and then plunged, head down, and twisted his hind end back and forth, back and forth, his tail held high.

"Release!" Daddy yelled at my brother.

[35]

Sonny slipped the rope off and they pushed the calf away and he bolted for the gate at the end of the barn, bucking and twisting against the pain. He bawled again and again.

Daddy called over the noise to Sonny, "Good job, Son."

Beston and I raced to the gate and let the calf run through. I knew when he found his mother because the crying stopped. Beston and I ran back to the grain bin and climbed on top. Sonny moved in among the scared, shifting calves and pulled the next one to the aisle, pressing the little head hard against his chest while Daddy loaded the pliers. I could see Sonny's lips moving as he tried to soothe the calf. Daddy stroked the calf's back as he moved behind him, and then the bucking and bawling started all over again. Sonny slipped the rope from the calf, and he and Daddy pushed the leaping calf away as Beston and I ran to the gate.

"You're doing a fine job," Daddy said to Sonny, and to Best and me.

The calves in the stanchion area were spooked and the sound was terrible. Beston held my hand as we sat waiting to do our job at the gate.

I called to my father, "Daddy, Beston could go back to the house now."

Daddy yelled back, without looking at us, "Beston will stay right here."

Sonny's eyes flicked from the calves to Daddy to the floor. His face was red, the heat and the noise and the frightened little heads against his chest, the soft necks and ears and the mothers' calling against this terrible forewarning. The steer calves' life on our farm would be short, six seasons of peaceable movement with their herd and no more.

Calf by calf. The barn grew hotter through the morning and the dust from the old floors rose.

Then Daddy was yelling at Sonny, "Hold him! Hold him hard, for Christ's sake!"

The calf twisted, bawling and bucking as Sonny tried to grab the loose rope and haul him back into his chest, but the calf broke free and screamed, wild and terrified and in pain, something gone wrong and the careful routine suddenly calamitous.

"Grab him!" my father yelled. "Goddamn it to hell, Sonny, grab him!"

But the calf bucked and leaped back over the feed trough, the rope tangling in the stanchion, and the calf fell forward, his jaw hitting the steel hard and his legs bent under him wrong and Sonny bending to him, trying to lift his head, his neck. The calf had stopped bawling and now the big eyes stared terrified and helpless. Daddy leaned over the calf, the others huddling in the far corner and Beston holding my hand, silent, and then drawing away, too, and Daddy tried to lift the little calf but one leg wasn't right, we could see that, the leg caught in the stanchion crooked and the calf refusing to be lifted upright, sagging onto the leg.

My father's voice was hard. "Bring me the gun!"

Sonny turned for the gun, the rifle my father had hooked over a nail by the door to the milk room as if he knew this could happen or would happen, but already it was Sonny's fault, his son's fault for not doing what he had done so well twenty times already today, the simple holding tight and the closing off of his heart against all this wild anguish and unknowability. Maybe Sonny forgot his hands and the rope for one moment of inattention while he turned inside to quiet his regret that this was what he had to do, a moment of tenderness or even love for these calves that could not be allowed.

"Run, goddamn it!" my father bellowed in the sudden quiet, the mother outside still thinking her calf would bolt through that gate, would return to her and her helpless protection, her nudging and moaning and licking and hot sweet comfort of milk.

Sonny lurched to my father and held out the gun to him.

"Are you going to do this?" my father yelled.

Sonny drew back, red-faced and just a boy, and he shook his head.

"I didn't think so," Daddy said fiercely and he clicked the metal and held the rifle pointing down.

Beston suddenly jerked away and ran to the gate where the beautiful green pasture slid away to the woods and the cows whose calves had returned grazed in contentment.

I turned to Sonny but he did not look at me or toward that opening through the gate to our peaceful childhood. He watched my father's face and the gun went off, a thunderous explosion. The calf slumped. The whole barn went silent.

"You drag this animal outside and then come back ready to work, you hear me?" Daddy asked.

Sonny bent low and reached under my father's arms and found the front legs and pulled the little calf along the floor and out the big door into the yard, a thin trail of blood marking the moment. Beston climbed over the gate and disappeared and Daddy let him go.

After, Sonny walked back into the barn and down the aisle, watching my father.

"Don't you dare drift into one of your goddamned daydreams again," Daddy said when my brother untangled the rope from the stanchion. "You just as well as killed that calf with your dreaming."

Sonny didn't answer, but he never took his eyes off my father's face, either. I felt so sorry for Sonny. It was clear that he had done a good job all morning and even this was just a very bad event, not his fault or the calf's or Daddy's. Sonny went back in among the calves that were milling again and calling out in panic to their mothers, and the moment was over, except for Beston hiding off somewhere and the calf lying dead outside the barn doors and Sonny's eyes suddenly distant with shame or anger or maybe some of both and my father not sweet-talking the baby calves anymore or telling Sonny that he was doing a good job, a man's job. I wanted to stand next to Sonny, to hold the rope, too, to stand against my father and this work and the noise of fear and aching that filled our farm.

[38]

But Daddy and Sonny started up again and one by one the exhausted calves returned to their waiting mothers and the barn quieted. Daddy told me to sweep the aisle and Sonny cleaned out the stanchion area and Daddy went to get the tractor. They used the same rope to tie the little legs together and dragged the calf across the road and through the field, all the way to the ledges where the woods start. Sonny stood on the hitch, watching behind him to make sure the body didn't break free. The barn was clean and quiet, the swallows flicking in and out of the shafts of light. One cow stood behind the barn waiting, longer and longer minutes between her calls for her calf, an acceptance settling in with all its dark weight. Daddy and Sonny returned half an hour later, silent, and did the milking, the other cows content again and their calves, both heifers and bulls, lay sleepily in the straw. I filled the water buckets and hayracks. Then we went in for supper.

Beston came down from his room, leaning against Mum as she laid our food on the table. Sonny and Daddy and I washed up and Sonny pulled his jersey back on. With his white chest hidden, he looked more like my brother, a young boy on a farm who tried hard every day.

"Daddy told me what happened," Mum said quietly to Sonny. "I'm sorry."

"Nothing to apologize to me about," Sonny said.

His voice was calm, and very sad, and we all knew that now he and Daddy were bound always by this day.

After supper, Mum and I did up the dishes. She told me about seeing Mrs. Underwood that afternoon when she went to Vernon in the truck for cloth and thread. When the dishes were all put away and the dish towels were laid over the sink to dry, we found Sonny and Beston and Daddy on the porch. They were all on the glider, one boy on each side of Daddy, leaned into him, tired and willing to sit in the darkening calm. Daddy was reading to them from a book he had loved as a boy, *Two Little Savages*, written by Ernest Thompson Seton. We loved it, too. He had to tilt the book to the yellow light of the lamp. I curled next to my mother in the big old wicker chair. Daddy stroked Sonny's thigh with his thumb as he read.

A whip-poor-will called again and again from across the road. It reminded us of the calf over by the ledges, but the call was tender, insistent. The cows were bedded down for the night, all of them silent now. Daddy would go out once more before bed to walk the aisle, checking. Sonny and Beston and I would make our way upstairs, released from all expectation. I heard Daddy come up the stairs, the quiet talk with Mum in their room. I could feel Sonny alone in his new room on the other side of the wall, could feel his hands holding the sheet to his neck, his eyes open in the dark as we all waited for sleep to come.

Tup

I ASKED DORIS to go to the July Fourth supper and dance with me and the children. I know that she is happiest at home, and not at ease in crowds. But I started this idea on her a month ago and it didn't take long for the children to pick up on it, so all the urgings and beggings finally bore fruit and she agreed to go. There are lessons in these gatherings about kindliness and generosity. I tell Doris this when she resists the children having friends over. To be fair, she submits, and it is possible that the children don't even realize her discomfort. But I can see the way she hovers, a certain intensity in her eyes and body that is a kind of wildness, a mother's love that claims too much.

"You have to let the world into their home," I tell her. "Nothing good will come of your holding too tight to them."

Sometimes she laughs and brushes off my comments, but sometimes she turns on me, her dark eyes bright and fearful, and says, "Tup, anything can happen and it will come from outside, not from us."

I cannot reason with her. She will not believe that our children can grow up whole and strong without her guarding our home from the world.

But she said yes. Doris and Dodie spent the morning making six pies for the church raffle and one for our own picnic supper. After Sonny and Beston and I did the morning barn chores, we left everything else that needed doing and went down cellar to my father's old workshop. I had bought a used band saw and lathe from Claude Baudoin a few years ago, and the boys and I spent the day making little band saw boxes for the raffle out of maple prunings. It was a pleasant time for us, the cutting and sanding and gluing and oiling, with a good purpose. We brushed the sawdust out of our hair before going upstairs, and laid out three little boxes on the kitchen table.

"Oh!" Doris said. "They are wonderful! Thomas Senter, I didn't know you could make such pretty little things! Why haven't you ever made one for me?"

The children watched us, uncertain smiles on their faces.

I didn't have an answer for my wife, but I said anyway, "I make a farm and I make a house and I repair the truck when it won't go. I didn't think I also had the job of making useless little boxes for my wife."

Of course, I felt like a fool the minute I started speaking but I could not stop. "What do you make for me that isn't necessary? You mend my shirts and make meals and paint the hallway, but I don't recall you ever sewing a little bag with a heart on it just for me."

The children watched me, and then looked to their mother. I was sorry for my foolishness, especially because Doris is a very good and thoughtful wife, and especially because I was blighting the special day.

Doris looked at me, and slowly nodded. "Well," she said calmly, "I will remember that you might like a little special something now and then."

I knew it cost her to respond that way, and to smile when she was done, and to reach out and put her arm around my waist. There was something I should say, but the moment for it was gone and it didn't seem vital by the time the children breathed out and smiled again and picked up their chatter.

Many times through that afternoon and evening, watching my wife in her friendly hellos with our neighbors, I wanted to catch her hand and draw her aside and tell her that tomorrow she would have a small box with her initials on it. Or at least I would tell her that I thought she looked very pretty tonight. But she was engaged with people and I did not find the moment. Is this what I will someday lie awake at night remembering, an old man's regrets? So common, an everyday misstep, a small withholding that will come to lie with me forever?

Rachel and Warren and his widowed sister, Ruthie, shared our blanket when we spread out our picnic supper. They are all older, their children grown, and soon Sonny and Dodie and Beston asked to take their plates to the blankets of their friends. I watched Doris.

"Eat here with us," she said, "and then you can go play. Come back and find us before the raffle. We will want to see who gets the boxes and pies."

This seemed to satisfy them and we had a good picnic. I could see that Doris was proud as she offered her own pickled beets and potted corned beef and soft fresh bread and farm butter to our friends. She did look very pretty in a red striped dress with a white collar, her strong legs tanned and her shoes kicked off because she was happy and relaxed, a proud wife and mother. The breeze caught in her hair and she swept it off her face. Rachel and Warren and Ruthie were very friendly and talkative, but Doris is from away and no one in this town ever forgets that.

Doris says to me sometimes, "This town is suspicious of me."

I tell her it has nothing to do with who she is. She was born in the wrong town and there's nothing she can ever do about that. But I know she will never have a real friend here. She is well-liked and respected. People know she is a good and hardworking wife and mother, and that's what they mostly care about. But I could have married Abbie Donahue or Gwen Chase or Evelyn Temple or any one of the town's daughters, and I didn't. I chose Doris. Doris will be judged for that for as long as she lives. It doesn't help one bit that she outshines every woman here with her cooking and gardening and homemaking and mothering. And her looks.

Sonny sat cross-legged as he ate two large plates of his mother's good food, and Dodie and Beston leaned against one another, asking for seconds. They responded politely to the questions and comments of these older people they have known from church since they were born. Then they were gone, and our friends told us that we were doing a fine job of raising such good and responsible children.

Later, I reached for Doris's hand, and later still I led her out onto the smooth grass where our local band was playing "Embraceable You" and we danced together, her body against mine, my hand on her back as if I were protecting her from some harm she didn't suspect. I felt her breath on my neck. She leaned back and looked at my face, and I saw her love and her goodness and understood that we are a pair forever.

Evening came. It was a warm, starless night. I danced with Dodie, and Sonny danced with his mother. Beston watched from a group of his friends. All the children played shrieking, whooping games of tag and red rover in the dark. The band closed with our national anthem, which everyone sang, and we all clapped and called into the dusk, "Hooray!"

All of the pies Dodie and Doris made went in the raffle, and all the boxes the boys and I made. Beston won a crocheted potholder, and he blushed hard when everyone laughed. We gathered our things and climbed into the truck. I drew my wife in next to me, the children squeezing in after, and I held her hand. Dodie and Sonny teased Beston about blushing until I told them to stop, and we rode home talking in a contented way about the outing.

Doris said, "That was a fine time. It was good to see everyone."

I was glad for the children to hear it.

Doris had left the light on in the hallway. She and the children climbed the stairs and I checked the barn. It made me uneasy to have been away, but the cows were quiet, rousing themselves just enough to make their soft, low greetings when I slid the door open. I was happy to be home.

I washed up in the kitchen sink and turned off the hallway light on my way upstairs. Doris was lying in our bed in the dark. I undressed and slid in next to her, and she reached for me. I was very grateful. The wind blew through the windows and across us. Our children slept. We gave in to each other, all the thoughts of the day insignificant.

AFTER SUPPER ONE night in late August, I asked Sonny if he wanted to get a deer. I saw his head jerk up and the quick look he gave Doris. She stayed quiet, attending to clearing the table.

"Can I come?" Dodie asked, and Beston asked with his eyes.

I said, "Next time maybe you two can come, but this time it is Sonny's turn, if he thinks he would like to come."

I wasn't sure if he would. Sonny is a different kind of boy. I sometimes think he is the better part of me, the way I think of myself and am not usually, I know. He has a very strong sense of what is right, and I do, too, but when you get older, you realize that those strict expectations have to give way once in a while. He has a hard time with that, and so I sometimes feel an uneasy shame as he watches me break some of the rules he holds so clearly. It is all the harder that he never says that he is disappointed. I just know my son and know that he is weaving all these moments together into an understanding, and sometimes things don't mesh together just right for him. I was not sure how he would respond to my invitation to get a deer out of season.

But he said clearly, "Okay. Can I shoot it?"

I responded seriously, although I felt laughter rising, "Yes, I think that is a good idea."

I had been watching two young does bothering the orchard trees and they were bedding down in the second cut grass, matting it so we would never get it to cut right. I wanted them out of there. I also like to hunt, like the quiet watching. This deer-getting in August, and after nightfall to boot, is considered poaching, but I do like the long, quiet slipping through the fields and woods of summer dark. By November, when the season opens, the land has gone cold and distant. In August, every creature is full of life, announcing itself in what seems like some sort of joy. I know that's what I feel when I move among them. I want Sonny to come to know that joy. It's a greedy kind of feeling, greed not for wanting the deer but for wanting the fullness of sounds and shadows and animals stalking animals in the summer night.

Sonny and I took our time, waiting for full dark to come. We stood before the gun rack in the hall and studied the guns. He was used to the four-ten shotgun, a good rabbit gun for a boy, but he reached out and touched the thirty-thirty.

"Think that's what will get us this deer?" I asked him.

"I would like to try," he said, and so he reached it down and cradled it in his arms.

I pulled down the box of bullets and we sat at the kitchen table and I told him to rub down the metal and stock with an old sock.

"Any way we could get caught?" he asked me.

I said there isn't a man in this neighborhood who doesn't clear his farm of the critters who cost us something—raccoons, weasels, coyotes, fox, deer, crows after the seedlings, dogs that come around our new calves.

"These laws work for the sports who come in from somewhere else, Sonny, but they have nothing to do with us. There are rhythms here and we are part of them. You never take a life needlessly. But if a deer is eating my apples and trampling my hay, I have a natural right to protect what's mine."

Sonny listened, his hand stroking the rifle, and he nodded.

I wanted more than that from him. "That sound reasonable to you?" I asked him.

"Yes, it sounds right," he said.

After Doris and the younger children had gone to bed, Sonny and I stepped out into the pool of light at the back of the house, and then into the black beyond that was so filled with the callings of the world. It was cricket time, their millions in the fields, and the whip-poor-wills called, and down the road beyond the bridge we could hear the yipping of a fox. We made our way along the fence and through the gates into the orchard, then through the west pasture and around into the field where the land starts to rise beyond the creek. I led the way, Sonny following behind, barely making a sound. Sonny knows how to handle a gun. He carried the rifle over his arm and pointing down, safety on. I teach my children that we have responsibilities for all that we do and don't do. We walked onto that rise with my son knowing that what he was about to do had weight and significance.

We crouched downwind in the new grass that was making up for our second cut. It was already soaked with dew and we could feel our feet getting wet through our work shoes. The half-moon was out behind milky clouds, just right to see the orchard below us. The light from the hallway in the house was dim, a calling of the family from far away, the familiar, the kitchen, the routines and cadences of our days. We settled on our knees and waited for this other world to forget we had entered, to remember itself without us. I laid my hand on Sonny's thin leg and we waited. Sonny never let his head drop with a boy's sleepiness. He watched with me, not eager, which would not have pleased me, but alert and ready, available to this night and this taking.

The two finally came as I knew they would. We watched them move among the trees and I felt Sonny's leg tighten. There is nothing more elegant in this world than the head of a white-tail deer, delicate as a story animal's, or her fine thin legs that look like they might snap under her weight but will carry her leaping and zigzagging through thick woods and away. Sonny raised the rifle to his shoulder, then waited, and silently eased off the safety. The does moved among the lower branches, ripping off my young apples, lowering their heads to chew. We could clearly hear the tear from the tree and the crunching as they ate. Another graceful step, another tear from the tree. They stayed in the night shadows of the branches, and we waited. Then they separated, and one moved slowly, deliberately, gracefully beyond the outer trees and looked toward us, her head raised, her big ears twitching forward and back.

I tapped Sonny's leg and I felt him gather himself, lay his cheek against the stock of the gun, and then the great shattering of the peace of the night, a momentary splintering of everything we knew. Sonny's young body jolted back and then forward, hard, a jolting that shocked me even though I should have predicted the effect of firing this gun. The doe pitched forward and was still. Sonny lifted his head and was still. The whole world was still. The booming echo of the shot quieted. The other deer, her sister perhaps, bolted noisily in the sudden silence. Sonny slowly dropped the rifle to his lap and I felt the letting down of his shoulders, the release of air from his young chest. He slipped the safety on and expelled the hot bullet case onto the wet grass. The light at the house glowed gently far off across the fields.

"That was a very good job, Son," I said, my voice breaking the stillness, and we stood stiffly in the cooling night. "Maybe another night this week we can get that other one."

"Dodie and Beston want it," he said.

But I understood that Sonny felt great pride carrying that rifle over his arm and that we would be here again once the remaining doe lost her spook. We made our way to the dead doe. We wrapped a rope around her thin hocks, binding her feet together, and I crouched beside her while Sonny wrestled her across my shoulders like a yoke. She was young, last year's fawn, and I easily carried her the distance back. Sonny led the way now, moving toward the soft light of home. When we came into the light of the yard, we searched the animal and found that Sonny had placed the shot nicely in her right shoulder.

We split and gutted her into a large bucket for the pigs in the morning. Sonny has done this with me a dozen times or more, but never a deer he has taken himself. He was confident, sure-handed. Everything about her seemed small, delicate, young—her small heart and liver and lungs, shining black with fresh blood in the light of the house, her teeth like a child's and her big soft eyes.

"We'll hang her for the rest of the night to cool," I said, "and cut her and get her into the freezer tomorrow morning first thing."

We hoisted her from a beam in the tractor shed, slit open and emptied, no longer seeming wild or beyond us.

Without turning on the lights, we washed at the kitchen sink, her blood black and then pink and then the water clear and clean. I cut slices of Doris's bread onto two plates and spread them thick with butter and the raspberry jam Doris and Dodie had just put up. We didn't talk. I saw that Sonny was still a boy, just thirteen, his arms smooth without muscle, his legs thin in his farm pants. His face was very fine, sensitive, but anyone could see already that he was becoming a good and strong young man. He ate his bread and butter, and we left the plates in the sink and climbed the stairs, turning out the hallway light as we went.

In bed, I could feel Sonny awake in the dark, his sister and little brother sleeping close by, untouched by that explosive division of the world or the hot young heart we pulled from the yearling doe's chest. I could feel Sonny moving in his thoughts back through the orchard and pasture and field, feel him crouching again, waiting, feel him closing on the trigger and calming his breath as the young animals came into our sight.

EARLY IN THE fall, on a cool night with a wind coming from the northeast, we moved our evening time from the porch back to the front room. Beston took out the dominoes from their old wooden box and spread them on the table. The children don't know how to play the game, and don't care to know. They spread the ebony pieces face up and made long trains across the table by number, dots matching dots, and then Sonny drifted to his book on the sofa.

The room glowed yellow and warm. Beston and Dodie started to clack the dominoes one against the other until I asked them to stop. Dodie sat next to Sonny and asked him what he was reading.

"*Robin Hood*," he said. "It's really good." He sat deep in the cushions, leaning on the arm of the sofa.

"Will you read to us?" his sister asked.

He hadn't for a long time. Sonny raised his eyes to her, and nodded. He moved over so Beston could fit on the other side of him and moved back to the first pages. "King Richard the First, Richard Coeur de Lyon, came to the throne in 1189," he read, "and very soon left his throne empty when he set off on the Crusade to free Jerusalem from the Saracens."

Beston and Dodie and Sonny leaned into each other, Sonny's voice clear and rhythmic, the quiet swish of the pages being turned like water behind his words. Doris and I put down our own books and listened. We felt the contentment of the early fall night soft among us in the room.

Sonny held us all in his story, his voice fuller and deeper than in his daily talk. "Prince John had ridden out to see the Sheriff at work, and at this moment he joined the little group round the glowing embers of the cottage."

This is fleeting, I thought. What we do is build a base for them, a good base for their start. I suddenly regretted whatever sharp words I may have spoken that day in the course of all the work that needed to be done. I couldn't remember if I had turned in impatience on any one of my children or my wife as they made their day. I regretted that I could not recall what I might have said. How could I tell them I was sorry if I could not say what I had done? I sat quietly, uneasy, my children and my wife happy for the moment, I knew, but I felt that I may somehow have stained the day and could not say when or how. "You are a very good father," Doris often says to me, and I am, I know that, but I remember the woundings of a child's feelings and suddenly felt a deep sadness that I must sometimes be the cause of hurt in my own children.

"All guests will be welcome and no close watch kept as to who they are," Sonny read.

The younger children were unembarrassed about lying across their older brother's legs, their heads on his shoulders.

I suddenly rose from my chair, moving too quickly, so the

children all looked up, startled. I turned and sat on the sofa next to Dodie, my arm across the shoulders of all three, an embrace. Sonny had stopped reading, and the room was quiet. I felt foolish, and helpless against something I felt pressing at us all.

Sonny looked across the room to his mother, and over his sister's head to me. "Have courage, my friends! cried Will Scarlet," he read, his voice still clear and steady.

I laid my head on the back of the couch, my eyes closed, my arm enfolding my children, and I listened. My farm lay with all its promise within our fence line. The creek moved at its will through the fields, into the pond and out again on its way. The hill in the far back rose to the edge of the woods, the little graveyard holding all the Senters who ever worked this land, who ever sat in this room on quiet evenings. I stopped trying to remember my trespasses. This is all that counts, I thought. Right here. This represents my love and the way I give it. Beston fell asleep. Sonny yawned, and we all stood. I picked up my sleeping child. Doris followed us out, switching off the lamps when she heard our feet start on the stairs.

The land is restless at night, even the tamed land of a farm. Doris and I lay side by side listening, wakened by the madwoman's shriek of a rabbit being killed. A fox, or bobcat, or a farmer's dog playing wild. Later, a barred owl in its own rhythm, and another's response from the woods across the road.

"What happened to you tonight?" Doris whispered in the dark.

"I don't know," I said. I reached for her warmth and pulled her to me, my face close to hers. "I don't want to ever have regrets."

I waited for her response but she stayed quiet.

"I go cold sometimes thinking that I will someday find that all the good I thought I was doing will appear to be all wrong. That I'll be blamed."

The night waited.

"That I will be rightly blamed."

Doris touched my lips with her fingers and allowed herself to settle against me.

"I am afraid that I won't be recognized," I said. "That my children will blame me for whatever might happen. That they'll believe I failed to try."

"Every parent worries about that," my wife said. "Your children know that you are a very good father. They know that you are a very good husband. I'll remind them when they are grown that their father was a very good man."

"Thank you, Doris." I rolled to my back and took her hand. "I'll remind them the same about you. We've gotten this far okay."

If anyone walked in the fields that night, they would see that the moon shadows of the fence posts stretched in long parallel lines across the pasture. The upper limbs of the hemlock and tamarack and pines swayed. This generation of Senters slept, unable to know what might ever come to us.

I woke in the morning at ease again, trusting that my effort would be the measure of judgment. Marion arrived after breakfast, and Dodie and her friend cleaned out the henhouse as if it were play. Best and Sonny and I had wood to get in from beyond the ledges across the road. Doris called us all to our noon dinner, and the kitchen filled with talk and laughter.

MY FATHER IS buried on the hill under the old pines, next to my mother and his parents and grandparents and great-grandparents. But some days I hear the voice of my father calling to me, small and faraway: "You scuttled the life I offered to you." I watch as if we are in a film that is fading. He is standing beside the horses, two good Belgians named Mick and Bonnie, and the mowing bar is silent for the moment. I am sitting in my father's seat on the Number 9, the same sickle mower my grandfather used on those tired old fields. Great long lines of cut clover and alfalfa lie out behind us, drying in the sun and wind. It is early June of a good year and the grass is thick and tall, nearly to my shoulders. I am just a boy, thin and willing but not of any real help to my tired father. My mother is still alive and understands that I will come in for supper tired out and satisfied, that my father will come in for supper tired out and made bitter by the long days of racing ahead of the rain and broken teeth on the mowing bar and the fox kits their mother couldn't move out of the way fast enough as we bore toward them. "Goddamn it!" he yelled as the mother danced her grief twenty feet from the soft whir and jingle of the scissoring bars. "Goddamn it!" A helpless man. I am a boy, and I share his shock of responsibility, but the wind is up, perfect for drying the hay, and Mick and Bonnie do their labor for us willingly and well, and the crows are gathering to glean their own meal from the stubble.

When I sleep, I will feel a boy's satisfaction, remembering the whir and the grasses falling and the chaff sticking to my sweating chest and neck and the sweet drunken smell of green and sun. I believe now there was never a time my father loved this land and these horses and this rhythm of jingle and whir and the heat and the promise of a winter coming with enough food for every creature we tended in the barn. I am made for this work and rise to it again in the morning, eager to be made tired, again and again. So these old films run, an effort to speak back to my dead father's accusations that some larger life was offered to me and I failed to seize it.

Several days ago it rained, and I stayed at the kitchen table making a mess of wood shavings that fell onto the canvas apron spread across my lap as I carved a new handle for my crook knife. Doris and Dodie spent the afternoon cooking down and canning pears from the tree beside the coop. Sonny and Beston were roughhousing in Best's room, their chores done, their shrieks of laughter and banging on the floor carrying all the way to the kitchen. Watching my wife, strong and thin, with our daughter at the stove, the thick sweet steam from our pears heavy around us, our sons thumping happy and free upstairs, the cows grazing the thick wet grass on the east pasture, everything fresh with paint inside and out—how could a man want more than this? I do not.

The green applewood carved easily, its sap wetting my hands even as I brought it to my use. I tested the fit of the new handle to my palm, whittling off more on the inside curve. It tucked in just right. Before supper, I drilled a hole into the wood with my smallest hand auger and inserted the tang of the blade, the same auger and blade my father used and my grandfather. Dodie left her chore and leaned against me, watching, her hair smelling of pears. Surely my father can see the quiet sort of peace I find here.

Someday, Doris and I will be the ghosts up on the hill, and Sonny and Dodie and Beston will be here on the land their great-great-grandfather cleared. This is my answer to my father's rebuke.

LAST WINTER, ON a cold, clear, early January day, Doris and I organized our chores so we could take the afternoon skating with the children on Johns River in South Brookfield. The ice was thick and we had had no snow since the cold weather really set in, so the ice was smooth and open. I truly love to skate, and the day felt as exciting to me as to my children. This was the place my father brought his own children when the drudgery of his work life overwhelmed him in the dark, early days of winter. That's not what drove me there, not too much work or the wrong work. But everyone needs a sense of cutting free once in a while, and Doris was quick to say yes.

She and Dodie put together thermoses of hot chocolate, and Beston and Sonny brought the sled from the shed. They waxed the steel runners with a candle stub and tied a new length of rope to the steering bar. All our outer clothes went behind the truck seat. Dodie got the place beside me and my hand, and the truck filled with happy nonsense and chatter.

Johns River is really just a wide, slow creek with overhanging trees and brush protecting muskrat and beaver bank dens. I've always thought it was a very good place, especially for children because it spools out forward, not like a pond or lake surrounding you, but a river of ice inviting you away. I love that illusion, that sense of the possibility of going on and away, turning your back and giving yourself over to what you can't see ahead.

The muddy landing was frozen, and someone, probably a trapper, had laid a good log down for sitting and a stone break for a small fire. Doris and I helped tighten the laces on the children's skates, Sonny always in new ones and Dodie and Beston in his hand-me-downs. Dodie complained at the start of each winter about wanting figure skates like her mother's, but she had mastered hockey skates and seemed content once she got on the ice the first time each year.

I seldom see Doris in slacks, but I complimented her, saying, "Well, Mr. Senter, you are looking very handsome today."

I could count on her to laugh, and the children, too.

"Oh, but I change into a beautiful princess at midnight," she said with her open smile, "if a handsome prince decides to kiss me."

My wife is a flirt, which no man ever complains about.

Off we went, the sun glinting from the ice and the bare trees and the blue sky itself. I was happy the minute my skates hit the ice. This is something we never forget, the feeling of ice carved by our skates with a rasping swoosh. It is a certain kind of freedom to not make steps, but instead to slide a leg forward, the other leg, the first again and find yourself suddenly almost free of the world, skimming smoothly and effortlessly into the light. I felt a kind of euphoria, a real elation, and wondered for a minute if my children knew this kind of freedom yet. We circled each other, Beston reaching sometimes for Doris's hand or mine, Sonny and Dodie breaking away and swooping along, their arms outstretched, their faces receiving the clean winter light. No one spoke or called out, our skate blades scraping loudly. The children dragged the sled down onto the ice and took turns, two of them stepping into the loop of rope like a harness and pulling the third fast along the river in wide, sweeping arcs, and now they shrieked and laughed and taunted one another. I watched Doris pull out of their way and start her silent remembering of a girl's ballet on ice, the twirls and little leaps and hips swishing side to side to go backward. She smiled, embarrassed to be watched, but didn't stop, which pleased me.

And I turned away and did my own remembering, the boy hard at hockey roaring low across the ice, feet pointing out to catch the ice and drive the body forward, faster and faster, and when I gained a curve in the river suddenly the sounds behind me became muffled and I slowly straightened and focused on the simple smooth glide of skates on good ice, the memory so strong I had nothing to say about it and I lifted my face to the sun and *soosh soosh*, *soosh soosh* in rhythm, I followed the shining ice. The noise and shouts fell behind me—"Daddy! Daddy! Where are you going?" Dodie called—and the memory of skating and this moment of skating became the same act and I was gone. I let myself be gone, Dodie's call left behind.

I went forward, and I was alone. *Soosh soosh, soosh soosh, soosh soosh.* The sun was ahead of me, nothing was behind me, there were no needs and no expectations and nothing waiting for me. The river curved right, and left, and farther right, a ribbon laid here for me alone. A crow called from the top of a towering old stave oak, and the sun shone purple against him. I did not rush, taking the river as mine, the silence as mine, the emancipating light as mine, my legs strong and the cold air now stinging my lungs, all mine with nothing secluding me or hindering me or binding me and so I did not stop.

Johns River winds smaller and smaller and finally I knew that I had come a very long way from my responsibilities and I felt a pang of worry that grew as I turned and pushed my way back. Now it felt like hard work, and the worry grew to a guilt that was crushing and that I resented and resisted. The light had changed, a warning.

And so I found my family seated on the log, the day gone and cold, the hot drinks gone, the truck keys in my pocket. Doris said nothing, and I resented that, too.

The children told me that they were very frightened that I had gone through the ice, and I said sharply, "I didn't go through the ice. I have more sense than that."

We rode home in silence, with no one's hand in mine, and although I knew that was a child's rebuke, I was not filled with sorrow about it as I might have been. Where had I gone, I wondered, that felt so distant from this family I love, and so sovereign?

We are always forgiven, and we made our way again and then again to an afternoon of skating, but we never returned to Johns River, as if keeping me from it would preserve us from some sort of sundering.

SONNY MUST HAVE been about ten when he really became aware of the war. A lot of men had left Alstead. I had three small children when we entered the war, but many of the men of this state who served also had small children. What kept me off those transports to Europe or the Pacific was this farm. There was a time early on that I wanted very much to join the effort, to offer my share, but Doris strongly objected. The draft board in Vernon gave her the reprieve she prayed for, giving me a II-C exemption and telling me to return to the farm. It was my duty, they said, to keep the land producing food. I felt a kind of shame at the time, especially as I watched men my age and much older leave their families and accept their obligation to fight. I suppose a lot of us who stayed on our farms carry a cloud of shame for the good years we have had raising our children on the land.

Sonny rode with me some mornings to Four Corners to pick something up at the hardware or get a load of oats from the granary. One day Jake Orne was coming out of Goff's as I pulled the truck up. He had volunteered, and he came home in bad shape. He stopped coming to church, and he was seldom seen in town.

"Hello, Jake," I said and shook his hand. "It is good to see you."

He nodded silently, not letting go of his grip on my hand. I could

[57]

feel Sonny staring at him but could not tell him to look away. Jake looked twenty years older than me, although he had a wife and two small sons and left this town my age.

"How are you doing?" I asked, dropping my hand to my side.

Without expression, Jake said slowly, "Not good. Not good, Tup. I know I am home but I can't seem to find my place again. It's hard."

"Yes," I said, careful with Sonny paying close attention. "I know you're right about that."

Jake stood before me, staring at me without saying another word, and finally I said, "Well, Jake, we have chores to get back to. Give Penny my best," and we parted.

"Who was that?" Sonny asked.

"That was Jake Orne," I said. "You know Michael and Dennis Orne from Sunday school. He is their father."

"Why is he sick?" Sonny asked.

"Sick? I don't think he is sick," I said.

"Yes, he is," my son said.

After that I heard people in town expressing discomfort about their conversations with Jake, and slowly, after the war ended, the discomfort became judgment, a kind of resentment that he couldn't or wouldn't allow us all to return to the tranquility we knew before the war. All he needs to do is be neighborly, they said. But Sonny was right, I think. Jake and a lot of men like him returned to Maine, and every other good place where they had been known, so hollowed out they could not recover. Sonny understood this in a way children do.

And then he started asking about war, and asking about this war, and asking for books from the library. Doris told me not to indulge his questions, but that is no way to raise a child.

"He has to know, Doris," I said. "This war is changing our country and the whole world. We can't pretend it isn't happening."

"On this farm," Doris pleaded with me, "we can separate ourselves from it. We can protect our children from it."

"But Sonny has already seen it," I said. "Every time we are in town or at church he sees that the war has come home to us."

I would not comply, and I allowed Sonny's conversations, even as Dodie and Beston listened.

Sonny had one question: "Will they ask me someday to kill other people?" And another: "What are they fighting over?" I did not have good answers.

"We are safe here," I told him, and my daughter and my youngest child.

The farm is a bulwark, I taught my children. This world, and then the world outside. We are safe on this land, in this home. Once gained, we can never turn from knowledge and its burdens. But we can find order here, and the freedom to love fiercely all we know.

ONE EVENING LAST winter I came in from milking and stripped to my underwear in the shed. For some reason, after all these years, this stripping down still amuses my wife and children. In fact, I enjoy this moment each evening. We all do. It marks the end of our work and the start of conversation, all of us together now with one purpose. And so I grin or growl or whip around in astonishment and the children scream and laugh and Doris comes beside me and fills the sink for me with hot water.

This night, Sonny showed me an article about tortoises that live one hundred years. The other children were interested and so he shared the photographs with them and read out loud. After supper, while Dodie and Doris cleared the table and did the dishes, Beston and Sonny went into the front room and I could hear the clatter of Chinese marbles on the tin board. Sonny moves between boy and man hour by hour. I am glad he has these younger children to invite him back to play.

I brought the carburetor from the tractor to the kitchen table and spread newspaper. I like evening chores. They have a beginning and an end, a clear-cut purpose. I like to use hand tools. I opened the old wooden box a Senter long before me had made to hold a basic set of tools, screwdrivers and pliers and rasps and a hammer with its handle carved from chestnut from this land. The screwdriver's tip is shiny from use. Dodie's chatter with Doris was like a chant behind my work. The slosh of dish water, the gentle clink of china, the click of seconds on the wall clock, the marbles on tin from another room. These tools in other men's hands in this room, at this table, their children at ease or troubled, the parents at ease or troubled, the seconds and minutes and hours and days and years. These evenings bring great peace and yet I was filled suddenly with an ache that startled me and then scared me. How could I not name its source? The tip of the screwdriver slipped and gouged my hand slightly and I watched as if it were someone else's hand as a tiny drop of blood rose and slid in a thin line down my palm. I raised my eyes to the kitchen, to my wife and my daughter, to the early dark of winter beyond, hearing the gentle lull of my sons' voices from down the hall, the water running at the sink, and I was so frightened I laid the tool on the table and moved quickly out the door to the shed and outside into the cold hard air, holding my bleeding hand apart from me, standing under the sweep of stars weeping, weeping from a place I did not know.

PART TWO

·····························

DURING

And the rain descended, and the floods came, and the
winds blew and beat upon that house; and it fell,
and great was the fall of it.

Matthew 7:27

[1948]

Doris

IT HAS BEEN two days now.
The noise of my wailing has finally ceased.
Now we enter our new story. The other one is over forever.

TUP'S SISTER, MAY, has brought me home again. She and Tup
tried to take me to the hospital. I have fallen far from myself. I
said I needed to return to Dodie and Beston. I couldn't recall who
took them.

Dodie ran outside to the car and stood silently as I got out. I felt
her hand reach for my skirt.

The great trees stand black against the gray sky.

I MADE MY way directly to the front room. May tried to pull me
back, whispering, *Let's hang your coat, Doris. The children. Don't
go in. Not yet.* I pushed past her and closed the door behind me.
The room smelled. Cleaners. Paint, turpentine. It was very cold.
Beston was there, sitting on the bare floor in the March gray. He
startled me, and I was unable to speak to him. I felt his eyes on
me and understood what he needed. There is nowhere to look for
such things. Love is not enough to help any of us now.

The sofa and old reading chairs are gone. The rug is gone. Some-one has painted over the wallpaper, white. I sat at the table, cleared of whatever we had been doing. I tried to hear my son's voice, and instead I heard only the whoosh of my own blood. Some time later Dodie opened the door and looked from me to her brother. From the kitchen I heard men's voices, the voices they use when they are helpless. I watched Dodie study the white walls, the floor, and then she closed the door again. Beston took a chair on the other side of the table. He is a very little boy.

SOMEONE PLACED ME at the kitchen table, and the children. Where is Tup?

TUP HAS BUILT a pine box for him. *Are his shoulders cramped?* I cried again and again. *Why did you make it so small?*

THE BOARDS HAVE been nailed into the top. My son sealed away. Where is his voice? Didn't he say quietly to me, *Listen to this, Mum.* Didn't I say to him, *Sonny, thank you for making up so much kin-dling.* Our voices are here, all the words, his soft laugh, here. I can't find them. Is this what's left to us?

TUP CRIED HARD in the night and came down to the kitchen for me. His cries collided with the terrible roar of my blood and I start-ed up and pulled away from him. *Doris,* he said again and again. *Doris, hold me. Please hold me.*

SPRING IS LATE. It snowed in the night, a muddy blanket.

THE THIRD DAY. Tup and his brother pulled me away from the body of my son. *It's time*, Tup said. *It's time, Doris.*

They put the box in the back of the truck and put Dodie and Beston in the cab with Tup. These are my children now. Everyone followed on foot as Tup carried him to the hill. I stood at the shed door and watched the truck cut dark lines in the new snow, people I know walking behind in their boots and black hats, their tracks a wavering line of mud across the white fields and up onto the hill under the pines. The mound of dirt, a mark against the thin snow. Our minister, Franklin Clough, wore his silk stole over his coat, the red angry against the morning. Who dug the hole? Tup and someone lifted the box out of the truck. My two children were very far away, small in the great expanse of white.

Franklin Clough kissed the end of his stole and let God put my son in the hole today. The son. The holy ghost.

Wind came and knocked the snow from the pines onto the stooped back of my husband as he bent to his shovel. I could see the wind, but I could not hear it.

TUP'S BROTHER, ALBERT, said to Beston, *You're the big man now, son. You need to fill Sonny's shoes and help your parents run this place. No more games.*

Tup lunged at him from the table. His chair tipped over. *That's horseshit!* he screamed at Albert. *That's horseshit! He's just a little boy! He isn't Sonny! Don't you ever say that to my son again!* And in the light we could see the spit at his mouth fly at his brother.

Beston leaned against my chair, watching the men. And then he cried, his face turned to my lap.

THE CHILDREN RETURNED to school this morning. I forgot to make them a lunch for their boxes, and Dodie packed bread and butter and apples from the cellar. They turned to me at the door and waved. The school bus door hissed as it always has. Tup never came to the kitchen for breakfast, and I threw his food to the pigs. *It was an accident, Doris. There was nothing you did wrong*, he begged me.

I REACHED UNDER my nightgown and felt the softness of my belly. I made three children.

Sonny lived here in me.

Beston cried in the night and Tup moved to his room, the first time in separate beds since our wedding night. In the cold silence came the winter owl.

TUP AND MAY tried again to take me to the hospital. I float above myself, watching.

TUP CAME TO our bed last night. We do not sleep.

We have routines here. Everything must still be done. Tup feeds and milks. I run the separator, then make breakfast while Tup loads the milk on the co-op truck. The children go off to school. Dishes. Laundry. Lunch for Tup. The tractor drones back and forth, back and forth in the fields, spreading the winter's manure. The cows mill around in the paddock, their legs crusted in mud while they wait for the pastures to dry. I stand at the window. I rebuild the fire I let go out in the kitchen.

"Do you want May to help getting the garden in?" Tup asked me.

But I shook my head no. I planted the seeds for the tender crops in the flats and laid them in the sun in the shed. Dodie wanted to help, but I got it done while she was at school. The children will be home for the summer soon. I am not ready.

I stooped, making my rows for the early crops, peas and cabbage

[66]

and spinach and carrots and beets. The soil was cold, my hands were cold. The spring sun weak on my back. This is the same soil.

Sweep. Sterilize the milk buckets. Scrub out the sink.

DODIE HOLDS BESTON's hand. I know these children are lost. I cannot find my way to them. I am wrong, I know this. I have always known my obligation to give my love. There is nothing here now. I feel a great wrenching when I see Dodie trying to comfort her brother. I mean to stand, to move to them, to draw them finally to my lap, to say words that will soften this for them. I mean to do this. I know we all hear that one terrible detonation, the explosion that took all of us. I watch them from this new land that is so far from the silenced house.

ONCE, SONNY ASKED if they could dig up the cat we had buried that spring to see what had happened to the body. I said yes.

Once, Sonny ran through the kitchen shrieking, with Dodie chasing him. *Get me! Get me!* he laughed.

Once, when we were all in the truck, Sonny had been quiet, not a word, and then suddenly he started to sing, a little song he learned at school. We all laughed, and he sang it through again and again.

"GO OUTSIDE NOW," I said to Dodie.

She stood still, waiting.

"I don't need your help today," I said. She went down the hall and I heard her climb the stairs. Beston followed her. Later, I watched them walk along the fences toward Tup in the west pasture.

I COOK WHAT we need for supper. There are five chairs at our table. I reach for five plates.

[67]

Sonny likes mustard on his meat loaf. Our kitchen is suddenly vacant and noisy with the scratching sounds of eating. I forgot to make coffee for Tup, but he said he didn't want any tonight.

What will we do with his chair? With the empty side of this table?

TUP TOLD ME this morning after the children left for school that he was drawing a bath for me.

"No. Do your work," I said.

"It will wait," he said.

He led me to the tub in the shed and put a towel on the clean floor. The boards are worn and scrubbed smooth as skin. Tup sat me on the side of the tub and pulled off my shoes and then my socks. I let him do this. He drew me up and unbuttoned my dress. His fingers were slow and clumsy. He lifted it over my head and put it in the basket to be washed. Then my slip, and my underwear. I could smell myself as I stepped out of my clothes. Tup did not talk to me. I was grateful. He held my hand as I stepped into the warm water. I lay back, the square of sun at the window coming behind my closed eyes. Tup sat in the chair. I could feel him, as if he were guarding me. He let me be. Later, before the water cooled, he knelt by the tub and slipped me down and poured water over my hair, his hand strong behind my neck. Tup's hands. Our old lives. I cried, the tears sliding down my neck to the water. He washed my hair and rinsed it and drew me up into a clean towel. The air was warm, spring coming.

Tup walked behind me up the stairs to our bedroom. He helped me dress, as if I were a child, buttoning a clean dress and brushing my wet hair.

"Doris," he said.

He led me to our bed, and we lay side by side with the window open.

THE SEEDS ARE coming up. All of this is so familiar, and so far away.

Tup cried last night, standing at the window in our room. His body heaved, a struggle to be freed.

The front room is closed. Its walls press out at us, a terrible pressure.

SUNDAY. TUP AND the children walked to the hill. No one told me and then they were moving across the field, Beston and Dodie holding Tup's hands. His fields are greening. He looked so small, tired and shuffling. It hurt me. My broken husband. A helpless man. Their shadows stretched thin and uncertain. They sat under the great pines, shimmering silver in the sun.

"We need to get a stone," Tup has said to me.

"No," I said. "No."

I can see that he has made a cross from wood, and laid a white rock on the raw soil. What would a marker say? Let the grass cover my son.

MAY CAME AND opened all the windows and swept and washed the floors. She cleared the sink counter and caught up on laundry. She is kindly, like Tup, but I did not ask her to come here.

Later, May said she would take the children to Vernon to the stores there. It felt very sad to me, but they arrived home pleased with their store-bought clothes, and relieved, I believe, to have had a break from home.

"Doris," May said, "I think it's time we go into Sonny's room. It has been three months. We could wash his bed linens."

I shouted at her, "No!"

She tried to move toward me to hold me in an embrace.

"Don't," I said.

Tup and May cornered me and told me there is a rest home in Grafton. No. I am doing what needs to be done here.

TUP AND BESTON cut the June hay this week. Beston wanted to help, and Tup said yes. My husband has been good to the children. I will come back to myself. The sickle bar jangled as it scissored back and forth, back and forth. Tup told me to include Dodie in my work in the garden today, and so she moved row to row beside me. She works too eagerly, as if she is afraid of me now. It started to rain so we came in with the baskets of pea pods. We sat together on the porch and shelled them, the crackle of the breaking pods all that bound us.

Dodie is twelve now. It is as if Sonny left and Dodie had to leap into his place. She does not resemble the child of last summer in any way, I see that. Her face is thin and strained. Her legs are long, and her feet have grown large. Her shoulders have widened, as if she prepared herself for all this. I see the woman in her now, a shadow coming.

"Mum," she said.

I could not answer.

"Mum," she said again. "Just answer one question."

I said, "I can't answer any of your questions, Dodie." I did not intend to sound harsh.

"But Mum."

We were quiet for a minute.

"Why did we want to play with the old gun?"

The peas rolled smooth and hard when I moved my fingers through the bowl, picking out bits of pod.

"Do you think he is in heaven?" Dodie asked. "Do you think he can hear us? Mum. We always played with that gun. Was it me? Mum, was it me?" and Dodie cried. "Did I do this?"

I stood and carried the peas to the kitchen. The blanching water was boiling and I poured the peas into the steaming pot. Dodie stood beside me, crying again and again, *Mum. Mum.*

TUP STOOD BEFORE me naked, stroking my hair. He is thin, emptied. What is here now will always be.

"Talk to me," he said. "Doris."

I turned away from his breath.

"You hate me for letting Sonny have that gun. But children have played with that gun in this house since before I was born," Tup cried. "Doris."

I know that my children and my husband are calling to me for help. I hear their voices, faint and indistinct, crying out to me from a distant shore. I want to respond. The wind and churning current carry me beyond them. When I turn to answer, all any of us hear is the roar of the storm.

DODIE ASKED IF Marion could come.

"There is no need for children to be coming here," I said.

Hovey and Daniel came here one day. If I had said no. The afternoon would have swerved into a different story if I had said what I knew was right.

Dodie asked if she could go to town to visit with Marion.

"You stay here," I said.

Tup argued for her, but then he said, "It's okay, Dodie. You stay here and play with Best."

ONCE, SONNY SAT on the well cover and braided long strands of sedge grass he had brought from the creek. He let Dodie and Beston watch him. It was a cloudy day, and windy, and the long grass blew gently across his thin legs, side to side. Sonny was a skinny boy. His pants hung loose from his bunched belt. His sharp little shoulder blades.

DANIEL AND HOVEY. Who took them home? Their childhoods gone, too, I know that.

SONNY HAD GOLDEN down on his arms, even when he was fourteen. We teased him. Baby duck, we said, and he was embarrassed and pulled his sleeves down. His skin was a child's skin, smooth and thin. He had a scar in his left eyebrow from falling off his bike. A scar under his chin from falling against the grain bins. A round, pecked scar on his right arm from his smallpox vaccination. A line across his right knee. On his collarbone. From what? I try to remember.

IN THE NIGHT, I woke Tup and asked, "Do you remember this?"

And I sang the lullaby Sonny heard as he nursed to sleep, and later Tup sang it to him in the dark as he went to sleep in his own little bed. My voice was uncertain, so unpracticed. *A candle, a candle, to light me to bed...*

Tup was still.

The moon is as sleepy as sleepy can be...

Tup said, "Don't. Don't do this, Doris. You can't do this."

I sang the whole song, it rising from far away, the aching sweet and unbearable.

"I WANT TO go in Sonny's room," Dodie said this morning.

"There is no need for that," I said.

Tup watched us. Beston moved to his father's side and waited.

My voice, I can hear, is hard now. I don't intend to be harsh with my children. Where have I gone?

ONCE TUP DROVE us all to the pond on our stream in Chase Mills. The children stripped off their clothes and jumped from the ledge, raising big spouts of water. Sonny was still a boy. This might have been the last summer he agreed to swim naked. After each jump, the children's heads popped above the surface, Sonny, Dodie, Beston. Their happy voices echoed against the old mill dam. *Watch this!* they cried. *Mum! Daddy! Watch this!* The water there is colored like tea from the tannin in all the fallen leaves. I could see their little legs churning to stay afloat, ghostly white limbs in the golden water.

Dodie

M UM ASKED ME to take Beston outside to play. She stood at the window looking out, and I waved to her, but she wasn't watching us. Daddy let us help him in the workshop stacking the new fence posts he was cutting. Best went into the paddock and lay in the sun against one of the sleeping cows.

I DREAMED LAST night that cars kept coming into the yard and too many people got out and came inside. I ran from room to room looking for Mum but I couldn't find her. All the doors were closed. It was sleeting outside.

BEST AND I went back to school today. We asked Mum and Daddy if we could stay home for another week, but they both said no. We don't want to talk to anyone, but no one wants to talk to us anymore, either. They made a wide circle around us. Daddy said that we need to remember that this town is a good town, that these are our friends, that they are just scared. I don't know what they could be scared of. They weren't there. Hovey and Daniel weren't in school. Mum and Daddy are asking too much of Best to go back so soon.

"Dodie, let us take care of Beston," Daddy said. "You have plenty to take care of yourself."

After school, we took our bikes down the road to the old stone bridge over the creek and sat with our legs hanging over. Beston held my hand the whole time. Daddy says we will forget some of this, that forgetting is a blessing hidden inside bad things. I don't know if Beston will ever forget. He was right beside Sonny, and something awful happened to him there. I can't tell the difference between forgetting and remembering. I think I was facing Sonny. Everyone was laughing and talking out loud. Beston wanted a turn. *My turn*, he called. But I wanted a turn, too. Did I reach across? I can see someone reaching across and I think it's me. A movie that jerks and rattles inside me.

When it started getting cold we went home and Daddy said, "Just the people I was hoping would come by. Will you help me feed the cows?"

It feels so much better when Daddy is with us. He tells us what to do. When we sit down on the porch after supper, he holds my hand. And Beston's hand. Mum doesn't like us to sit near her. She stays in the kitchen and stares. Daddy says that she is sick and will get better when she's had some time.

One thing I always loved in this house was lying in bed and knowing that each of us was there, in our place, while the dark came into our rooms and bound us together for the night. Sonny in his room, Beston in his, Mum and Daddy in theirs, me in mine. No one had to stand guard. Now we all do. Some nights I go to Mum and Daddy's door and look in. Mum lies straight in bed next to Daddy. He isn't touching her hair, she isn't lying across his legs. Some nights Daddy is already in Beston's room and Mum lies on her side facing the wall, her back to me. I wait, hoping she will sense me there and lift the covers and call me to her.

I WATERED THE seedlings in the shed to help Mum, and when I told her she just nodded. This time she let me hang out the laundry with her. I shook each thing out and handed it to her.

When we were done, she said, "Thank you, Dodie." Then she stood looking at me. She wears the same clothes each day. "Thank you," she said. "Now you go play."

On Saturday I sprinkled and ironed the clothes. I set up the board myself, and gathered all the clothes from the basket in the kitchen, still left from before. In the bottom I found two of Sonny's shirts and a pair of pants. I could feel the sharpness in my chest, and it wouldn't go away. I found Mum sterilizing the milk separator and held them out to her. She looked from me to my hands and to me, and then she reached slowly across and pulled them from me and turned away. I wanted to ask for them back, to bring them inside and sprinkle them and put them in the cold bin in the refrigerator and later open the damp pile and I would spread each sleeve tight and straight and the iron would hiss across the plaid cloth saying *yes, yes, yes* and I would turn the sleeve over and then the cuffs and the collar and the button placket and the left side, then the right side, the sun out on a nice morning and the iron heavy and balanced and sliding across the cloth the way it always does. I would walk up the stairs with each pile, Best's and mine and Mum's and Daddy's and then Sonny's, into his open room and I would lay his things in his drawers with all his other clothes that I know by heart and I would go back downstairs and put the hot iron on the sink to cool and take down the creaking ironing board and hang it back in the cellar stairway and Sonny and Beston and I would have the rest of the day to play. We would ride down to the creek and see if the pickerel weed was blooming and we would lie in the cool damp grass and talk. Our creek would make its own talk as it made its way to us and past us and on, like a hymn.

IT WAS SLEETING that day. Hovey and Daniel came to play. We came in from the barn and Mum told us to take our boots off in the shed before we went into the front room.

The boys called out, laughing and shouting. Sonny was always the center, like a shining sun, drawing everyone to him. Calm, like Daddy.

We got the old gun we liked to play with, the gun Daddy and his brothers played with. *No, me!* yelled Hovey, or Daniel. *My turn!*

Or was it Beston? I see an arm reaching. But not mine. Was it? I don't know.

Mum says *God forsook us*. Forsook. God forsook us. But I don't think God knows anything about a broken old gun we have played with a hundred times, or what might come next.

Is that how we are forsaken?

I remember the tiny clatter of sleet against the big windows. Mum had turned the lamps on for us. The warm bright room held us against the cold and stormy day. We were happy, children playing. We didn't need to believe we were beyond the reach of harm. We didn't understand it is close to us every minute.

Once Sonny asked me if I believed in heaven. I said yes. In Sunday school we sang "Jesus Loves Me." Sonny's voice was full, carrying over the rest of us. Forsook.

DADDY SAYS TO say our prayers. *Our father, who art in Heaven, hallowed be thy name. Forgive us our trespasses. God bless Sonny and Mum and Daddy and Beston.*

No one sleeps in our house now. Mum stays down in the kitchen and Daddy goes in with Beston.

"Son," I hear Daddy say. "It's okay, Son. I'm here."

I go in, too, and Daddy lifts the covers and we all lie tight together. In the morning, Daddy has moved to Sonny's old bed, where Sonny was a little boy. I can feel us all awake before the light even comes. Beston holds my hand against his chest. Then Daddy climbs back in with us and I lay my head on his chest and listen to the roar of his heart.

Aunt May came to clean the house and change the beds and do laundry. She hugged me and asked, "Are you doing okay, Dodie?"

Mum watched us, then turned away. Sometimes I think she hates me because it was Sonny who died and not me. She would have traded me in a minute. I know that. I will always believe that.

The bindweed is curling through the tall grass along the barn.

The calves nurse, their sloppy wet sucking sounds coming across the pasture.

WHEN DADDY AND Best went out early to start cutting the hay, he said, "Doris."

She turned to look at him.

"Doris, Dodie is ready to work today. She can help you in the garden. Are the potatoes ready for hilling again? She's good at that." His voice was gentle, as if he knew he was asking for something arduous.

My mother studied me and said, "Let her play."

"No, Doris," he said. "You take her into the garden and let her work with you today." My father reached over and laid his hand on my mother's wrist. "You hear me, Doris? You let Dodie spend the day with you today."

We worked in the sun and wind, hilling up the potatoes and putting in more brush for the peas. It has been cold this summer and the garden is slow. The hens pecked in the rows as we moved along. Mum didn't talk with me. Bees hummed in the honeysuckle bushes, and the silent wind moved through the hayfields in waves. The sickle bar's jangle came across the fields to us, our farm.

"Take this to your father and Beston," Mum said.

I carried the bag with our lunch out to them beyond the creek. The new-cut hay lay over, glistening in the sun, and the air filled with its greenness. Daddy took us to the hill and we sat in the warm pine needles under the trees. It smelled good, the wind lifting the heavy pine resin into the hot air. Beston leaned against Daddy.

Daddy said again and again to him, "You are doing a fine job today, Son. That wind is a blessing, isn't it?"

We all watched for Mum in the garden, bent to her work, but she had gone inside. The yard looked empty, the hens just visible working along the pasture fence.

It felt good to be on the hill. Like a visit, a way to say to ourselves that what we all remembered from last summer, and every summer before that, really was, once.

Daddy said, "I've always thought that this is the prettiest place on the farm. It is a good place for us to come to."

Once, Sonny and Beston and I rode our bikes here. It was hot and windy. Big soft clouds raced on the wind and their shadows flashed, light dark light dark, all afternoon. I don't remember what we did first, but then we were lying in the sun on the hill among the grave markers and we had stopped talking because the day was so good. We let the clouds open and close the light and warmth of the sun on our bodies, the lift and fall that comes with sun and its absence, as if it were on a switch. I could feel my back laid out on the rough ground. I tried to name which cloud was causing this sudden darkness, but I could not. First the sun and the billows of white racing over our heads and then the shadow dropping over us as if we were falling out of the light, and then the sun again, too fast to predict, the chill and then the warmth again. I took the grass in my hands, an anchor, and I gave myself over, this shifting sense of brilliant sky and darkening earth, sky and earth, sky and earth, light and dark. I looked over at Beston and Sonny and saw that sometimes they were in light just as I slipped under the dark, and then here I was again and they were sliding into the dark shadow, and then here we all were, the great summer light. And I thought, I will remember this. This is beauty, and I am in it. I will remember this hour.

On this hot, sunny day with Daddy and Beston, this day without Sonny, we ate the food that Mum had packed and we stayed in the shadow of the huge pines. I asked Daddy if he cut hay with his father.

"Yes," he said. "That was a long time ago."

We know which marker is his father's, *Emmett Senter, died December 18, 1933, AE 53.* And his mother is here, *Eleanor Webb Senter,* who died in 1924 when Daddy was just about my age, and Sonny's age. We know these markers, a play place for me and my brothers, mysterious and quiet but nothing to be frightened of, familiar, mooring us to this farm. But here was my father, whose mother died when he was like me, and then his father, and now his son lying under a white wooden cross. I climbed into my father's lap as we sat, too big for this now, I knew, and he held me while I cried for him. For all of us.

"I'm sorry everyone died," I cried.

"Yes, I am, too," my father said.

Tup

THE RAIN SET in this morning. The cows were in, the pastures too muddy. The barn was heavy with their smells. I have rhythms here that rescue me. Pitch their manure to the outer aisles, scrape it down into the pit. My great-grandfather forged this manure fork. The handle is hardened smooth with the sweat and grip of five generations of Senter men. The cows are patient, standing off as I lean into their smooth sides to pitch out the soiled straw. They know me, and trust me. They give to me, and I give to them. I work hard. This is my barn.

These are my cows. These are my fields and pastures, my fences and creek. This is my farm. This is my family. This is my home. This is my wife, Doris. These are my children, Dodie and Beston. My son, Sonny, gone now.

My work. Shake out fresh hay into the racks. Swirl and dump the water from every bucket into the pit. Fresh water. Wash down the outer aisles. Sweep the center aisle. Restack the toppled bales in the lower loft. Study the feed and milk records for every cow. Check Trudy's left eye. Check Sally's front right hoof. Trim it back. Replace the light bulb over the grain bins. Check for signs of rats. Feed the cats some milk. Remember to tell Beston and Dodie we have two litters of kittens. Rub down the halters with saddle soap. Adjust the radio. The goddamned static will put these animals on edge. Change the oil in the tractor. Check the hydraulic fluid.

Straighten up the tools in the workshop. The rescue of order.

The rain thundered on the roof and echoed through the lofts as I worked. I moved to the open door and stood in the rain. Lightning flashed in the distance over the hill. The roll of thunder came slowly. The wind had picked up and drove the rain. Water dripped from my face, my hands. My hands that do the work that supports this farm and this family. My hands that enfold my children. My hands that touch my wife. My hands that laid out my son, bloodied and ravaged by a gun I allowed him, that laid out my son on the rug, my goddamned hands that lifted him to my chest, his mother moaning at the door. The rain beat against the roof. I stepped outside, pulling the door behind me against the storm, and I moved toward the darkening fields.

The gate swung heavy against the wet grass. The children were inside with Doris, the house closed and silent. I was without my jacket, my barn clothes soaked through. My wet pants pulled at my legs, as if to hold me close to home. The lightning came, and the thunder, closer now. The sky and the fields and the fences and the pines were all the same color, like an old photograph of something I was trying to recall. Water seeped inside my boots, my feet heavy. Across the fields, the creek, the west pasture, back away from the house, up the slope beyond the orchard. But here was the place Sonny shot his deer, the great blast that shocked his young body. There is no place on this farm that is without Sonny. The lightning came, and the rain, and the thunder moved toward me. I lay down above the orchard, my house and my barn so far away it scared me, distant and unknown, and I spread myself to this rage. It came. Doris had screamed across the fields as she ran for me that day, wild. *Sonny!* I heard her scream. *Sonny!*

Lightning seared the land. The rain beat upon my face, my chest, my groin. Thunder shuddered through me, and my cries were lost.

WHEN DODIE WAS born, at home in our bed, Sonny waited downstairs with May. He was just two years old. As soon as we invited him to see his sister, he wanted to hold her. I have always believed that something stitched them together in that moment. Sonny watched her without saying a word. And then he said, *My baby*. And he smiled, and our bed, our beautiful room, our home was filled with whatever this big thing is that has bound us all so closely. Love, but it is something more than that. Love, and light. It has always felt to me that Sonny brought light to the world.

And now what? I want to return that light, for my poor, poor wife, and my children.

THE LEAVES ARE coming on the trees.

I woke in the night and Doris was not with me. I left our bed and stood in the darkened hall. My wife sat in the kitchen with the lamp off, the glow from the lights in the barn softening the room. She sat stiffly, her shoulders straight and square, and stared into the dark. There was no tea, no open book, no handkerchief. I will remember this night, I thought. My wife. I am helpless.

I sat at the table with her. She let me take her hand, and we sat. Our house asleep, two children left to raise.

"We can do this, Doris," I said. She didn't look at me. "We will do this, Doris," I said.

"Yes," she said. "I know that."

Later, I said, "Doris, I will always love you."

Later, "Come to bed now," I said.

"I can't," my wife said to me.

"But Doris. This is all we have now. We need this."

She turned and looked at me, perhaps for the first time since it happened. "None of us can afford to need anything anymore," she said.

"That isn't a choice you get to make," I said. "You have a family, Doris. You have me. I need you. You need me. You need Dodie and Beston. These are your children. They need you. Come with me now."

And she followed me upstairs and into our bedroom. I led my wife to our bed and untied her robe. She lay down, and I beside her. The bed had cooled. I pulled her to my chest. I felt her silent tears slipping across my skin to the sheets. And my tears. She let me pull her hands under my chin, and the night slid on. Later, Beston called out, a sob that makes me feel each night that he has gone on alone as long as he can bear.

"I will bring him here to sleep with us," I had said the first night.

"No," she had said. "I can't."

And so I went to my son's room, with the little empty bed so still and neat beside us. When I rose in the morning, Doris was putting on her clothes. I stopped her, and offered her a different slip and dress. The sun was familiar, its big slanted blocks across our bed and floor starting the day.

SONNY'S HANDS LOOKED like mine when I was a boy. His fingers long and straight, his thumb joint large, suggesting already the man.

BESTON IS A lost boy. He follows me, mostly silent, trying to do the work Sonny was taking on. After breakfast I returned to the barn, and there was Best.

"Well, Son," I said. "It looks as if you are here just in time to give me some help."

I tried to sound as if this was a new kind of game shared between us. I reached for him but he said, in a voice that never existed before this season, "Please don't call me Son. You never called me that before."

He stood before me, somehow frightened and brave all at once. I stepped back, deeply stung, and then I understood that he was right. Son. Sonny. He is not and never can be Sonny. He can never be asked to become Sonny.

"Beston," I said, and I cupped my hand to his shoulder. It fit so easily in my palm. "Beston. Do you think you could throw down six bales of hay?"

There is no game here, not now. But he and Dodie are children still. No matter whether Doris can allow them that.

The cows were out in the east pasture, which drains early and already has good grass. The barn swallows swooped low with their chittering. Best threw down the hay and clipped the baling wire, two-handed on the cutters. The bales burst open, the tension always there until it is unloosed. And with the unloosing, the sweet, protected smell of the summer before. This will soon be the last of the hay we put up last summer. To everything now, there is the before and the after. The before feels like a dream, the now and the tomorrow demanding something we don't yet possess.

But the work requires us.

"Good, Beston," I said. "Let's get everything set up for this evening when the girls come back in. Give everyone a flake of hay. Shake it out well in the racks."

And then I said, "From now on, let's make this your chore each afternoon after school. Right now, we'll sweep, and then I could use some help loading the manure spreader. After that, you can go find Dodie or stay with me."

He stayed, sweeping the aisle carefully, and then we brought the tractor and spreader below the barn. Steam rose from the manure pit in the cold of the morning.

Beston leaned against me on the tractor as I filled the bucket with the winter's manure and dumped it in the spreader. His hands wrapped around my shoulders so I had to be careful not to move my arms too much and make him think he shouldn't hold on so hard. It comforts me, this holding on, and should not. I need to be the comfort for my children and wife.

LAST WINTER THERE was a storming day when the children and Doris and I headed out to the hill to sled. The no-school fire horn had blasted from Four Corners at dawn, and we knew without talking that it was going to be a holiday for all of us.

After chores, I said, "Games in the front room or sledding?"

And the children yelled, "Both! Both!" as I knew they would.

Doris smiled her happiness, the day handed over entirely to her family. We spent a lot of time dressing in boots and outer pants and waxing the sled runners in the yard, and then we trudged in a line across our fields and the creek and the west pasture and through the orchard, me breaking the route and then Sonny and Dodie and Beston, and Doris holding guard in the rear. Doris was always a very good playmate, ready for fun and knowing, too, when it was time to haul things back to calm.

The snow was heavy in the air and deep, and our boots squeaked with every step in the perfect silence. The land I knew so well lay under that heavy white cloak, mysterious now, apart from me and my ownership, my husbandry. The long sleds slid smooth, humming behind us on their skim of wax. Sonny was overflowing with the happiness he always felt when he was outside, and he sang out bits of songs that we all jumped into. Our voices carried across the still fields, the fence posts lining out ahead and the house and barn behind marking the vast white country as ours.

What comes now from that day is our voices, like bells in their cold clarity, and the light. What comes now is Doris on her sled, Sonny and Dodie and Beston clinging together in front, Doris's feet catching the snow like small brakes to keep things under control. Her laughter rising, released in full trust of what might come. And now I see that the hill we loved for sledding is also, of course, the place where our son lies among the men and women of our family long dead. This sickens me suddenly, such transgression. Play and death confused. Winter is going to come again to this place, and my son will lie beneath the snows, further removed from me. How can Sonny's laughter and Doris's terrible screams on that day bind themselves equally to this land? How can I slide back before that moment and keep from my child an old gun I never feared? But these are the things I tell Doris she cannot afford to consider.

Beston was there, on that tractor beside me, his arms wrapping my shoulders, his watchfulness tensing his little body, and I know it is my one and single duty now to be present, to help this boy make the fearsome and hurried journey from child to man. And Dodie. On her own unflinching course. And Doris, the mother, swept away by the flood, and believing what of her husband's failure? These thoughts wait for the unbearable dark of night.

I throttled up hard on the tractor and told Best to hold on. His arms tightened and we scooped the next steaming load into the spreader. By midday we had loaded and spread five loads and we returned to the house for noon dinner, the late spring sun hanging bright and warm above us. The front fields were nearly spread.

"You and Dodie go play now," I said. "I can work alone for the afternoon. Tomorrow, we'll spread the fields across the road."

He nodded and attached himself to Dodie. She cleared the table with her silent mother and filled the dishpan with hot water.

"Help me do these up, Best," she said, and he took up each dish and wiped it and placed it on the table for his sister to lift to the shelves.

I should have made my way back to my work. But Doris sat watching, and I stayed for a while, holding her hand in my lap. The ordinariness of a day, an almost impossible charge to get through this. If there were no Dodie, no Beston? The obligation would lessen, and Doris and I might each choose to succumb. But there is no choice. Our brave and desperate children washed the dinner dishes. The sun flooded our kitchen as it always has at midday. My wife's hand rested in mine, in supplication or abnegation, I could not know.

Later, I saw Dodie and Beston making their familiar way to the creek. When the day was closing they followed the cows home for milking and they watched them pull at the fresh loose hay Beston had laid in for them in the morning. I did my work, the washing of hands, the heat and weight of udder and milk. The shadows lengthening, the swallows returning for the night.

My father did not know Sonny. They lie side by side, strangers on this shared land.

DORIS HAS ALWAYS said that I live inside my mind too much. There is no sanctuary there now.

All that can help us is finding a way to allow the past and my terrible error to ride down this pitiless river. Finding a way, Tup and Doris and Dodie and Beston Senter, to turn for home.

SUMMER HAS COME. Dodie has been reading to Beston in the evenings after supper. The door to the front room stays shut. We sit now on the porch, an outpost. Twilight comes to us with all its sadness, and we speak out loud as a declaration, like petitioners making another appeal. But Dodie, every night, calls Beston to the settee and makes room for me between them. She has grown this long summer, and I see Doris more and more in her determined, energetic gestures. Last night, after doing dishes, we settled around *The Last of the Mohicans*. Dodie hesitated at some words, but her brother was patient. Mostly silent, as ever. Dodie spread the book across her lap so Beston could see the occasional illustrations. The children allowed me to hold their hands, or lay my arm across their shoulders. As I listened, bats flicked after insects in the dim evening light beyond the screens.

Doris does not join us anymore during these evenings on the porch. But last night she came in, an insubstantial body somehow, and sat in her worn old chair, her face turned to us as if she, too, were listening.

In the quiet before Dodie started the next chapter, Doris said suddenly, "I know that I cost my son his life. I know I have been very..."

In her hesitation we all watched her, the storm across her eyes. She said, "I have not been present to any of you as I should be. As I want to be." She looked out into the dark yard, and then to her hands in her lap. "This is harder than I ever could have imagined," she said. "We think we are going to be heroes. I see that I am no hero. I am very sorry for that, because I know what each of you needs from me and how little of that you are receiving. I will come back to myself. Soon. I will come back to you all."

Dodie said, so quick to comfort us, "We know, Mum."

Beston lay back against my chest.

"Doris," I started to say.

She turned to me abruptly. "Don't say it, Tup. Whatever it is you think is going to help me, don't say it."

Dodie and Beston watched my face, and then Dodie said, "Chapter seven." Her voice was small.

Doris didn't speak again.

When we went up the stairs to bed, Dodie moved ahead of us as she does each night now, turning on the light in Beston's room before going into her own. Doris followed us. I said goodnight to each of the children and walked in the dark to our bedroom. When I lay under the summer blanket, Doris reached for my hand.

"I am sorry," she said.

Insects clicked at the screens. The moon had come nearly full, already in another cycle.

"I am sorry for everything," she said.

Far across the fields and pastures, across the creek, on the lonely hill lay our son. Under us, around us, our house breathed its great and unbearable sadness.

I ONCE GAVE Sonny a crook knife for carving. It was very sharp and he understood that I was saying we trusted him. It wasn't his birthday or Christmas. He was very pleased and sat immediately at the table with a short piece of green apple wood. I gave him my leather palm and showed him how to draw the knife toward his hand. He sat for a couple of hours, so serious and earnest, making his mother a wooden spoon, the curls of glistening wood peeling up and away as he worked. She still has it, an uneven and unbalanced tool he sometimes pulled from the drawer and laughed at, though proud.

DORIS AND I lay awake.

"Come with me," I said, taking her hand in mine.

She followed me down the hall to Sonny's closed door.

"Come in, Doris. It's time."

I opened the door. The cold, dull air spilled out as if it had been pressing for release. A vague shadowy light from the barnyard made the bed seem too small. Sonny's sweater was still over the chair, four months since he laid it there. I felt negligent, careless, answerable. Doris turned away but I held her.

"It's time, Doris. Be with me."

But she was gone, closing the door as she went. I stood at my son's window and watched the world he knew from this room, the great elms in front, the dirt road running past, the fields across the road with their high ledges. We dragged a dead calf there last spring during castrations. Sonny was thirteen years old. Now that felt shamefully young, a boy so sharply chastised by his angry father. There is no escaping. What we do stays in the world. We hope that we are forgiven. Who am I asking for forgiveness? The son I allowed to play with an old gun? God? Doris? Dodie and Beston? And what does it matter, now, if any of them forgive me? We live our days hoping we do not harm, and then we are left to reckon with ourselves.

I opened the window wide, the cool damp air, smelling of grass and Doris's roses, spilling into the deadened room. A cleansing, finally.

I sat in the gloomy light for a long time, a man in a boy's chair. Sonny's small objects, brought in from the wild to be studied and exhibited on the shelves we made. The morning light would show the imperfections of a boy's efforts, but in this unlit time there seemed perfect order. Finally I rose, closed the window to the night's calls and stirring air. I closed Sonny's door and moved down the hall past my sleeping children. Doris was awake, not waiting for me, I knew. Waiting, instead, for what? The soft nighttime light of the moon off the fields glowed in our room. I lay close to Doris and pulled her hand to me. I could see that her eyes were open, the strain of her face.

"Doris."

I kissed her hand, and then moved on top of her and kissed her neck and her throat. She closed her eyes and lifted her arms to me.

"Thank you, Doris," I said and we kissed, uncertain after so long.

I stroked her leg and we kissed, and her breasts, the crushing sweetness of memory, her breasts, her belly, us in our bed, and she wrapped me with her legs and held me tight to her hips, and we remembered how to move and found each other's mouths and we were for a few moments on a different river and this necessity was from our bodies and our exhausted hearts, and our fields reflected their light to us, our room, my wife.

"Doris," I said, "Doris," and then she cried out her anguish and she sobbed, my wife holding me to her hard and crying.

I quieted her, "Hush, Doris, hush."

And her legs fell from me and her arms and she rolled away from me, lost again. I lay on my back, the sheets tangled at our feet, aware of the cool dark air that blew down to us from the hill, across the fields and pastures with its own unceasing news. We lay apart and the night circled on.

SONNY. SOMETIMES THE summer wind hums in the rafters of the barn and I hear in it his voice calling. *Mum! Daddy!*

I am here, I call back. *I am here, Son! What do you need?* The foolishness, a man alone in his old barn.

BESTON CALLED OUT to me in the night. I lay in the little bed with my son, my clothes twisted and hot, and he lay with his head on my shoulder, his breaths small and uneven like a calf learning to live outside its mother. I drifted into thoughts I could not fend off and then, later, I heard Dodie come down the dark hall. She slid the covers back on the other bed and I felt her hand reaching for me across the little aisle. With Best on my shoulder and Dodie holding my hand, all of us awake, I felt marooned in a terrible stillness.

Finally my children slept. I rose carefully, pulling the blankets up for the nighttime cool that was setting in. It was late. I checked my bed and it was empty. I looked out over the fields and orchard and pastures, the fence posts standing in the dim moonlight like helpless little sentinels in the wide space. I studied the tractor road to the hill, the slope under the old trees, hoping to see my wife making her way finally to our son. But no one moved in that place. The house was absolutely still. I listened for Doris downstairs and heard only the yelp of foxes running the creek.

I found her sitting on the floor in the hall outside the door to the front room. She turned to me when I approached, her face distorted with grief. I reached for her to stand and she pulled away sharply.

"Come to bed, Doris," I said. My voice was too harsh, but I felt harsh at that moment. "Your children are upstairs," I said. "Come."

Doris tucked her head between her knees and a thin high wail filled the echoing hallway.

"Doris!" I said, my voice hushed for my sleeping children. "Stop right now!"

Her body shook with her cries.

"Doris!"

I tried to lift her to her feet, to make my wife stand to her purpose but she slumped back against the wall.

I leaned down to her and pulled her face to mine. "You listen to me, Doris Senter." My voice frightened me, a loud hiss tamped down tight. "You have obligations in this home! I am goddamned exhausted from trying to do your job here. Goddamned to hell tired of it. Do you think you are the only one suffering? Do you?

[94]

Do you for Christ's sake? Goddamn you!" My voice had become a wail like hers.

I grabbed her arm and lifted her from the floor, whispering low and hard, "What happened to you? Where the Christ have you gone? You either walk away from this room and get on with the life you agreed to make in this house with these remaining children or you walk into it and fight God to your end. I don't care which the hell you do but it isn't going to be this, Doris. Do you hear me? It isn't for Christ going to be this."

I pulled her up the stairs and along the hall to our room, and she resisted and cried. I pushed her hard onto the bed and she sat covering her face with her hands as if I might strike her, and I was enraged.

"Don't you hide from me! You are my wife! My wife! Goddamn it, my wife! You do not get to do this!" And I loomed over her, and suddenly I wondered if I was going to hit her, and I pushed her down across the bed and turned and walked out of our room.

"Tup!" she called. "Tup!" her cry faint across the sea between us.

I turned back and yelled, "Don't you ask me to give you one goddamned thing more, Doris! Where are your children? What do you offer them? What, Doris? You make Dodie raise Beston and make me take care of everyone! I am done!"

She rose to me and cried, "Where do you think my child is?"

I took her arms hard and pulled her to my face and said, "And you want to join him! Well, I don't give a goddamn if that's what you do. Do it. You are the walking dead in this house. You want to go join Sonny on that hill? Then go. I don't care. I'll raise your other two children myself. It will be easier than what we are all doing here now."

I remember saying this. I said this to my wife. My children heard this. Our house trembled in the quiet summer night. What we do and what we say stays.

I WALKED THE shadowed fields, my fields. Our fields. Doris and I made this farm. It was already cricket time, and they filled the air with their small entreaties. As my legs parted the grass, they silenced, a pool of quiet, and then I passed and they returned to their incessant work. I could not walk to the hill. I lay back in the cool wet grass by the creek and watched the clouds drifting over this darkened land. Stars winked and blurred. Slowly I calmed, and then came fear and shame. I had not known that I was capable of doing such harm.

The creek followed its unchanged course. Only the small lamp was on in the house in the distance, such a tentative claim. The crickets allowed me to enter the constantly shifting pool of quiet as I walked home. Doris met me at the kitchen door, her night-gown and bare feet reminding me of another life. She reached for me, and we held each other, standing in the fragile light, our arms enclosing. Doris. Tup. The words I said will be here between us forever, I know that. We love each other. We are suffering. There is only one road, and we have barely started.

PART THREE

....

AFTER

There will be rest, and sure stars shining
Over the rooftops crowned with snow,
A reign of rest, serene forgetting,
The music of stillness holy and low.

Sara Teasdale

[1950]

Doris

I HAVE NOT entered Sonny's room since last year. I have no need to do that again.

Tup had urged me to put this behind me, a breaching finally. I stood outside the door for a long time. I could smell the cold neglect even from there. The door opened noiselessly, no roar of lament.

The winter light filling the room was grayed, as if the light had stood still since that frigid, sleeting day. My son made his bed the morning he died. He tucked in his sheets and blankets. The nights were still cold then. He needed two blankets.

My son leaned over this bed and pulled his covers tight. My son was fourteen years old. He folded the cover over his pillow. I turned the cover back and drew Sonny's pillow to me, breathing him in. He was not there. I pulled the sheets open and sat on the bed, touching the place my son had slept until six o'clock that last morning. He could not know that. He could not have known. Is there rest at all in that? He could not have known.

Over the chair by Sonny's desk, his green sweater. A casual toss, saying *I will be back.*

One of the sweaters I knitted. So many sweaters. So much attention paid, day after day. How could I have failed at that one moment to pay attention? I knit sweaters stitch by stitch by stitch and still I allowed my son to die. The last sound my child heard was a blast that obliterated all of us. Did he have time to be afraid? I believe he had time to understand everything.

Sonny's small, careful handwriting. *Clemmys guttata.* Spotted turtle. *Solanum dulcamara.* Nightshade. *Celastrina ladon.* Spring azure butterfly. *Pyrrharctia isabella.* Banded woolly bear. There is perfect order here. A containment, a bulwark. Safety. *Mantis religiosa.* Praying mantis. Forgive me, God. God forgive me.

The large squares of light swung across the floor. It has grown dusty here, layers settling, sediments, the slow entombment. I opened his window for a minute and felt the air stir, Sonny's breath blowing away, and I closed it again quickly.

Tup uses this room now.

WINTER HAS PERSISTED long this year.

Tup works all day whether there is work to do or not. I will feel better when the sun returns. The rounds of gardening and canning and new chicks and painting will help.

Dodie and Beston are at May's for several days for their school break. It wasn't necessary.

When they are away, I am aware of Tup in the night, awake in Sonny's room. I am sure he feels my presence, too. A current runs between us, never quiet, never allowing us any ease. We are calmer with the children here, when the coming of night brings the sleep we are due.

On these mornings, Tup and I sit quietly at the kitchen table alone. There has been no sun for weeks. The woodstove hisses its heat. I provide a good breakfast. Tup sits over his coffee, talking to me about what needs to be done for the day. Sometimes he reaches for my hand and we sit in the heaving room. We have been here for so long tending the ruptured ship. Heaving. Heaven. "Heavy," I say to Tup. "Heaving. Heavenly," I say. "Heat. Heart."

"Doris," he says, and I quiet.

"Come with me to the barn and help me with the milking," he says, and brings my heavy coat, but I have work to do in the house and he knows it. I need to do the dishes and clean out the ashes from the stove and sweep the kitchen and the shed and wash the clothes and hang them on the porch if there is rain or snow and scrub the wood floors upstairs. But today all that will have to wait. I need to empty the drawers in the bureaus and wash them out and refold the clothes. There is too much to do when Dodie is not here. Tup sits again and watches me as I clear the pantry shelves onto the table. "You did those yesterday, Doris," he says. "Leave them alone today."

Tup works in the barn. He doesn't come in for noon dinner anymore. Each day when the children return from school, they do their chores. Then Dodie and I cook a supper and we sit together at the table, the children and Tup making conversation about their day. The dark returns.

Tup takes his children into the front room to read or take out a game. I prefer to sit in the quiet on the stoop. I prefer to walk in the yard, the big light making heavy shadows of the house and barn that lie like rooms I can enter or not, rooms of light and rooms of dark.

Dodie

Beston works with Daddy in the barn. I help Mum in the house. Rather, I try to get my mother to help me in the house. There is too much work here. If I look in the mirror over my bureau, I see that I am like her. We used to sit all together on the sofa in the front room and go through the old photographs in the albums. Mum had a coat once with a big shawl collar. She was about my age. She is looking straight at us, as if she knew even then that we would be this family, as if all she was doing was waiting for us to come. She is alight, attentive, anticipating the happiness that she expects to arrive. When I look in the mirror, I feel a rush of anger. The young girl in the photograph and the one in the mirror have the same features, but in me there is no light burning, waiting for joy. When my teacher or May or Mr. Whalen at church says to me, "Dodie Senter, you look just like your mother," I remember the expectant girl in the coat and wonder what it is they see in me.

No one takes pictures now. If they did, if someone asked my mother to face the camera in her coat, she would look like a forsaken woman. Her eyes look inward. She cannot see me.

Sleet today. There is no school. Here is the awful gray light, the rapid little ticking against the windows that stays forever in my ear. Daddy is in from the barn. We are all restless, moving room to room as if we are praying at stations, praying that this story will have a different ending this time. *Once upon a time. A sleeting day. One day, it was sleeting and Sonny and Beston and Dodie played in the front room with their friends, Daniel and Hovey, and their mother heard laughter as she worked in the kitchen. On that day, the children made up a game of scouting a new continent with its tall*

*swaying trees and graceful animals that roamed the high meadows
and Sonny was the leader. He took his travelers off to the new world
and then they returned home, heroes with this new knowledge. On
that sleeting day, five children played and the day closed quietly, and
the dark came, and their father returned from the fields and drove
their friends safely home. Over supper, the children told their parents what they saw in that faraway country, and they sat in the yellow
lamplight in the front room, and then they slept, and then the next
morning came, like any other.*

BESTON IS TEN years old.

He is silent. He smiles all the time, no matter what is being said
or not said. He is helpful and kind and never argues back. His
room is very neat. He reads a great deal, books we get from the big
Vernon library when Aunt May takes us there. After supper in the
evening, Beston and I do the dishes while Mum walks in the yard
or sits on the shed steps. When Daddy says, "All right, my young
soldiers, is it a game or books tonight?" Best asks me what I want
to do, and whatever that is he joins in. We have become very good
friends. Does Beston look in the mirror and wonder who he sees?
No one dares to say to him, *Beston Senter, you are looking more
and more like your brother, Sonny.*

Daddy moved the shelves and all Sonny's specimens into Best's
room last fall. That was when Daddy started sleeping in Sonny's
room each night. Daddy said he thought that Best might like to
have the shelves and specimens for himself. That is possible, although I believe that Daddy did not want to see them last thing
every night before he turned off the lamp on the desk. At any rate,
they have suited Best. He has the same eye as Sonny did, and brings
home objects to name and study. He practices Sonny's small handwriting and makes the little cards for each one. *Coprinus comatus*
and *Amphipoda gammaridea* and *Carex appalachica*. Shaggy mane
and pond scuds and sedge grass. All fall, we wandered the fields

[104]

and orchard and creek and found what pleased him, and then he brought the treasures home and he made order here. Mum cleans out the closets and the drawers all over the house, day after day, but she does not touch these shelves. She does not touch Sonny's room.

AND I AM fourteen.

MY FATHER IS very tired. His light stays on late in Sonny's room.

Once, not long ago, on a Sunday afternoon in late winter like this, when the light still left early, Daddy teased Mum until she agreed to do a play for us in the front room. We heard them upstairs laughing and whispering so we could almost hear what they were saying, Daddy's voice low and soft and excited, Mum's high, giggling. Sonny and Best and I stood at the bottom of the stairs until Daddy called out, "Okay, you three!" and the whole house filled up that day with our happiness. Mum had on a pair of Daddy's pants rolled up to her knees and bunched at her waist in a belt, and a big blue church hat from the shelf in her closet. Daddy wore only his long underwear and his father's pocket watch, which he lifted and looked at often. Their lines were nonsense. They moved around the room as if they were pirates on a ship, or maybe pilgrims lost in the desert, and they sang old songs we all knew from the radio in the barn, what they could remember, and we three watched from the sofa and thought it was wonderful, our mother and our father free and in love. That afternoon must still be held in these walls. Stories don't go away, I have learned that. Whatever happens is with us forever. Whatever has ever happened in this house and in this room is with us forever. That other life endures in these walls, all of it. We are a family. We love each other deeply. We will return to ourselves. We hold to that longing.

My father has a very good singing voice. He used to sing along with Caruso on the radio in the barn. He said the cows liked Caruso very much. Once, when I was little, I came into the barn and saw him standing still, his arms at his sides, silent, as Caruso's voice filled the great empty barn, and my father was weeping. It didn't scare me. Daddy says that our love for beauty is one of God's greatest gifts. Sometimes now I hear Daddy and Beston singing a song as they work, Daddy's big gentle voice and Best's high girlish voice, and from the kitchen or the barnyard their song muffles and then emerges, quiets and then lifts as they turn, bend, move down the aisle, and I hear the song like a flock of swifts shifting in the light, silver-dark, silver-dark, and all the joy of this farm returns for a few minutes.

I HAVE MADE myself three skirts this winter from wool Aunt May and I bought at the Dunbar Mill in Grafton. She has taught me that I should always buy good cloth, even if that means I have one less skirt for school. She showed me how to drape the cloth from the bolt over my arm to see how it hangs, and to hold it to the light to see how dense the weave is. I looked at zippers and buttonholes in the skirts Mum had made before and I figured out how to put them in myself. I am quite proud wearing these skirts I made without help, and I like the feeling of the smooth wool swaying from the pleats when I walk.

I have also made a light wool shirt for Daddy, which he wears when he changes into his house clothes. The button placket bunches some but he has never said anything but a very pleased thank you. I also made a new flannel nightgown for Mum, which she needed very much. I haven't tried to make a school shirt for Best, and May is careful to keep the right clothes for him in his bureau drawers. This is all work I enjoy, especially the quiet sound of the machine running its thread through the good cloth. I like to feel Best and Daddy reading on the sofa behind me, the quiet, measured hum of my sewing filling in all the new silences of this old house, the breathing rhythms of the sewing machine in this room of so much held breath.

Mum finds it hard to have Best and me near her. She started allowing me again to spend the night sometimes at Marion's. Marion has a gray plastic radio on her bureau and we listen to the station out of Portland. We take off our shoes and make up dances, pretending we are girls at a dance at the high school and the boys are lining up hoping we'll pick them. Marion has no father. He died in France when she was seven. I knew her then, but somehow I can't remember learning that he died, or that Marion was having trouble. I am only lately thinking about this. She was my best friend, and still whatever she and her mother had to come to bear, it was theirs alone. No one can be of help.

Marion plays the piano. She is teaching me a simple little song by Mozart. Marion told me it is part of an opera he wrote when he was just our age. I think it is very beautiful when Marion's mother plays it, and Marion is very good. I feel like a girl from the back country. I love this music, and want to play it in its beauty. But I seem much better at planting gardens and canning peas. I have spoken to Daddy about this, and he told me that he will consider buying me a piano if I choose to stay with the effort. A piano in the front room. I think Best would like that very much.

Daddy spoke to me last night about Mum. I have dreaded these words, but they came finally as a relief.

Winter is closing and the hard work of running the farm will start up again. We will be setting the early seeds in the flats soon, and then the garden needs to be turned and planted. Then the weeding, the watering, and then the harvesting and preserving through the summer and fall. It is time to put thirty chickens in the freezer. Mum makes lists and lists of the chores she thinks she will do, but only tends to shelves and drawers. The house has grown dirty, although I keep it tidy, and everything will need to be washed and aired. The floors need to be scrubbed down hard and oiled. The outhouse needs its paint refreshed, and the kitchen. The yearling pigs will be slaughtered and butchered and put in the freezer. The flower beds have been neglected for these two years and should be dug out hard. Mum's flowering quince and mock orange and lilacs haven't been pruned and are overtaking the yard. The root cellar is blooming in mold in the corners from lack of attention and needs to be bleached and dried out to start fresh, or we will lose this coming year's potatoes and carrots and turnips and cabbage.

"A woman is needed on a farm," my father said to me. "There is always work here for a woman. A woman who is at home all day."

"I can do this," I told him.

"When, Dodie?" he asked me. "You are in school. You are a fourteen-year-old girl in school."

He was scared, and his fear filled me. "I can do it," I insisted.

"When?"

"After school and on weekends," I said.

"And when would you be a girl, a growing girl with time to yourself?"

"I don't need time, Daddy," I said. "I can do this work. I'll quit school. I can run this farm. I can do Mum's work."

"You're not quitting school!" Daddy yelled, turning from me. We stood in the shed, the door open to the sunny yard, the cold air of winter still caught inside. "Jesus Christ," he said. "You are not quitting school, Dodie. How does a thought like that even come to you?"

And when he turned back he was crying, and I was not certain I could fill the place of his wife on this farm. He did not stop the tears. This will be the hardest moment of all of this, I thought, my father's fear and dread larger than anything I might fix, no matter how powerful my longing to correct all that has happened since that gray, sleeting afternoon when we lifted our eyes to this new terrain. This land on which my father cannot run his farm without the help of his wife, without the help of a son coming of age, a son who loved the work and the land and the sight of the cows grazing in the late afternoon before they turned for home to be milked and the sweet clean order of the barn. His wife, his son, and I am neither.

"I'll get Mum to do more," I said.

But he shook his head and said, "Your mother has gone inside herself, Dodie, and does not want to come out."

"I think she is getting better," I said, and my father moaned and drew me to his chest.

He held me, his arms the same as I have always known and the chaff caught in the wool of his barn coat the same and the sweet smell of cow and milk the same, but my father now weeping.

"Daddy," I tell him. "Daddy. It's not too much. We can do the work. I can do everything that needs to be done, Daddy. I know everything Mum does on this farm. Daddy. Best can help. I'm going to tell Mum what she needs to do."

The sun slanted across the old worn floor of the shed. The hens, their black feathers iridescent blue in the light, pecked in the new grass starting to come in the yard. My father's tears wet my face. He stood away from me and ran his palm across my cheek and then his own.

I RISE BEFORE the sun each morning when I hear Mum and Daddy say hello in the hall. I made a list, and I am making my way through. It is not as hard as Daddy thought it would be. School will be out soon for summer. There is satisfaction in learning to be the woman of a house. Beston is adrift with me so busy. He is just a little boy. Daddy holds him close every night while they play a game or read, and they work together every day, even when I know it takes longer for Daddy with Best there. Sometimes Daddy tells him to help me in the garden, to drag away brush or hang laundry with me. He needs a stool still to reach the lines, and so I tease him. I like his presence. He is very quiet, but he smiles easily and it feels at times as if we are still children together. Sometimes while I work in the garden I see him walking down the tractor road to the creek, a skinny boy all alone.

Mum still does the cooking, and makes endless order in the closets and drawers. She is there somewhere, Doris Senter. My mother. It is hard now for me to remember. Sometimes I feel angry with her, and then I understand that she must feel a greater anger with me, that she must know what happened in that room. I believe that is why she keeps herself so apart. I would like to ask Daddy about this, about how I might be forgiven. I do not know if forgiveness can ever come to me.

But the work is before us, Daddy and me, and we match ourselves to those rhythms.

There is no talk of forgiveness or condemnation.

"We are stealing your childhood from you," he said to me. *I believe I stole your son from you*, I want to say.

There is a great deal of time for this kind of thinking while I work. I did not understand that men and women at their work have so much time to consider the questions that trouble the night. I remember that the long hours of quiet while we used to play were like light pouring down on us, a river of wonder without end. We did not yet have thoughts we struggled to avoid.

But I have a very good garden started. We are already eating spinach and beet greens. Daddy asked Carl to help with the pig slaughter, and then we all stood at the bench along the back side of the shed and the men cut the meat and I wrapped it, and Beston carried it, piece by piece, to the chest freezer. He is always anxious, wanting to be of help. I had to repack it, but it got frozen in good time and will feed us through the year. Mum stood holding her elbows in each hand, watching silently from a distance. I make sure she wears clean dresses that I keep ironed, and aprons. I use her aprons now, like a housewife. My mother's golden hair slips loose from her bun and strands flicker across her face in the breeze. She does not sweep them back. For a few days after Daddy runs a bath for her and washes her hair, it catches the light and shines.

I have learned to bleach the root cellar and oil and buff the floors and sand and paint the outhouse and the walls of the kitchen. Daddy stood on his stepladder and painted the ceiling for me. I do my homework before bed, and stay in from our recess if I need to catch up. I am a good student and my marks haven't slipped. I am able to do all that needs attention here. Daddy sometimes says to Mum, "Our daughter is a very big help, isn't she, Doris?" and Mum nods. I have been practicing whistling like Mr. Britton does when he works at the granary. I sing to myself and whistle and hum while I work. I am afraid I will become silent, too. I refuse to be a silent mother, no matter what ever happens to me. No matter what my child might do, I will tell her that she is good. I will hold my daughter, no matter what she may ever have done.

Mum and Daddy argued when Daddy finally put a stone on Sonny's grave. Mr. Goodale carved the letters into the rock. *We thank our God upon every remembrance of you.* Beston and I stood with our father while he told Mr. Goodale what he wanted on the stone. Daddy was very calm, withheld, and Mr. Goodale accorded my father that grace. *Every remembrance.* Forever.

Mum had yelled, "You will not weigh my son with stone. You will not place that weight on him."

"Doris," my father said, tender, always, the remnants of love. "Sonny lies in an unmarked grave," he said. "It has been two years, Doris. It is not right."

"The words are for us," he said. "Let's find words that bring us comfort."

"I have wondered," he said, "about saying *Blessed are the pure in heart.* Doris, we owe this to Sonny," but Mum slapped her hand hard on the table and slammed the shed door and did not come back inside until after we all went to bed. I don't think Daddy goes out after her anymore.

In the night I heard them talking in Mum's room, and the next morning Daddy asked Beston and me what we would like to say. "It's like a message you are sending to your brother," he said, "like a note you are writing to him."

"We don't go to church now," I said. "Why would we talk about God?"

Daddy was quiet, and then said, "God is here with us every minute, Dodie, no matter what. He is here in what we love and what we find beautiful and good, and he is here in every hard and terrible thing. It is all God. Your brother knows that. He knows God."

"Are you telling me a children's story?" I asked, and he watched me and then shook his head.

"No, Dodie, I would not do that to you. If we do not have God, what do we have?" He watched me. "Find Him, Dodie," my father finally said to me, his voice beseeching.

Beston told Daddy he liked the one about remembering Sonny, and I said yes, and so Daddy set the big stone deep into the soil over my brother. He asked Mum to come, too, but Mum will not walk to the hill. Daddy prised the heavy stone upright and it slid down into its trough.

"Sonny"
Thomas Edward Senter
Beloved Son of Thomas Arlen and Doris Canton Senter
Born January 12, 1934
Died March 3, 1948, aged 14 years
We thank our God upon every remembrance of you.

DADDY PACKED THE dark soil at the base of the stone, and stepped on it gently with his boot, all around, a new stone risen among the ancestors. "Well, Son," he said.

Later he said, "Forgive me. I pray that you forgive me."

My father seeks Sonny's forgiveness. Is it Sonny I should be asking for forgiveness? Or Mum and Daddy? Or God?

Daddy and I held Beston's hands for the long walk home. It was a cool, cloudy day, and the grass that was making up in the hay-fields ran like rivers in the wind. The swallows swooped ahead of us in their great freedom. Beston told us that he had found a large spotted salamander under the board he lays in the grass along the cellar wall to attract them. He was easy with his talk, relieved perhaps that Sonny's place was finally signified. Relieved perhaps that Sonny has been named among the other ancient names on that hill. What lies beneath the soil is still ours.

That night, after supper, I sat outside with Mum. Although she doesn't like to be touched, she allowed me to lean against her, and we sat as the thin waning moon rose cold and pure from behind the barn. *Find God*, my father had said.

"Mum, have we lost God?" I asked.

She stared out across the yard. She let me put my hand in hers and we sat in the quiet of the night. Daddy and Beston washed the dishes, and I felt guilty that Daddy still had work to face at the end of his hard day. But I did not leave my mother's side.

The next morning came with all its routines and requirements. My father worked, I worked, my mother worked at what she could see, my brother worked at his bravery. We love each other. Every remembrance. The gentle, distant rumble of the tractor came on the wind as my father and Best started cutting the hay. I was at my chores, washing and canning the rhubarb. The door to the clean milk room stood open, and the cows roamed thoughtless across our land. The sun shone on us, on our little island in this vast world of innocence and harm.

Tup

I STOOD AT the shed door and watched my wife in her nighttime circuit of the floodlit barnyard. As she entered shadow she disappeared, and then the great blocks of light and there she was again, as if she had walked out of the world and back into it. Even invisible, her footsteps came to me in uneasy rhythm.

The spring air was soft, carrying the sweetness of the cows and the coming green of the pastures and fields. Doris looked up and saw me in the light of the door. She stopped in her place and held my face in her gaze. My wife has emptied. She looked down and returned to her devoted act of being and not being, her ghost walk.

AFTER MY FATHER died and before Sonny came, Doris and I moved from our little apartment in Claremont and onto the farm. It was a dirty and worn-out place then, all of it, my father too tired and too lonely and too uninterested to have kept this farm as his father and his grandfather kept it. I was worried about Doris, but she said, "Tup Senter, I am happy to make this our home."

Her mother and father visited us sometimes back then, town people from Colebrook who could not imagine, I think, their daughter in a life like this. But Doris was always loved by the people near her, she earned that, and they were very kind to us. I know that Doris must miss her mother and her father.

One June day when they visited, we all drove late in the afternoon, after the chores were done, to the beach at Munson Lake. This was before Sonny was born, when I was still at the college. The families were mostly gone for the day, and we spread our blanket and a supper picnic and then Doris and Celia swam. It was a windless evening, and the setting sun made its long golden road from the horizon to my wife as she drifted easily in the still water. She and Celia laughed and talked, their words rising away over the lake, indistinct, carrying only kindliness without complication. Lester and I sat talking on the blanket, watching our wives in the light of the closing day. Then Doris stood and turned toward me, smiling and beckoning *Come, Come*, and I could hear her laughter, and then she came out of the water dripping and pulled me by the hand, teasing, luminous, unashamed of our love before her mother and father, and we splashed together into the water, Doris's hair tangling across my shoulder, her face turned to the radiant sky.

Tup Senter allowed an old gun to stay in the house, a toy. Allowed his son, Doris Senter's son, to play with an old gun. My wife has never said those words to me. My wife's fury is a lightlessness, and my longing for forgiveness a supplication against the dark.

That day at the lake, with Celia and Lester watching, Doris wrapped her arms around my neck in the gold water and our feet left the bottom, me pulling us away from land, Doris's face to mine, the closing sun caught in the water drops in her hair. She lay alongside me, attached, watching me, her strong arms sweeping slowly back and forth, and we were weightless.

DODIE RUNS THIS house now, and the milk room and the garden and the hens, and she does it well. The work on this farm protects us, the hard work that is there every day without finish.

Even Doris, with her endless drawers and shelves, seems to understand that. We work, and keep the current slowed for hours at a time. It is two years now.

I am coming to believe that my wife will not ever return.

I am working at my limit, too little sleep, a sleep that offers no rest, and the work of the cows and their calves and the milking and the fields and pastures and fences and equipment to keep running and the hay and the corn, without real help, and the firewood and the house paint and the heavy work of the house Dodie can't do.

The roof of the barn is going to need to be reshingled. If I allow myself to study it all, I feel a low sickness of discouragement. This is a business, a constant flow of effort in, milk and meat out, the prices low or high, the gamble. My father came to hate this farm. I do not. I hold this farm as blessed land, and now my son sanctifies its soil. But my father dogs me. *You are becoming me*, he says, as I struggle with teeth that snap on the hay rake while Beston and I race the weather. *You are coming to know why a man would dream of any other kind of work,* my father calls to me. *Why a father would send his son away to college to prepare for any other kind of work.*

On the days the equipment runs without failing and the sun warms the growing grass and corn, when the calves move with their contented mothers on the south pasture, I have a solid answer for my father. But there are days, I am coming to see, that I am less convincing, to him and to myself. And then the question comes, what else could I ever do to support this farm? Running a dairy herd or not, this is home to me and to my family. It is either this work, this constant effort, or the barn standing empty, the haylofts barren, the fields and pastures running to thistle and juniper. I offer myself no choice. I will come out of this difficulty, this disheartenment, and find again the satisfaction that resides here. My father is kindly but insistent. *My son,* he says, *you do not have a wife. It is not failure for a man to say I have had enough.*

But I am not my father.

Beston stands behind me on the tractor, engaging the power take-off in and out, in and out at my command, and we make our long straight lines down and back, down and back across the great fields, the hay raked into mounded windrows, the air filling with the wild sweet scent of green. My son finds comfort here. This will be his farm, and Dodie's. In four more years Beston will be the age Sonny was. Sonny did a man's work here, and Beston will. Dodie does a woman's work already. We will be all right.

DEER HAVE BEDDED in the drying rows of cut hay beyond the pond.

"I don't like deer in my fields and orchard," I said to Best over supper. "Maybe we should come out tonight and shoot one of the buggers," and Dodie froze.

Best turned his small face to me and stared. Doris laid her fork on her plate in a startled clatter and I, too, was stopped by my words, by the idea of carrying a gun across this land, and I was silenced.

But I cannot run this farm a scared man, cowed, and I said loudly, "For Christ's sake! There are deer in my orchard eating everything they can reach! They are ruining the hay I just cut!"

The children looked down but Doris stood and left the kitchen, her chair scraping as she pushed away. I was left, as I always am, alone with our children.

"I am going to clean my guns," I said loudly, "and I am going to shoot a deer tonight and put it in our freezer." I know my voice was hard and cold. "You wanted to hunt with your brother and me," I said to my young boy. "Do you want to do this with me?" and of course he nodded yes, his silent acquiescence to anything I ask of him. "Then good," I said. "We can't go on our whole lives running away from things. Can we?" I asked Dodie.

She reached for Beston's hand.

"Can we?" I asked Beston, and my son shook his head no. I felt the cruelty of what I was asking of my children and could not stop myself. "No," I said, "it's time we face this goddamned thing down. We aren't prisoners."

We drifted from each other after supper, unwilling to sit in the front room. I did not go after the deer. The house was awake in the night. The morning came and slowly my children relaxed with me again. I know that I do not have many of these awful breaches left to me before my children will believe they cannot rely on me.

DORIS SAT IN the sun on the shed stoop this morning watching the hens peck and preen in the yard. It looked like any day in our lives here together, the house and yard and barn tidy and cared for, my wife taking a moment from her work. I sat beside her. Dodie whistled in the kitchen, her new skill, uneven and thin, a young girl's sound but cheerful and assuring. Beston was, I believe, in the hayloft with kittens born a few days ago. Two have already disappeared, and he is keeping desperate watch on the rest. Dust rose in little sunlit clouds from the hens' scratching and settled again. The cows wandered slowly in the front pasture, their calves full of milk and dozing in the coming heat of day. My wife did not resist my presence, and we sat together for a few minutes, our shoulders touching. We have all worked hard this year, making up for the two before when we could barely move forward. The farm and the garden and the house are in order again. I can see our work, completed well. For that short moment, in the warmth and brightness of the summer sun, the dread of memory and the dread of whatever is coming abated.

ELWYN PEABODY MENTIONED to me that Dunbar Mill in Grafton was looking for a man to work nights keeping the machinery in good order. I started there when the children returned to school in September. It is an odd thing, going to a wage job. I am a thirty-seven-year-old man who has never held a job off the farm.

It is not a necessity. We have all that we need here. The children have made it very clear they do not like the idea. I have no answer for them. I want to do this.

I do not want to do this. But I do not want to lie through the long nights in a small bed that once held my son. I do not want to lie through the long nights in a room down a dark hall from my reproving and absent wife.

THE DRIVE TO the mill is a rare time free of responsibility. Driving away from home, I listen to the radio, usually the farm reports out of Augusta, and I give myself over to the rhythm of the truck tires and the beam of the headlights on the empty roads. This going away feels well-earned. An indulgence, I suppose, but I believe it has come to be my due. The headlights open the road fifty feet before me, no more, and for thirty minutes going and thirty minutes returning that is all there is to the world. A great comfort, the voice of a stranger coming through the air with his lists of milk and oat and corn and meat prices, and this limitation of lighted space bounding me and what I must consider. For this time there is no farm and there is no wife and there is no daughter or son. There is no guilt, not for these few minutes.

I take the River Road along the Androscoggin. Sometimes I pull over and stand in the dark for a few minutes, the heavy river running within its banks through the indifference of the night. I imagine a dream I might have, leaning to remove my shoes, stepping out of my clothes and walking into the lightless turbulence. The water rises around my legs and my chest, more powerful than I. The river banks, the truck, the road that leads back home, all in silent obscurity. I am released.

But I am a man on his way to a night of plain labor in a woolen mill owned by someone named Glasser. I work alone in the mill after the second shift leaves. The work is clear: keep the machinery in good order. I met the floor manager the day I introduced myself and was hired. I haven't seen him or any other worker since.

He said to me, "This equipment needs to run. Can you do that?"

And I said I was certain I could figure it out, and that was that.

I have figured it out, night by night. The scouring machines and openers are quite direct in their design and tolerate inexact settings. They require simply a routine cleaning of the accumulated stock and dirt, a simple enough procedure. That is not true of the carding machines, which are likely to dip and vary in their rotary movements and require constant calibration, or the spinning machines that must draw the wool strands with even tension and provide the proper turns of twist, whether right-hand or left. It is these machines that call for my attention most nights, and which I find most fulfilling to attend to. What has been a surprise to me is that the great looms themselves do not require a lot of my time. Their function is actually quite direct and they need little attention from me. I admire the dark silent bulk of the looms. Their ability to do their work shift after shift, reliable and unwearying.

Tonight when I arrived at the mill, I nodded to the security guard and walked straight upstairs to the spinning floor. I stood in the half-dark, the long hall with its hulking machines hushed finally after two shifts of clatter and punch and whine. The floors had been swept, but still tufts of wool floated around my feet as I made my way down the long aisles. These aisles are as far from those of my barn as they could be, small dark alleyways just large enough to capture the labor of men and women and hold it here for the long hours exacted. The bright wide aisles of my barn announce the labor a man does for himself.

Somehow I have come to this new work not feeling obligated or bound. I have good skills. I come into this immense brick barn and use those skills and earn some pay beyond what we bring in on the farm. I allow myself these nights alone, moving without humiliation from machine to incognizant machine. I admire the precision, the rigorous exactitude demanded in this business. I get it right and it works. I get it wrong and there are problems. I work until I get it right, and then move on to the next solvable problem. Everything can be fixed here.

THE WOOL SCRAPS that float across the floors rise and drift and float like little clouds in the yellow gloom. Last night I gathered fistfuls and stuffed them in my pockets. This morning at the breakfast table I told Beston and Dodie to reach into the pockets of my jacket on the hook and see what was there. There was a moment of satisfaction as their fingers met the downy nest and struggled to identify it. They both yelped with surprise and withdrew the pure white fleece. Then Dodie dropped hers on the table and turned from me.

"That's from the mill," she said.

"Yes, these scraps float all over the floors," I said.

"I don't need anything like that," she said, and she got busy packing Beston's and her lunch into their boxes.

"I didn't think you needed anything," I said. My voice came out slow and heavy, reproaching. "I just thought you and Beston would like it. If you don't want it, it means nothing to me, Dodie. Do what you want."

"Do what I want?" she hissed at me. "What do you think I want?"

Beston held his little ball of wool to his face, watching his sister. She filled their thermoses and said, "The bus is coming," and she went out the shed door without saying goodbye.

I rose from my chair. I could feel the anger rising and followed her into the yard. "You have no right to have an opinion of what I do, Dodie," I called to her back.

She spun around and said, "Yes, I do. You ask me to carry this farm and this house for Mum and then leave me here every night as if I am the head of this family. You leave me here with Mum awake in her bed and Beston awake in his bed. I am fourteen years old." Her voice caught and I stopped following her.

"You don't need to do a goddamned thing at night and you know it," I yelled, shame rising even as I shouted at my daughter.

She spun around and faced me. I have never seen Dodie purely angry.

"You ask too much of me!" she cried, her voice shrill and high, a child's. "I can't do all this!" And she turned back to the road as the bus drew up. Beston ran past me from the kitchen with his lunchbox. When he was seated he waved at me, a disquieted and scared boy. I could not see Dodie, and was left with her unreasonable scolding for the rest of the day. Doris watched me pour my coffee down the sink and take my jacket from the hook. She turned from me and we started our separate days without speaking.

Dodie was quiet at supper, the supper she helped her mother provide for us before she started her homework.

"You make a good meal for us, Dodie," I said, but she would not look at me.

She did not join Beston and me in the front room, both women in my family now hovering beyond the circle of lamplight, and I felt adrift. At one point I went into the kitchen and stood by her chair as she worked on her studies. She did not look up.

"Dodie, you are being unreasonable," I started. She would not speak. "I don't see that working at the mill a few hours each night should have this effect on you," I said. When she would not answer, I felt anger rise again in me.

"I don't know what else you want from me! I do more work than any man I know. I have taken on a new job! I run this farm and I run it well. What else is it you want from me? You and your mother!" I said in disgust, and that did it.

My daughter rose from her chair and faced me. I felt a shock at how tall she has become, and how defined her features have become. I could feel myself react to this vanished child, a wave of grief and the measureless guilt lifting into fury.

"Me and my mother?" she whispered at me.

Our breaths met in the space between us. The good order of our kitchen stood against our turmoil. Dodie stood fearless.

"You wonder what it is I want from you? What I want is this," she said in a tight, low voice. "What I want is for at least one of my parents to agree to finish raising their children. I have finished the job on myself, but you still have a little boy that needs you. Playing with your machines at the mill all night suits you but it does not suit Beston." She stood silent for a minute, holding my eyes. "You are asking too much of me. Both of you. You are asking too much of Beston and me."

She sat back down and picked up her pencil and was gone from me. When I returned to the front room, Beston looked up and smiled at me, a release. We will be all right. Dodie is at a difficult age, and she carries a large load. I need to make certain that she has more time with her friends. But we have come through the nightmare all right. Beston held the wool ball in his small sweaty hand and while we read he brushed it again and again across his lips.

"Would you like one night to come to the mill with me and see the machines that make cloth of that wool?" I asked him, and he said yes.

Doris finally came inside and Dodie led us all upstairs. I left the lamp on by the kitchen sink so that when I came back down after my nap to head to the mill I would not feel so solitary.

[1952]

Doris

I WATCH MYSELF. I am not who I am. I am not a wife. I am not a mother. I want to be. It is my obligation. I speak from a hundred miles away. My hands reach out before me and nothing is there. My husband sits beside me on my bed in the dark and tells me stories. The light from the hallway marks his face in planes. We know each other. I know his stories are true. *Do you remember?* he asks. *The front room smelled of the cement Sonny used on his models. Do you remember, Doris? You held my hand in the truck and we sang that Benny Goodman song. Sonny and Dodie and Best on lay on their bellies in the muddy grass by the creek catching cider bugs. Do you remember? You were wearing the yellow sweater I always liked. Dodie gathered eggs and made us egg salad sandwiches on your bread. You slipped off the stepladder and bruised your shin so badly I wanted you to see the doctor. You told me once,* he says, *that you lost the children while you did laundry, lost Sonny and Dodie before Best came, lost them for a few minutes and you were still in a panic telling me all those hours later, I could hear it even when you laughed at yourself. Do you remember?* he asks.

I remember it all, the dream of it all.

I AM WORKING much harder at sparing Dodie. She is just a girl. The children are back in school for the new year, Dodie in her second year in high school now. She has too much to do. I try to get some of the laundry and the canning done before the bus returns each day, but it is difficult to get to everything. Dodie scolds me sometimes, pressing me to help her as if I am her child and she is my mother.

"You allow yourself to become distracted," she rebukes me.

I earn this castigation, and make greater resolve. She is a very good girl. Beston is a very good boy. Tup says that I am not well. That I am sick and need to see a doctor in Portland. I do not feel sick. I just need time to return to myself. Tup says that I have had time to do that and need help. I am certain that no one outside me can fix this.

Do I remember? I float among us. We are small and distant, a family tableau, and I watch from the corner of the ceiling. I love us and cannot speak. Pull me home, pull me home.

Dodie

THE FREEZER IS nearly full for the winter, and the canning shelves. I did that. I told my father I could and I did.

I have two lives now, this one at home and the one at school. The bus takes us all to the grammar school and then we older students stay on and go to the consolidated high school in Sheldon. There are twenty-seven students in my grade now, a much larger class, and I am very glad of it. They interest me, and I seem to interest them. Marion and Flora and I made a pact when we moved to the high school last year that we would be friendly with everyone and make new friends. It was hard at first to watch Beston get off the bus alone at our little school, but I am glad to be among these new people, teachers and students. I have felt for over four years that all of Alstead's eyes were on the Senter children, and now I am simply one among others. They probably all know the story, but there are a lot of stories in this building and no one seems to need to consider mine, or maybe and more likely this story feels to them something to avoid, to turn away from. Let them turn away. A relief to me. And the classes at this grade level ask a lot more of me, also a relief. I am studying Latin. After supper, Daddy listens to me reading my Latin. Flora hates it and says it is a dead language, and what good is a dead language? But I love the words that carry the roots of our own, and I love the nobility of the speeches, calling us to be bigger than we are.

I have Mr. Creighton for English. He sent a note home for my mother suggesting that she might use the state library to get books for me. I showed it to my father and he helped me write a letter to the library in Augusta asking for a card. Mr. Creighton gives me the names of books he thinks I might like and I send off a request. Within a week a book comes in the mail. It is as if Mr. Creighton opened a great locked door and pushed me over the threshold. Now

Daddy and Beston get books, too, and we read together in the circles of lamplight in the front room. These are happy hours for all of us at the end of our long days. This fall, I have already read *Uncle Tom's Cabin* and *Anna Karenina* and *Jane Eyre*, my favorite. I got *The Iliad* but Daddy suggested we read it together, so he is reading it out loud each night in his soft, steady voice, a story of love and violence and regret. Daddy has a book of plays by Shakespeare and we are going to try some of those next. The world has opened to me and I am grateful. It is very strange to me that all this has been here all along and I did not know. What else is in this world?

"Is it all right for Best to hear these stories?" I asked Daddy.

"There is nothing Beston does not already know," my father said.

I know he is right. I wish I could erase what he has learned and make him again a boy.

THERE WILL BE a Harvest Dance at school in October, with a hay wagon ride from the school to the Odd Fellows Hall where the dance will be. I am sixteen now and allowed to attend. I can't wait. There are three boys already who speak to me in the hall, Donald and Paul and George. Marion and I practice dancing when we stay over, taking turns leading and following. We are not sure if we have to wait for a boy to ask us or if we can ask a boy. Flora says the boy has to ask. I am not afraid of asking.

Sonny's friend Daniel is two years ahead of me at school. We ride the bus together and pass in the hall, but he still does not look at me or speak. I know what he is thinking. That I was the one who took the gun from Sonny's hand and created this world. If he would speak to me, I would accept this. I would say, *Yes, I believe you are right.* I would say, *We all came out of that room into this world, except Sonny. My brother. Your friend. Yes. You are right about me.*

But we pass each other and he looks away.

My other life is here.

Daddy still works nights at the Dunbar Mill in Grafton. He says we need the extra money, but I don't see that we need that income for anything beyond what we have. I think he doesn't sleep, and this is a way to stay occupied day and night. I asked him not to do this job, but he says he will continue unless it becomes a problem. It has been a problem from the first night, at least for Best, who is left alone now in the darkness of his dreams.

At the end of the day, Daddy and Best do the milking and the barn chores and then come in to supper. Daddy is in good spirits and jokes with us and with Mum. She goes outside while I do up the dishes, and then Best and Daddy and I go to our places in the front room to read or play a game of cribbage or checkers. Everything is the same. But when Mum comes inside and we go upstairs to get ready for bed, Daddy goes into Sonny's room and lies on top of the covers for a nap. In the night, he changes into a pair of green cotton coveralls without putting on his light and he goes down the stairs in the dark. We can hear him getting from the icebox the nighttime lunch I have made for him and then the door to the shed opens and closes and his truck starts and he is gone. I feel a terrible space of emptiness as I watch his lights travel across the walls of my room, down our road and away.

But it is always Beston who faces the hardest time. His light stays on now into the night.

He was accustomed to Daddy going in to him if he called out. He is too old now for that. But he must feel acutely that there is no one here to ease the night for him, certainly not our mother, and it is not me Best needs. I don't know if he sleeps with the light on or prevents himself from going to sleep.

Parts of us seem to be falling away, piece by piece. Maybe if Daddy could go back to sleeping in his own room with Mum he wouldn't need to leave all of us alone here. He works through the night, a man rescuing himself from the dark. But we are all awake, waiting for Tup Senter to return, to supply ballast, the empty rooms in this house heaving and accusing of us all.

And then before dawn Daddy drives back into the yard and shuts off the truck and comes into the kitchen. I hear him washing up at the sink and then he climbs the stairs and moves to his room and lies in the last of the dark. We all finally sleep, and then the first morning light comes and the next day starts.

MARION ALWAYS MOVES over when our afternoon bus picks up the younger children so Beston can sit down beside me. He is so thin he looks like a smaller boy, smaller than the other boys in his grade and watchful, apart. Each time he comes into the new life I am making and we meet again, brother and sister, and we start back home to this other world, each time I feel a rush of protectiveness. He trusts me. That trust sits hard on me and makes me lonely. We sit side by side and make our way across the six miles that return us to our beautiful island of such light and such dark.

Yesterday he asked quietly if we could walk home from school together in the afternoon. He sometimes asks this and each time I feel I have to say no.

"I have so many chores to do, Best, and then so much homework, I need to get home," I say.

But yesterday morning the second cut of hay gleamed in the early light, the green stretching across our land, across and beyond the creek and the orchard, across the road on the other side to the ledges. That shining grass speaks of more work coming for Dad and Best, the cutting and raking and tedding and baling and hauling to the barn and hoisting to the lofts, the timing critical before frost takes the grass. But that is not my work, and while I stood at the kitchen sink looking out on our land, I felt for the first time in a very long time the simple and perfect beauty of our land, its beneficence, and I said yes to Beston, tomorrow.

I got off the bus at the little school and we took the route so familiar to us across the Munfords' fields, shutting the gates behind us as we moved down the long slope to our stream, Senter Creek, and followed it to the rocks where the bugs collect. Beston held my hand in the privacy of this big land, a boy too old for this, and still a necessity. The sun and cool air swept us clean. Mr. Munford's black cows watched us without caring.

I felt patient and contented lying next to Beston as he searched for bugs in the creek. We used our thermoses to hold them. Everything is known to us in this place. We carry it inside us. I believe Sonny carried it inside him. My father says that we have no choice but to believe in God, that we have no evidence against him. I think we surely do. Daddy says that God doesn't pay attention to each one of us. That he gave us this grace, and it is up to us to be human inside it.

"Everything is here for us," he says.

"But why would God allow us to suffer?" I ask my father.

"I think," he says, "that he doesn't allow suffering. He provides it. It is a vital part of the great gift."

I resist this. I have not found one thing better coming from suffering than from happiness. If heaven waits for us, then a place of no suffering is the prize.

Daddy says heaven is here with us now. He tells me, "Dodie, you don't know this yet, but you are forming around all that you have known and you are going to be a very large person. God is in you."

Lying with my brother by the creek that runs through our farm and on to the sea that is waiting for it, lying in this sun, in this soft wind, stirring my fingers among myriad creatures none of us can ever imagine, I might believe in my father's God. But then Beston holds a backswimmer in his small palm, and his eyes lift to mine, and here in this sun and this wind and this growing green grass, here by this noisy shallow stream named for us, is the face of unspeakable terror carved forever into a little boy. Here is the absence of our brother, a child himself, and I am certain there can be no God.

I am angry. I am an angry girl, I know that. At my mother and my father and at whatever my father calls God. At myself. Mostly myself. I never meant to do harm in my life, I am certain of that. My father says we each choose, every minute of every day, to do good or bad. I did not know I was choosing anything in that warm room filled with children's laughter on a sleeting, forbidding day when I was just twelve years old.

But I did not speak of these questions with Beston. Instead I admired the backswimmers and the mayfly nymphs and the crane fly larvae he offered for my appreciation. Hemiptera and Ephemeroptera and Diptera, he said. Latin. The poetry of these names, belonging to me in a new way. This was respite. Beston smiled at the little creatures he found as if he were greeting them, *Hello! I have missed you all. We are back!* And so we accepted this peace. My father is right in this part of it, that we receive great gifts. I know this, too. Beston and I lay in the damp grass all afternoon, warmed by the sun. After supper, he poured the water and his strange creatures into a big bowl and my father carried it to the old table on the screen porch. Beston lifted each one onto a piece of cardboard and let the water soak away. When they have dried out, he will make a small card for each one in the tiny handwriting he has learned, and he will add them to the others that Sonny once found. If Beston attached any sentiment to this dying—this killing, really—he did not show it.

When we went to bed, Daddy lay down for his nap before leaving for the mill. My mother came up to her room, nodding to each of us as she passed our doors. The sun and the creek and the familiar walk and the black cows and the constant sound of water heading to its home and the Latin names and the intricacy of legs and gills and feathery antennae had entered the house with Beston and me, a balm, a remembrance, a thread stitching us to Sonny, to this family's life before, and we slept.

I heard my father return to his room before dawn. When we rose with the light, my father was waking from his early morning nap. It was Saturday, a day filled with its usual necessities and obligations, an armature we rely on. I felt free all day. Beston asked if we could walk home again on Monday. I said maybe, we'd see. Maybe, like a great promise to us.

"Maybe we can go over to the ledges next time," I said, "and see if anything is denning in the rocks."

"We could ride our bikes to the pond," Beston said.

"Yes, we'll see how much work I have."

The great trees at the front of the house stood over my work all day, their cool shade dappling the walls inside and out in the fall breeze. I felt prepared, ready. The sense that a dark train was headed at me from somewhere unseen was gone for a time. No surprises. I am Dodie Senter. I am sixteen years old. I help my father run our farm. I have a little brother. I attend Sheldon High School. Every day I choose to try to do good. Much of the garden is harvested and put away for the winter. I will not forget again that we can walk across this land in all its constancy and return more certain.

Tup

DODIE WENT TO her first dance last night. Of course I was struck hard with a father's questions of how his daughter could be old enough to attend a dance, and especially to want so eagerly to attend a dance with the boys from these towns around. But I was struck hardest with an understanding that the child who learned great suffering in this house is making her way with courage toward her womanhood, which has come already in such large measure and so early.

The house has hummed for two weeks or more with Dodie's concern about this dance. She sewed each evening, putting together a pretty dress of soft velvet, chosen for the colors of our fields in the fall. I was concerned about stockings and shoes, but my sister took her to Vernon without Beston, a girls' day, and Dodie came back pleased and confident. She tried on her finished dress and the new shoes for us that night, and Doris stood in the doorway smiling, a vestige of an earlier time. Dodie stopped in front of her as she went upstairs to change back into her house clothes and smiled, too. Her mother reached out her hand and adjusted the short sleeve, and then turned away and left us. Dodie turned back to me, still smiling, unable to understand the shocked pleasure and sadness such a milestone in a girl's life brings to a parent, but able to understand fully the momentousness of the smile and touch from her mother. I saw Doris in this young girl, the disarmed radiance and readiness and generosity of heart. My love felt crushing for a moment, and then I brought myself back to a daughter's first dance.

"You are going to have to fight off the boys, you know that," I said to her, and she laughed in a way that told me she believed so, also. I was very happy for her, sixteen years old and so full of expectation.

On the night of the dance, Dodie allowed Beston to ride along in the truck. We picked up Marion, the four of us squeezed in close with the heater running at our feet. Dodie was in a jubilant mood.

The mood was unlessened when I returned for them later. I asked a lot of questions about their evening and teased the girls, but I received no answers. Marion spent the night with us, and I listened to their voices, lightened with happiness, until I left for the mill.

The silence of the mill did not suit me. Generally I find a loosening, an unbinding, as I move among the machines, drawing them to precise action. Last night as I worked, I listened again and again to the memory of Dodie's laughter. It seemed to come back over her shoulder as she got out of the truck and walked away from me, a willful turning away it seemed, and I sensed the closure that was coming forever on any kind of undoing, of repairing, of compensating. She was changed on that sleeting day. I allowed my children to play with a gun.

I cannot recast this history. What I can do, what I am assigned to do, is to pay attention, to bear full witness, the only help I can give. The lightness and the burden of her sudden laughter, of her radiant face and pretty dress, her stockings and stylish shoes—all I can do to help her is to bear witness.

When I rose from my nap this early morning to start my day, Doris was already in the kitchen putting together a Saturday breakfast.

When the girls came down, Beston asked Dodie, "Did you dance with a boy last night?" Dodie laughed and said, "Of course I did. Marion did, too. It was a dance, silly."

"Your sister had a lot of fun last night," I said to Beston.

"And today we dig potatoes and get them into the root cellar," she said, still laughing but making a face of mock disgust. Marion had borrowed work clothes from Dodie, and the two girls spent the day moving down the rows with the potato forks, laying the potatoes out in the air to dry for a couple of hours before picking them up in baskets and carrying them, one at each handle, to the cellar. They chattered and laughed as they worked, but the emancipation of last night was already cinching closed with the hard, dirty work of the day.

Beston helped, of course. He stacked the wood I was splitting and then wandered into the garden with the girls to dig potatoes with his hands, and then back to the woodpile. It was the kind of day that I like, when your work is evident at the end of the day, bins of potatoes and piles of firewood stored and ready. My children were cheerful in their chores. Doris watched sometimes from the stoop, elbows in her hands, and then slipped indoors. The weather has turned, the sun without the warmth of August and September, the closing of the season.

After supper, we drove Marion home. Dodie and Beston and I rode home in contented silence, the gift of hard work. But I also understood that Dodie has taken one step into her life apart from her mother and her father.

I HAVE MET Mrs. Helen Glasser, the widow of Leonard Glasser and now the sole owner of Dunbar Mill. I admire her.

She is a good businesswoman. She has none of Doris's vitality. The vitality I remember. Or her intelligence, and certainly not her looks. But she is good to her workers, and has managed to keep this mill open when others are closing down one after another all over this state. She buys raw wool from Maine sheep farms. Orders for wool for uniforms have disappeared since the war, but Mrs. Glasser has figured out how to keep her expenditures down and sell a good product to the clothing industry, gabardines and worsteds. Maine workers have a very good reputation, and Dunbar wool, too. Mrs. Glasser pays the men and women who work the machines decent wages. Unlike most mill owners, she lives unpretentiously, in a small house on Taft Street close to her office at the mill. She has means greater than that, I am certain, but her moderation and evenness earn the loyalty of her help, and she seems at ease in that modesty.

I met her one night when I thought I was alone with my work. Suddenly I sensed that someone was watching me, and there she was, fifteen feet from me in the gloom. It was an intrusion.

"I am not accustomed to having my work overseen," I said, and I knew I sounded insolent.

She stood where she was and simply said, "I am not checking on you. I just wanted to meet you. You keep my equipment running. You keep it running well."

My equipment. I am able to feel in these dark quiet nights that these great machines are somehow mine. Not the enormous mill spanning the river and its old dam works, not the cloth that leaves this place and makes something of a profit, but these old kindly machines that have allowed me to find peace through the nights. My equipment, she said. Mrs. Glasser owns everything in Dunbar Mill by herself. Whatever happens here is of her doing. I recognize that this is not unlike my work on my land, my farm. Success comes or not by her own decisions. She is younger than I am, but her voice is of an older person, attentive, sympathetic. She looks to be an ordinary woman. She appeared steady, constant among her great imperturbable machines. I have not seen her since.

AT NIGHT, IN the mill, I tell myself stories of my son. I am always ready to move back to him. *Once,* I say, *once Sonny was walking into the barn and he caught me singing with the radio. We stood at opposite ends of the center aisle, the song between us. Sonny paused, and then he sang with me, moving along the stanchions with the water hose. A man's voice and a boy's voice, the afternoon sun slanting across the aisle, Sonny in the light and then the shadow.* I want to remember the song, but I cannot. He resides. Our song, awkward and uncertain, the yellow light across his strong young body. For this moment in this forgiving mill, he is alive to me, a brief visit.

I WAITED UNTIL the snow was gone from the yard, and asked Reuben Gilley to deliver the piano while Dodie was at school. I should have done this a long time ago. It fits in the front room between the windows. She is very pleased, and sits for a half hour most evenings, making up songs. Beston has been the surprise. He spends every minute that he is free from chores teaching himself to play. He has an exceptional sense of music. Dodie likes to sing along to her made-up songs, spilling out her full heart, this land and love and hope. Beston does not. Whatever he hears on the radio during the day becomes a song he can play by nightfall. He finds the music in his memory and there it is. "We Kiss in a Shadow." "Happy Trails." "Nobody Knows the Trouble I've Seen." "Till the End of Time." "Rock My Soul." A revelation. Beston is a musician. My son who works alongside me, willing and devoted every day. How is it possible we did not know this lives in him? Doris comes inside from her nighttime pacings some evenings and stands alone in the kitchen, listening. When Beston carefully closes the lid over the keys, his mother turns back through the shed and resumes her solitary journey.

I always believed that love is joy. That if we are bound by love, we are assured of grace. The Senters are bound by love. But it has assured us only of itself. We love each other. Anything can happen.

When I leave the house each night, the great and limitless sky over the fields and pastures and orchard and hill looses me again. Beauty is God, I tell my children. We love beauty. This is a great gift from God. He allows us to feel ourselves transformed by beauty. We are made good by beauty. Beauty, I say to my disbelieving children, is in every moment of every life.

MARCH BROUGHT AN early thaw and now, in April, the fields are dry. Beston helped me load the manure spreader last evening. Tomorrow is Saturday. We will have the fields dressed and the equipment washed down by supper Sunday. Dodie has started her seed

[139]

flats, and is cleaning the house and the coop and the milk room from the winter's use. Doris is paying her usual silent attention to the shelves and drawers, but continues to prepare our very good meals, three times a day. I do not understand why it is our food that lifts her to attention when nothing else can.

I found myself stopping at Helen Glasser's house last night on my way to the mill. I have noticed that her light is on late. I did not have an explanation for my presence at her door when she came, but she asked for none. She was in her housecoat and slippers.

"Would you like a cup of coffee before you go to work?" she asked simply.

Her kitchen is modern, with linoleum floors and countertops and a white electric range. She herself is modest, an unexceptional but kindly face, the stature of a woman who sits at a desk, who does not work on a farm. Her brown hair is kept short and practical. Our conversation was of nothing. She is serious, and agreeable. I did not speak of the farm, and she did not speak of her dead husband. The hour felt like a small reprieve, a rest I did not know I needed.

"Come again," she said as I rose.

"Yes," I said. "I will."

Of course, that longing came home with me and I went into my wife's bedroom in the early dark of the morning. I have not entered this room for a very long time, or its familiar light. The chair with Doris's slip and dress and sweater waiting for tomorrow stabbed me. I lay beside her. She sleeps still at one side of the bed, my place empty all these years as if she might allow me to come home to her. We knew a rare love in this bed. I empty myself each day, with no filling of this depleting well. I was a good husband. I am a good husband. I am loyal, and hardworking, and hold this family together. Doris was a good wife.

I lay along her back and pulled her to me, my wife. My face in her loose thick hair. I felt her stiffen. We lay in our bed, a man and a separate woman, lost to each other. Spring peepers filled the land with their desperate calls. The light of the half-moon rested in soft squares on the floor.

"Doris," I said. "I am here."

My breath and the breath of my wife could not find rhythm. I swept her hair from her neck and kissed her softness. She rolled from me and sat on the edge of the bed, then rose and put her housecoat on. Before she could open the door I was beside her, grabbing her arm, which I had not imagined doing, no matter what came.

"Doris!" I breathed into her still face. "Doris! I need you! I cannot do this anymore!"

But my wife waited quietly, pulling from me, until I let her arm go.

"You don't need to leave your room," I said. "I am going. I will leave you alone."

I lay in my small bed in Sonny's old room, in the dark of early morning memory. Doris coming to our bed unclothed and lying along the length of my body. She kissed me, my mouth and my neck and my chest and my hands. She offered to me her closeness, her smell, her willingness to give up for a while the boundaries that secure us all. I remember this as if it were one night, *once*, a night I might return to. In this memory, we made love. And then we held each other while the night sky spun over us, while our children slept, while the cows and the hens and the fields and the creatures in the stream rested. The deer slept at the edge of the woods. In this time there had been no harm. Doris and Tup Senter held each other.

The first light arrived without solace. My wife and children found me in the kitchen, lighting the fire in the range against the springtime cold. There is work waiting. Doris served my breakfast, well-made and sufficient, without a word. Dodie and Best joked about the stink of the loaded spreader joining us for breakfast. The new calves bellowed for their mothers, and the cows called to be relieved of their heavy bags of milk. The April sun has warmth and the land surges awake. This is what there is.

The tractor started and its roar echoed over the fields. Beston climbed onto the take-off bar and leaned against my back. He is not a scared boy anymore. Dodie hung the first load of laundry in the shimmering morning sun. Doris stood on the stoop watching her, and she turned to us as Beston and I moved out of the barnyard and through the gate to our work. Beston waved. This is the Senter farm. We are a family. We love each other. We live every day in beauty. Our hard work brings us plenty. The calves follow their mothers out into the greening pasture. This is what there is. It is a lot.

[1953]

Doris

Tup said that it is enough that he be here at five o'clock every morning, even though he had risen from bed that morning in another house.

"The economy of this home is no different than if I slept here," he yelled at me. "I will keep the farm as I always have. It is still the best goddamned farm in this county. I have met my obligations. That's a lot Christly more than you can say."

I felt roused, drawn suddenly into an agitation I have not allowed for a very long time. I was angry with my husband, an anger I had not known until that moment. I wanted to tell him that, to tell him that he is making harm here now, that the harm he has believed he made five years ago is not his, it is mine alone, but this, this is harm he is choosing to make. But I could not make these ideas come clear, and then I started to cry.

Tup turned at me and said, his voice low and hard, "This is what is finally going to make you cry? Where in God's name have you been?"

He put his face close to mine. I pulled away from him and moved to the door. He was quiet, and finally he said to me, "I am a loyal husband, Doris Senter." His voice was shaking. He sounded very tired. "I have been a very loyal husband to you. This is the time for you to tell me that you are ready to return to me. To your children. This is the time, Doris."

I felt the imperative. I understood my obligation. More than that, I understood my love, which has not diminished, no matter what my husband has known. But neither has it released me home to myself. This is not Tup's failing.

I could not find a way to say yes, to say I made a choice and now I will make a different choice.

I want to return. But wanting has not been enough for these long years.

I could not speak.

Tup stood close behind me, pressing against me. "I am so goddamned tired of your silence," he said. "I am so goddamned tired of your burying this family in grief. I am alive, Doris Senter! I am alive! Dodie and Beston are alive. Sonny is dead! Dead, and he always will be. I cannot bring him back! You have exhausted me! I owe you nothing more! There is nothing but the children and the land binding me here now. I have no wife. I am gone from you."

He left the kitchen and now we are in a new realm.

TUP SLEEPS IN Grafton now. I don't know what the children have heard in town, or how they might answer those rumors. We are no stranger to rumors about this family. But this is a family matter. This is a marriage matter, between a husband and his wife. Between a husband and his wife and the past, when a husband kept a gun in his house as a toy and a wife allowed a child to take it up in one moment of inattention. That is what we reckon with, my husband and I. Tup imagines a God who forgives us, a freeing, an exoneration. There is no such God. It is our hand that shapes all that comes. Those are decisions we make. We will spend our lives in regret, or worse, because we did not pay sufficient attention at one moment. We have no safeguarding from God.

Tup charged Dodie to find God. Once, I knew that God. I was thankful, every day I was thankful. I was loved. Tup loved me. We created three children. We lived on this farm. The Senter Farm bound us. Beneficence. Benefaction. Benediction. Benevolence. Beauty. Beatific. The Beatitudes.

Blessed are the poor in spirit, for theirs is the kingdom of heaven. Blessed are those who mourn, for they will be comforted.

But I am poor in spirit. I mourn. And I am not comforted.

I want to escape myself. I am very tired, and carry a great barrenness, a universe emptied.

THE SPRING MOON is nearly full, the full light hard on the dark land. It is the time that the calves are separated from their mothers. The calling from the barn, the calling back from the pasture, the terrible incomprehension. Our will imposed.

The nights are cold. I stood last night in the door of the barn, the calves and their mothers separated for the night in the containment of the pens. There was such stillness under the cries of the calves, like wailing supplicants in a hushed cathedral. The night's light lay across the aisles and the backs and necks of the stiff-legged, weaning calves. They could not comfort each other.

There, I said, *there. Your mothers are gone. This yearning will come to an end, and you will no longer need what you once had.* I stroked their shining necks and stood beside one, and then another. This is a forgotten song, the hushing and comforting. I watched this woman, a stranger. The silence of the lofts above, the wild fear of the young animals, the unpracticed voice of the woman in her husband's old coat.

The helpless mothers called from the far end of the barn. *There,* I heard the woman say slowly. *I know. I know.* The swallows sat on their nests in the great darkened eaves of the barn. The cats and the mice and the rats and the weasels hunted in the hay overhead. An ordered world. The woman moved among the calves, spending tenderness. She stood in the cool flooding moonlight, turning, turning, the barn and its old walls and stanchions and bins and ladders, the ropes hanging in loose loops. The night deepened and the light shifted, dissolving shadow, and the stillness, the deep wailing of the calves. I watched this woman turn back to them and reach her hand to them, and she wanted to say to them, *It will be all right,* but she could not.

YES, I REMEMBER before. My husband drew me to him. Night, the window opened to the clamorous petitions of spring, Tup's legs stretched long between mine, his weight and his sweet breath and our entrance to something full, a covenant. When the light came again each morning, we rose from our bed and looked across to each other, we looked out the windows to our barn and fields and orchard and creek, we parted. At any moment in the day, we lifted our eyes from our work and searched for each other. There you are. The grace of this binding.

Tup will return in the truck at five o'clock tomorrow morning to his wife of twenty years come June. He will change into his barn clothes and refuse breakfast, a man already fed. He will make his familiar walk to the barn, and for twelve hours he will tend this farm again. After supper, he will leave us.

I find a territory that is apart. I roam inside, searching for the way to break free. I am cornered. The roaming is wild, and still I cannot find release. Release. Relief. Relinquish. Retreat. Retreat, retreat. I drift, out of reach.

Once, I believed that I have a good soul. I do not. I know that now. I press at the edge of the endless circuit. My daughter and my son and my husband float in a line at the far horizon of my sight, shadows in communion with each other. There is no language that crosses this frontier. I long for them, a desperate and powerful yearning. Awake. Awake, Doris Senter.

Dodie

I AM A very good student. Latin continues to be my favorite sub-
ject, and English. We are reading *The Good Soldier*, which I am
not very interested in with all its justifications and self-delusions.
But the first line promised something to me: *This is the saddest
story I have ever heard.* We are living a very sad story and still we
plant the garden and plow the fields and fill the root cellar and still
we eat noon dinner and supper together and still my mother and
my father stand side by side in the open shed doorway looking out
over this farm and all the work they have given to this land. Still
we castrate calves and send milk each morning on the co-op truck.
Still we paint the west side of the house again and still we load the
heavy green bales of new hay into our lofts. Still we watch Beston,
grown into a young boy and no longer a child, and still we listen for
his music. Still we sit across from each other at the kitchen table
and we find words to share, simple words and few, but we speak.
What we do not do is move together after supper to the porch or
the front room to sit with our father and read and play cribbage
and then say goodnight and rise together to our adjoining rooms,
the sense of the father nearby, the weight and ballast of him. That
is gone forever.

Now my father comes in from his hard work as he has always
done and he strips off his barn clothes and washes at the kitchen
sink as he has always done and he sits with this family and shares
the food we have grown from this Senter land and then he rises
and says, *Well, goodnight, I will be back in the morning,* and he
goes. What we do then is the saddest part of this long story. Our
mother rises from the table to her nighttime wanderings in the

yard, as if she is searching in the light and in the dark for a passage out, and Beston and I do the dishes and we go together to the porch or the front room and do our schoolwork. I sew and Beston sketches out songs in his notebook or plays the piano and sings quietly and then we read, to ourselves with no father's strong voice sharing books with us and opening up the world. Later, without a word, I rise and turn off the light and I feel my brother rise and follow me up the stairs. Our mother will sit out most of the night on the dark stoop. The empty rooms upstairs draw our breaths into them, extracting far more than any mother and father have a right to ask of their children. The night spins.

THE SCHOOL BUS shuttles me between my two worlds every day. It is harder and harder to face the friends I have known all these years. What are they saying about me and my family? My mother I could defend, if anyone ever dared to say a word to me. *I pray you never lose a child,* I would say. *Then you judge the dark corners of a mother's grief. She has stayed with us, doing her best,* I would say. *She loves us,* I would say. I would not speak of her silence, or her wanderings so apart from us.

But my father? Yes, I would have to say. *Yes. He has chosen to give himself two lives, there and here. Yes, he works at the mill and then he goes to what he must call home to sleep the night in another woman's bed. Yes, as if he has taken a second wife. Yes, he returns to Senter Farm at five o'clock every morning, and throughout the day you would think he is still my father, still husband to my mother. He works his farm and works the mill owned by his other wife and eats his food at both tables. Yes. Yes. This is true.*

Beston is thirteen years old, and these are the only stories he will remember.

I have one more year in school. I would walk away from this place and never once look back over my shoulder. But Best would have another four years here alone. I have no choice. Let the mother and the father do that. I will not. No matter what happens in my life, I will not abandon my brother. Find God? Just where would I look?

I KNOW THERE is a lot of talk around town. But at school I have friends, and I can spend the hours forgetting my other life. I am still a happy person, or at least a cheerful person, and my friends and I laugh and talk about our schoolwork and make big plans for the future. We flirt and hold hands. I like boys. I like their thin bony shoulders and the hard nub of their knees against the cloth of their pants when they sit. I like the way they look at the floor and then get up their courage to look me right in the eyes. I like their ideas in class, the hold justice still has on them. I like being around people, boys and girls, who live simpler lives than I do. It is a relief, a rest. I am able to return to myself, to remember the faith I have always had in goodness.

Mrs. Hamlin is having us write poems. At home, at the table in the front room as Beston and I try to fill the emptied space, my words seem silly and excessive. But when I stand in front of my classmates to read, I sense their kind attention and my poems seem sincere and important. I wrote about lying in the wet grass with my brothers at the creek: *Shoulder to shoulder, we were three / and home waited faultlessly.* Mrs. Hamlin encourages me. I would like to show my father these poems, but we seem to have lost the way to do that anymore.

Beston is going to be in a play. It is hard to imagine my shy brother speaking to a room filled with people when he does not speak to the people in his own home. The students in seventh and eighth grade wrote the play and are making the costumes. Beston is going to be the main character, a preacher, a man he says is clumsy and bumbling but kind at heart. It falls to him to rescue children who have for some reason become lost in a strange city. Beston says it is a comedy, and he is eager and pleased. Beston, the maker of music and imagined characters. He asks me each night to help him learn his lines. It is astonishing to watch my quiet brother stride back and forth across the room, reciting his part in confidence. I see a suggestion of the man he might become, quiet but certain, serious but capable of good humor, smart and able. Like our father. How much of himself my father has betrayed.

I started my monthlies last summer, later than a lot of the girls. I had been waiting, not dreading or anticipating. I knew what to expect, and where to find Mum's supplies, so I thought I was ready. But that first flow of blood from my body frightened me, and every month since I have braced myself against this shock. Every farm knows blood. But this farm knows blood as a stain on all memory. I wanted Mum to sit with me, to let me lean against her for a little while. Instead, she wailed when I brought the soiled and folded napkin to the kitchen to ask what I should do with it. Her hands fluttered and she turned from me, her strange tight cry filling the room. I put the napkin in the cookstove and lit a match to it. Blood, my blood, dark and smelling of the earth. On the moon's cycle, blood now appears and reminds me of that sleeting day.

One day when we were in Marion's kitchen doing supper dishes, Marion spoke to her mother about getting monthlies. I was humiliated, knowing that she was hoping to help me. Mrs. Barton is always kind.

This time she turned to me and said, "What, Dodie, have you gotten your monthlies? Well, that's wonderful! This means that you are becoming a woman."

I felt a terrible weight settle. I have felt like a woman for so many years now, a mother, a mother to Beston and to my mother. To myself. Blood, shifting me away from childhood forever. Mrs. Barton saw something in my face that I tried to hide, and she drew me to her. It has been a very long time since I was held by anyone.

I do not want to be an angry person. I was a happy and grateful child.

Here I am again, in my mind instead of in whatever task is at hand. Work is respite.

Tup

I AM BEING pulled under the terrible, dark current by Doris's refusal to struggle with me to shore. She chooses a silent drowning. I don't feel that I have a choice. One of us must remain for our children. I make every effort at that devotion.

This morning I came home from Grafton and did my morning's work and then sat down to noon dinner with Doris and Dodie and Beston as usual and as usual Doris served me and her children a good hot dinner with beets and greens from Dodie's garden and as usual Best nodded hello to me but never said another word to any of us and as usual Dodie carried on about the chores she was going to do today and, as usual, Doris didn't eat, sitting across from me with her head hung, her mouth brittle.

Dodie is finishing school next year and I know she hopes to go to the state school at Orono. We can afford this now, and for Beston. The farm will not survive their absence. They are smart and need a chance to go to school. But I am doing too much of this all alone now. I'm very tired. I think every day when I am out on that tractor or milking on a cold morning, I think I'll sell this place and be done with it. There was a time I loved it but now it is a yoke around my neck I'd as soon shed if it weren't for Doris and the children. And my father. It's a bountiful place. I have one of the best herds in the county, maybe the best, which is what I believe, and every farmer in this area knows that. Nothing has changed. I do my work from five in the morning to six at night seven days a week. That's what this farm requires and that's what I give.

I would be happy to do that with my wife.

For now, Dodie refuses to accept my arrangement. I know this is hard on the children. It has been very hard on all of us. But it could not go on forever the way it was going. I have chosen to stick this out, returning every day to too much work and a silent, gone wife and two polite but remote children. I resent this judgment. I have earned my peace.

I asked Best at supper if he would play a few songs before I had to leave, but he just shook his head and said not tonight. I am not going to beg my children for a few small gestures of kindliness and love. I am not going to beg anyone, in this house or outside it, for their approval. I don't need it. I certainly do not need their judgment. Goddamn everyone.

HELEN AND I have rearranged the schedule at the mill so that I am home through the evening with the new baby and Helen. I have trained Alvie Brower to keep the machinery. He worked the carders and looms for fifteen years and is a good man. Helen is happy with this change.

Walking into her bright kitchen is, of course, a great relief. She invariably looks up from her papers at the table, or from washing up her supper dishes at the sink, and she smiles and gives me a small kiss on the cheek and takes my jacket. She asks once if things were okay today at the farm and I say, *Yes, yes, everything is in good shape.* I take up Grace and sit with her at the table, her joy at seeing her father evident. Helen watches, smiling, and tells me the small events of the day with her child, the larger events of the mill—Gary Clement's arm injury at the carding machine, an order for sixty bolts of gabardine canceled or called in, tensions among the girls on the second loom, an older woman she should let go because of her need to sit so much during the day. I might say that I laid in the corn seed in the field across the road, or I finished replacing the old separator in the milk room, a two-day job, or that I heard her favorite song, "Till the End of Time," on the radio on my way here. She doesn't ask anything more.

Helen understands that I have eaten supper and so she offers me a cup of coffee. Grace is still at her mother's breast, a sweet baby. Helen bathes and puts her to bed and returns to her own affairs, allowing me to read by the lamp in the living room, books that come from the library. Helen is not a reader. She spends the evenings doing the accounts and inventory and payroll. I admire her. When I look up from my book, she is bent to her paperwork. Her first husband left her in the dark when he died and she has taught herself everything needed to keep the mill running and thirty-two people at work. She handles her own money and hires and fires and drums up the accounts she needs. She is not a cook or gardener, and does not enjoy being outdoors. She is a practical person, very steady. She asks no questions and makes no demands on me.

I told her once at the start, without her asking, that I go each morning to my sister's farm in Alstead. That her husband died many years ago and I have always lived there and kept the farm for her. That it is home for her and her children and I am obligated. Helen is trusting and that was the end of the conversation. I do not consider this a lie. I consider it a kindness to Helen, and perhaps to Doris, who deserves some dignity in all this. Who could explain this story? No one. So this explanation is as good as any. A woman and two children need my work to keep them on the farm. That is not a lie. I do not have to justify any of this, and least of all to myself.

It is a comfort to hear her in the other room moving her papers, sometimes making a telephone call, putting together a small lunch for me to eat before I go to bed. She stays up beyond me every night, but has not once chastised me for climbing the stairs early and on my own. *Running the farm tires you out,* she says sometimes. She is a kind and sensible woman. But she is also a grateful woman. I have come into this home asking nothing of her except a quiet recognition that I exist. That I am. That I might rest here beyond the guilt I carry about my son. She knows nothing of that. What Helen Glasser knows is that a decent man has entered her life, given her a child she never dared to hope might come to her, and breathed the loneliness out of the corners of this house.

When Helen comes into her bed at the end of her long day, she is clothed in her nightgown. She comes quietly in the dark and parts the covers. She lies on her back, breathing softly and smoothly. Sometimes she pats my arm, and we slip into our necessary and separate sleep. If there is anything I might remember in the dark of night, her uncomplicated sleep allows me to turn away, leaving the past in Alstead.

I do not divorce Doris, because it would compromise our family. But any witness will attest that I have not had a wife for five years. I have to admit to myself that the news Helen brought to me that a child was coming distressed me. She saw that, I am afraid, an impression I worry she will never be able to shake. Her joy was absolute. *My miracle baby*, she says of Grace. Forty-one years old, and now a child. If I could take back the sense I know I gave her that I did not want this child, that this arrangement was not to be that sort of union, that I did not share a dream of making a family together—but all this she certainly now discerns. A man who has devoted his life to his sister and her children should be ready and grateful to finally have a wife and child of his own. Then why, she must wonder, is he not? Surely there are rumors, and so I am certain that Helen has made her bargain: a kind, if aloof, man, and a baby.

There are complications and contradictions and distinctions in every decision we make.

I have resisted all my life the judgment of other men. I am an honorable man. No one works harder than Tup Senter. And no one, no one can know what any man must do to secure calm and rest. I do not expect Doris or Dodie or Beston to feel gratitude toward me. Or Helen, or this new child she named Grace. But neither will I allow judgment from any of them.

BEFORE SHE COMES to bed each night, Helen leaves a cold breakfast on the table for me. I rise very early and eat in the half-dark of the streetlight shining through the kitchen window. I drive back to the farm. I am rested. Waiting for me is my silent wife, her indictment of me five years long now. Waiting for me is a bedroom I am no longer allowed to consider. Waiting for me are mistrusting children. My son's grave, a child among old men. The words of stories we have read, a room with new furniture and paint. What waits for me is weight. But as I drive in the early morning dark around the long corner and past the stone wall, and the great old elms like guardians in front of the house come into view, that weight and some sort of awful thing like joy, the joy of seeing home again after a very long absence, collide. I think I am ready every morning, but there it is. Senter Farm. Dodie and Beston Senter. Sonny Senter. Doris, and that terrible anticipation as I near her, as I near the woman who made this home and made these children with me in the sweet warmth of our bed. The woman who turned to me with the light from the dashboard on her cheeks and sang with me to a song on the radio. The woman who smiled as I entered the kitchen at the end of the day and put her arms around my neck, flirting, and told me that I smelled good. The woman, my wife, who turned from her garden, the sun caught in her hair, and waved to me as I crossed the yard, a beckoning.

This morning, I passed the dark house and pulled into the square of light in the barnyard. The lamp went on in my wife's room, and a minute later in the kitchen. I turned off the truck, preparing for the day, resisting this old drama. I have saved myself, at great cost to the children sleeping in this house, I am sure, although they understand I will not abandon them. The cows made the start of their early morning greetings. Doris's shadow moved across the kitchen. I wanted to walk into the shed and into my house and to this wife. I wanted to rewrite all of this. This is my one life. I wanted to walk inside and wreck everything we have ever touched, I wanted to pull Doris to me and hold her no matter how she fought, until she spent her anger at me and her children and this house and this soil for holding her boy. Fall is coming, with its chill and its

[155]

slow-dawning light. This morning, I was caught off guard. These longings will carry us nowhere. The river has receded, and we are each left in our place, stranded on the naked shore.

HELEN KNOWS NOTHING of Dodie or Beston or Sonny, of my wife Doris, a separate country. There are no names for the parts of me that have been lost. I ask for little. A sanctuary, that is all. Helen receives as much as I do, I am certain of that. We have made an arrangement, and we both accept its terms.

[1954]

Doris

I T HAS BEEN cold and very wet this month. The anniversary is coming, March third. Dread fills the rooms. Fills us. Dodie keeps the cookstove burning hot against the dampness, against the foreboding. This morning, after she put the dishes away, after Tup and Beston went out the door to their chores, she damped it down and went out to the coop to feed and water the hens and spread fresh straw. I was upstairs preparing to sort through the sheets and towels in the hall closet, the quiet filled with the incessant pulse in my ears.

The shed door opened again and I heard her cry out at the same moment. I found her in the darkened kitchen, smoke billowing along the ceiling in great coils.

She grabbed a towel and threw open the stove damper and opened the window and the door, yelling at me, "Mum! Didn't you smell it? Didn't you smell it?" and Dodie turned her back to me and stood in the shed door. "I can't do it all, Mum. I can't do everything myself," she said.

The smoke drifted past her as it cleared, and Dodie started to cry, a quiet cry, her shoulders heaving.

I moved closer to her. "No," I said. "I didn't smell it. I was upstairs. I was busy at my chores."

The smoke whitened and subsided, and the room emerged again, our kitchen. Beyond the open window, the hens scratched in the turned garden.

Finally, Dodie turned back to me and said, "Mum. You haven't talked to me like that for a very long time. I think you are getting better. Let me get a doctor who can help you." She watched me for a long while, and then went out through the shed to the yard.

May has told me there is now a child, a girl. Tup did not tell us.

THE SWALLOWS HAVE returned. The yard is muddy, and the paths to the barn and the coop and the work shed. I am waiting, impatient. Impatient. Impotent. Impoverished. Impious.

Beston sings his songs in the front room, songs filled with his own impatience. I cannot say what any of us is waiting for. We are on the rim of a wheel, spinning slowly, the landscape stilled around us. There is no one beyond this land watching.

When Dodie was three or four years old, Tup took her hand and walked with her to the fence and he lifted her to sit on the post. I could see them pointing at the cows, Dodie leaning against her father's shoulder. It was spring or summer, everything green and full, the air pulsing with the warmth of the sun. At supper, Dodie recited the names of the cows she had learned, Ginger and Ada and Caramel and Lolly and Daisy. Sonny joined in and added the names he knew, a list like a poem, and Dodie repeated each name in a singsong, turning to her father for his approval. He was pleased, the naming making its claims. I hear the children's voices sometimes, like hymns we once sang. The days will ease for all of us when March third passes for another year.

Dodie

O<small>N A COLD</small>, sleeting day in early spring, Daniel was standing by the front entrance when I came out of school. We have not exchanged one word in six years, and I did not expect that we ever would again. He graduated two years ago. As Sonny would have. And immediately Sonny is between us, and the front room and the great convulsion. Daniel works now for the dairy co-op delivering milk, house to house. I have asked Beston if Daniel is doing all right and Best shrugs.

I came out through the door in my own thoughts and Daniel stepped toward me, hunched into his jacket against the sleet. I looked behind, wondering whom he might be approaching, why he had returned to his old school.

"Dodie," he said, and reached for my arm.

All the students were coming behind us in their end-of-school chattering. I stepped aside toward Daniel and we looked at each other.

"Daniel," I said. "Are you all right?"

But he did not answer. We walked around to the side of the building, out of the wind. I waited for him to speak, shifting my load of books. Finally he took them from me and started to walk to the parking lot. He held the door open to his old sedan and then closed it carefully behind me. This is a part of the story that feels as if it has been waiting a long time.

B<small>ESTON IS ALMOST</small> fifteen years old and comes now to the high school. I do not like the boys he spends his time with. They are the lost children in our school. I have tried to speak with him about the company he is keeping but he will not agree to that discussion.

He laughs a new offhanded laugh and shrugs his shoulders and draws on the cigarette that is always lit.

"You have been raised in a family that teaches discipline," I say to him. "That teaches hard work and attention."

Beston relies on his surprising charm, even with me. "They're just fun," he says easily. "I like them."

I have spoken to my father about my worries, but he says each time, "Best will find his own way."

Best is nearly as tall as his father, still a very skinny boy, still ready with a smile, but this is now a smile that holds me at a distance. It is as if there is one response for Beston, amusement. As if he cannot afford a conversation that disallows this smile. The songs he plays on the piano, the words to his songs sound like a man crying. Beston knows more than any boy should ever know. Still, he is my brother, my little brother. I wash his clothes and mend them and ask Aunt May to keep him in pants as he grows. I pack his lunch each day, nag him to polish his shoes. I scold him about his homework, which he will let go if I do not pay close attention. He refuses to address his father at meals, and to work with him. He will do any chore and well, but he will do it alone. My father can say, "Beston, will you grain the cows in the morning?" and Best will nod. When my father drives into the yard at dawn, the cows are watered and grained and Best has dropped hay from the loft into the racks. All that is left is the milking and the cows to be sent out. Beston walks past my father with a nod, and my father finishes the morning chores. Beston does not shirk his share here.

Last night I cornered him and said that it was time for a haircut. I had been bothering him about this for three weeks.

"Your hair is over your eyes and ears, Best," I said.

"So?" he asked with his smile.

But he acquiesced. He drew off his shirt and undershirt and sat on a kitchen chair in the middle of the room. How many times have I cut my brother's hair? How many times have I bothered him, a fussing mother, to sit down for me? We had done the dishes together, as we do each night. The wall lamp by the sink makes the kitchen a welcoming room. Our mother came in from outside and stood at the door. Our father had driven away as he does every day after supper.

Best clutched the towel at his neck and sat still, whistling softly, "Please Love Me" and "Mess Around," songs he taught himself on the piano. Songs too old and knowing for a fifteen-year-old boy. I combed through his soft straight hair and lifted it to the scissors. His ears, his neck, his forehead. He has the Senter head, long and wide at the eyes. My brother, without a mother to cut his hair. I do a good job after so many years of learning. When I was done, he leaned forward over his long legs and I ran my fingers hard through his hair, shaking the cut ends onto the floor. He stood in the quiet light and pulled his shirts back on. While I swept, he took the towel outside and shook it hard. I could hear the soft snap again and again, and saw my mother turn to the sound.

"Play me a song," I said, and we sat together in the big front room, the piano and the sewing machine in their uneven rhythms, the songs of orphans.

ONE EVENING IN May, after we had done our chores, we were together at the kitchen table eating the supper my mother had prepared for us. The early evening light softened the corners of our old kitchen. My father has settled into an acceptance of our silence with him. He returns to this old life each morning, does his work and leaves. There is nothing to say. My mother's familiar food, the old plates and bowls and blue tablecloth with the yellow roses in the center, these are what we have to steady ourselves during these lifeless meals at our table. My father asked me for the butter, and my mother rose in the hot kitchen to open the window. As she returned, a terrible crack, an explosive crack and boom blew apart the silence and we all leaped from our chairs, that crack and boom from another time and the one of this moment the same for one terrible moment, the same incomprehension, the same shattering of who we had believed we were and would be.

A rifle shot.

My father was out the shed door looking down our lane beyond the barn and here came a blue truck skidding back past us as we stared in the yard, skidding dust and then the whooping of two men in the cab and a rifle held high out the window like a torch, the horn an uneven stutter above the jeering and yelling of the men who looked straight at us as they sped past the house on our narrow road shouting *Fornicator! Fornicator!* and then their tail-lights in the evening dusk and they were gone.

"Sons of bitches!" my father screamed after them.

"You filthy sons of bitches! Drunks!" Beston yelled and then came a bellow I have never heard, low and rising, coming from the east pasture beyond the barn and my father started to run, yelling back at Beston, "Goddamn it! Goddamn it! I need my guns! Get a goddamn knife! Get me a knife!"

Beston stood slowly turning toward the bellowing and watching my father's back and my father yelled over his shoulder, "Get a goddamned knife!" and Beston suddenly lifted into a run and came from the work shed with the big knife in its sheath and he and I ran to where my father stood in the pasture by one of the cows, her leg blown out at the knee, the cow on her side scrabbling in the grass in tight screaming circles, the leg dragging along by muscle and tendons, the bones splintered and white, the blood smearing a circle beneath her. Her eyes stared at my father, the good and hardworking farmer who tended these animals with kindness and even with love, she stared at him as she bellowed, spinning around in that helpless circle, the leg bones catching in the grass, and her calf stood apart, stiff legged, head down.

"Sons of bitches!" my father screamed as Beston ran to him and held out the knife. "Those filthy cowards killing my animal! Suffering my animal like this!" his spit flying as he yelled. He knelt, his knee pinning the cow's head and he pierced the neck below the jaw with the cow's scream and he sawed the knife across, the blood let loose now and gushing, the cow suddenly silent and watching, her eyes trying to lift to my father's eyes, and she scrabbled still in her circle, the legs pumping and the blood pumping. My father knelt away and stroked her blooded neck, soothing her with soft cooing sounds, "It's all right. There, there now, it is over, it is over," and the cow spun across the red grass and then stopped and the eyes stared and she stilled. My father stood, the knife and his arms and his pants and his boots blooded and he looked back up the road and my father roared, "I will goddamned kill you sons of bitches!"

And Beston rushed at my father and pushed him and screamed, crying, "You are the son of a bitch that did this to us! You are getting paid back for what you are, you bastard!"

My father stood stunned, arms hanging, the knife hanging and then he lunged and I believed he was going to stab his son, he lunged and pushed Beston and screamed, "You blame me? You goddamn blame me? I am a good man!"

Pushing himself close against his father, Beston said, low and hard, "You are a selfish bastard who takes exactly what he wants in the world, to hell with anyone else, and this is what you'll get," and he turned away.

My father dropped to his knees and wailed, the heavy dark of the spring evening now finally coming. My father toppled forward on his side and held his knees to his chest and he cried, hard sobs, and Beston walked past the barn and past the house and away along the road.

"Beston!" I called. "Beston!" as I tried to catch up with him, my father lying near his dead animal, his wailing carrying across the silenced fields.

Later in the night, we sat together again at the table, my mother also, silent, the uneaten supper still on our plates, and my father said, "Would you help me drag her?" and Beston nodded and they walked out together. The tractor started and my mother and I could hear it working out by the fence line across the road and past the ledges. My mother went out into the barnyard light and shadow and I did the dishes and sat on the porch, chilled and insubstantial. Beston and I climbed the stairs, my mother following as she always does, my father alone at the table in the tender light of the wall lamp. He stayed the night, sitting downstairs. I felt him in the house, a strange sort of relief, the bringer of this harm and the only true comfort against it. He had started the fire when I came down at dawn, had put coffee on to boil, and our day went on.

Daniel picks me up every day after school now, his milk run finished. We wait for Beston and the three of us drive through Four Corners and onto Doggett Road and we turn onto our dirt road over Crocket's Hill and Daniel delivers us home. We listen to music and Beston sings along and Daniel asks me about every class, what I learned. He misses being in school and scolds me every day because I have not made plans to apply to college. My father says it is my decision but he prefers that I attend. He says that not having an education bothered my mother.

But I ask him, "What would be different now if either of you graduated from college?"

He says that is an impossible question, that the events of our lives are a complex web of chance and decision. Daniel pushes me on my decision, and urges Beston to get good grades and look toward college. I know that Daniel cannot afford to pay the tuition, and that he feels trapped in his job. I encourage him to save his money and start in a year or two. He nods, but he deflects the conversation back to Best and me.

Each day, Daniel gets out of the car and says hello, a kind and respectful hello, to my father who comes from his work when he hears us drive in, and I watch my father rise to it and he shakes Daniel's hand each time and says, "Welcome, Daniel," a formal way of telling this boy that he has a place here, which we all believe. He fits here, as if that day opened up a space that has always been his. Some days he drives out of the yard and Beston and I will see him waiting again the next day when school lets out. But more and more, he stays, following my father to whatever chore he is on, and I can hear their voices across the yard. I don't recall Daniel ever helping out with Sonny when we were young, but he seems to have learned how to work a farm through just his intelligence and instincts. He fits smoothly with my father's pace and habits. Sometimes I watch them far off in the field, Daniel sitting on the fender as the tractor makes its way up and back the endless rows. Or leaning over the take-off to throw the planter or the rake or the tedder into the racket of its work. Sometimes he sits with us at the end of the day, a chair placed again on that empty side of the kitchen table.

No one pretends that Daniel is a replacement. But he is a kind and tender boy, very smart, with soft gray eyes that pay close attention. He was Sonny's friend, and is like Sonny in certain ways. On the days he joins us at our table, Beston and I are drawn into conversation with my father. The room eases. He helps Best and me wash up the dishes, and those evenings my mother stays inside, in her chair, listening to our talk, and my father sits over his coffee.

Daniel is a very serious boy. We have never once spoken about that day. But he sometimes speaks Sonny's name, part of a story or remembrance. At first we all went stiff with—with what? Fear? Shame? Grief too large to have words spoken around it? But Daniel persisted, a matter of fact, and slowly we have become accustomed to having our son, our brother, alive again in our shared memory. Some evenings when Daniel leaves, my mother follows him through the shed and Daniel turns and she accepts a hug from him, silent, both of them. When we move to the porch or the front room, some evenings now my father joins us for an hour. I sense that we have been unburdened for a little while and we sit with each other again as a family, attuned and accepting. Then my father rises without comment and walks down the hall to the kitchen and the door closes and the truck starts up. We can hear it making the rise and then it rounds the corner and is gone.

Tup

Helen knows I need to be here during calving. I am careful to do the breeding so the calves all come close together in March, so I am not away from Helen and Grace for weeks on end, although no farmer chooses to be up nights with two or three cows birthing at once. It had worked out all right until last night when Carrie started her labor. She is a good birther, so I expected no trouble. Haddie was in the next pen and she was coming fine, I wasn't concerned, although she's a bawler and it puts the whole barn on edge.

I stayed here at the farm and was up several times checking the cows in the calving pens and there was Carrie down on her side with the sac broken and the calf's hind leg out and I knew we had trouble. Carrie wasn't all right and I ran into the house, calling up to Doris in her dark room that I was going to need her. I have managed calving for six years alone and probably could have managed again this time. But the idea of Doris awake in her room and me in the barn trying to save a good cow and a good calf got to me suddenly after all the nights alone in that barn, and so I called up to her that I would like her help.

There was no response at first.

Dodie came out on the landing and whispered, "I'll help, Dad. Let Mum sleep."

But I said, "Dodie, you go back to bed. I need your mother to come down and help out with this."

Dodie stood looking down at me, her bare feet making her look like a little girl again. She went back to her room and the house was silent.

I waited without moving and my wife slowly opened her door and came out. She had pulled her dungarees on under her nightgown and was buttoning her old red sweater. She came down the stairs and walked past me without a word, but I was satisfied that my wife and I were headed to the barn together to bring this calf out alive, or at least without losing my good cow. I got two buckets of hot water at the stove. Doris took down her old chore jacket, not worn for so many years, and, hunched down the way she does now, she walked behind me to the barn.

The cows crowded together in their pens, all of them turned toward Haddie's bellowing. Doris stopped and watched her strain and then lunge forward, strain and lunge.

"It's not her I'm worried about," I said. "Carrie has a breech calf."

But Doris had not been in the barn for so long she didn't know anymore the names of the cows that give everything we need to live on.

I led her into Carrie's calving pen and she stood watching the poor cow stretch on her side, her legs stiff and her head and neck straining upward, her eyes rolling white. A small, wet hind leg hung from her backside, not a thing a dairy farmer wants to see. Doris knelt at the head of the cow until I said, "I'll need your help, Doris."

We took off our jackets and scrubbed our hands and arms and then the cow's opening, the steam rising into our faces, Doris holding the calf's leg aside.

"It's alive?" I asked her. She jerked her head up to me, then back to the leg, and stroking it, nodded.

"Then let's get it out now," I said.

Doris knows how to help a weak cow deliver her calf. She has done it many times. She squatted in the hay and took hold of the leg just inside the cow, pushing it aside for me. I slid my hand inside, running it up along the leg to the hip, searching for the other leg. Carrie raised her head and dropped it hard on the hay but didn't make a sound.

"Wait," I told Doris. "Push it in some."

I found the hock and then the tiny hoof of the other leg and pushed hard into the cow. Air whooshed from her open mouth, but she didn't bellow. I believed we were not going to save this calf but I sure as hell wanted to save this cow.

Doris was beside me in our barn. Haddie bawling, the kind of bellow I like to hear, the mother's loud complaint before the calf slips front legs and head and shoulders onto the hay and then the bellowing is over and the cow turns several times in the pen and then the lowered head and the tongue pulling off the sac from the nose and mouth of the calf and then along the back and over the neck again and again and again, rough and insistent and then the calf finally, weak with the exhaustion of entering the world, wobbles to its feet and the milk flows.

Carrie didn't make a sound. I slid the second leg down until I could catch the other with it between my fingers, the two legs in the same direction now.

"Okay, Doris," I said. "Help me pull."

Doris knew how to do this pulling, hard but slow. She got onto her knees and wrapped the slick little hooves in a clean rag and I said, "Okay, here we go," and we pulled together.

We are a very good team. We have done this many times. Of course I would not wish for one of my cows to be in this kind of trouble but it felt better to be there with my wife hauling on this limp calf than just about anything had for a long, long while. It felt as if maybe this was a grace offered by God to draw things back to their right order, and so there was almost a joy in the awful work together in the night barn, Haddie settled and happy with her calf, and Doris knowing just what to do.

Our bodies pressed to each other as we did the straining for Carrie, our shoulders and hips and feet braced together. There was terrible resistance at first and we grunted together and I watched Carrie's eyes roll. She was too weak to fight any of this barbarity, and then suddenly the release and the legs came and the hips in a flow of water and blood. Doris and I reached forward to the girth and adjusted our legs against each other and pulled again and the calf slipped with its fluids to our feet, a pile of very sad dead animal.

Doris fell back against the pen wall with a terrible look and I said, "I knew it was a dead calf."

She looked down at the calf, pressing herself against the pen boards, and up at me with what had to be accusation and my wife cried out, her eyes on me, her cry loud and full in the dark barn. Carrie lay still, needing me, needing water and a hard shout to get up, get up, get moving, and Doris there against the boards staring at me with wild eyes and a moan of horror.

"Doris!" I shouted. "Doris!" I tried to move toward her, I thought I would hold her but she stood and struggled with the pen latch and ran from the barn to the house.

I poured water into Carrie's mouth and shouted and pushed until she rose to her feet, swaying, her head hung low and drooling. I pulled the calf, perfectly formed, out of the pen and laid his body by the barn door. I would haul him in the morning across the road and let the coyotes and crows have him. An awful sight, a perfect calf, dead. I washed Carrie's backside and gave her a shot of antibiotics. I convinced her to move to a fresh pen and gave her a large measure of grain and watched her for an hour to make certain she wouldn't go down again. Then I went up to the house. The hope I had felt was gone, absolutely gone. I knew what I would find.

Doris was at the kitchen sink, the wall lamp on, rinsing out the barn rags again and again. She didn't turn when I came in.

"Doris, I'm sorry," I said. I stood behind her, feeling pity and tiredness. I said, "I knew soon enough the calf was dead. I thought you knew. I think it surprised you." I touched her shoulders with my hands but she tightened and I dropped them to my sides.

Still I stood against her back. "She's on her feet," I said. "If we can keep infection off, I think she will be okay."

Then Doris turned to me and leaned her head in against my chest, the first time in all these years that she has approached me. I found her hands at her sides and we interlaced our fingers, and we stood together in the lamplight of our old kitchen.

"Doris," I said, and she lifted her face to me and I kissed her softly. I pulled her to me. She let me hold her for a moment, then turned back to the sink.

I pulled off my barn clothes in the shed and washed up at the tub faucet and walked, mostly naked, past her and climbed the stairs. Those calving nights I stayed in Sonny's room, lying on my side through the night in his narrow bed. I kept my eyes closed so the shape of everything in his room stayed blind to me.

When I heard Doris finally come upstairs, I went to my door and said into the dark, "Are you all right, Doris?" but she did not answer.

Her door closed and I returned to the small bed. Dodie and Beston might be pleased to see me here first thing in the morning, but uneasy, too, the way we all are now.

The owls called for a while. Beyond that, silence. The night was dark, no stars, nothing crying out its hunt across the fields.

I rose in a few hours to check on Carrie and Haddie and her new calf, and to see if any other calves were coming. I had left the aisle lamps on in the barn, their light spilling through the windows and doors onto the land. There is a great peace that comes from being among new calves and their contented mothers. I did not return to the cold bed in the dark house. I lay down in the clean hay of the waiting calving pen and listened through the night to the stirrings and breath of the farm.

GRACE IS A sweet girl. She is walking now, and toddles after me when I come in the door. Helen keeps her up until I arrive, and always has her bathed and in her pajamas. She holds her to me for a kiss goodnight. Grace leans her face to mine, such expectancy. Every child wants a father's love and affection.

Her mother carries her up the stairs, and I hear Helen's coaxing laughter as she reads the bedtime book to her daughter. I should do this myself. It is surely a great pleasure to hold a child and share a book. I remember holding each of my children on my lap, Sonny and then Dodie and then Beston, the end of the tired day and the reward of the sweet-smelling soft hair below my chin, the concentration of the child, the lamplight, my voice. I feel shame that I do not feel deeply attached to this girl. She is Helen's daughter. I seem to have only two children, Dodie and Beston. I am a good man. I care about this kind woman and her child. But I am neither husband nor father in this house, and Helen, I am certain, knows that. We each extract what we need from the other. Helen finally has her family. The man who spends his nights in her house is benevolent, or at least benign. Is it true that is all I offer here? And what is it I take? Helen's soft chatter. Her cheerfulness. The warmth of her unneeding body next to me in bed each night.

Asylum from accusation. Do we love each other? We are each grateful. We have become accustomed. I spend my love each day at Senter Farm, my home, the home of the family Doris and I made. I spend my love on Doris. It is not a happy or a safe spending. I cannot seem to find the way to staunch its flow.

Do I take more here in Grafton than I give? I believe I do. But Helen allows it, and it rescues me.

I am slowly collecting books here. I am solitary in Helen's parlor these evenings. Living room, Helen calls it, but there is little living that happens here beyond that done by the people on the pages I turn. I am reading a great deal these evenings about people who live in primitive societies. Claude Lévi-Strauss and Franz Boas and Malinowski. Books the librarian in Augusta finds for me. There are ideas here that are challenging. I have always believed that I live as most men do. But there are no laws. I see that clearly now. It would be comforting to have a guide to follow. I have none. I am not like any other man. Every family makes up its own rules. Doris decides her own course. Dodie, and Beston. Helen. Grace will as she moves through her life. There is no map. The sun appears at the horizon, and in its sudden terrifying flare we start to build a ship we hope will float us home.

I pass these books along to Beston. He nods and places them on the big table in the front room. I believe he reads them. He hands them back to me without comment. I would like to speak with him about these ideas. With Sonny. Some evenings in Helen Glasser's sheltered home, I am caught off-balance. The loneliness works at me. I no longer maintain the machines at the mill. Why am I here? Why did I come here? I am a man watching myself.

Helen comes down the stairs, her child heedless and drifting as she gives herself over to sleep. Helen sits with her papers at the table, looking up sometimes and watching me as I read.

[1955]

Doris

WE ATTENDED DODIE'S graduation tonight as a family, an awkward charade. Tup continues to leave his clothes here, as if he is away on a visit somewhere. He brought his suit from the back of our closet after noon dinner yesterday and suggested to Dodie that she might iron it for him. She did that, hanging it over the chair in Sonny's room. She went into the closet and pulled out my green dress with the flowered belt and collar that I made when the children were small. Seeing it was a surprise. She ironed that, too, and polished my good shoes. These vestiges of a previous life we all lived. And so there was a sadness to the preparations that I am certain she did not escape.

May took Beston to Vernon last week and bought him a new suit jacket and black leather shoes. He borrowed a white shirt and tie from Tup. Beston is slight, but he is almost as tall as his father. When they walked down the stairs to leave for the high school, they looked so much alike I knew Tup could not have missed it. This is not a time for that sort of wonder. I believe Beston resists it. He walked ahead of his father and right out the door, waiting alone in the yard by the truck. He has taken up smoking, and kept his back to us while he waited, looking out over the east pasture as if there was something to find there.

Dodie sewed her own dress. I am aware that there is a tradition of a mother making what may be the last dress at home for a young girl. But Dodie went with Marion and her mother to Vernon

[175]

late in the winter and picked out cloth for herself. Soft, yellow cotton challis with a pale blue stripe. She has made a good dress, three-quarter sleeves with a fitted bodice and a small collar with piping, not an easy dress to sew. She came downstairs looking uncertain. I had an urge to hold her, to say that she looked very grown up, that she had made a very nice dress for her graduation. But we are no longer accustomed to that sort of engagement and the moment did not come.

Tup said to her, "You look very nice tonight, Dodie. You look like a young woman about to graduate into the world."

She stood at the door looking back at him and said, "And what kind of world is that?"

She and her father and I went out silently and met Beston at the truck. I can't think when I last left this place. I had spoken to myself many times about this as Dodie's graduation day came closer. I have an urgent dread of driving away from this house, from these fields and the barn and the hill with its stone. My vigilance is required. Tup has chosen to go away. That leaves me, guardian of the past that is held in this world. But I made the decision that Dodie's mother would see her graduate.

No one wanted to get into the truck. It was like an ache just waiting for us all.

Then Tup said, "Squeeze in, everybody. We'll still fit." He sounded excited, as if this five-mile ride was going to deliver us back to something.

Dodie climbed in first, and then Beston, and then me. Tup closed his door and we all shifted, the children grown now and without enough room. We were aware of Dodie's skirt, which she spread over our laps like a shawl. Beston stretched his long thin arms over the back of the seat behind us.

"Off we go a-wandering," Tup said in his old singsong voice, and he seemed to wait for our response, *Let's hope we don't get lost*, but the children sat stiff and silent. Tup became quiet.

Then he said cheerfully, the effort clear in his voice, "Okay. We have a girl here who wants to graduate from high school tonight. Let's get her there on time," and he opened the choke and turned over the engine.

It was a sweet sound, the breathing of the old motor familiar. It was a beautiful June evening, warm, and Tup had put the cows and calves back out after the milking. Looking across the farm, it was hard to believe the story has slid along so far.

We drove out our road, the dust swirling behind us. Through the break in the stone wall. Up the rise and around the sharp corner that lets you look back across the farm, our barn and our house and the big elms like sentries. The cows scattered across Tup's good fields. The hill beyond the orchard with its great pines and lonely sepulcher. With the next curve, it all disappeared. We passed through the woods and fields, the farms, Four Corners. Past Goff's, and the feedstore. Nothing has changed. The church, our old church with its vehement white steeple. The side door to the vestry was open to the evening. Past the children's old school, the yard bare dirt from play over so many years. This was once Tup's school, and his mother's and his father's. I do not imagine that any more Senter children will run in that yard. Then on to County Road, Tup's hands loose on the steering wheel. I suddenly saw that they are not the bony hands of a young man. We have leaped ahead somehow. They have thickened, and the graying hair on his arms showed below his cuff. "Going to the River" and "A Little Bird Told Me" played on the radio. I could feel Best's fingers tapping out the songs on the seat back. Over the road I have not traveled for a long time. Familiar, and a dream. This part of Maine is very pretty. We slipped through it in silence.

Daniel was waiting to say hello to Dodie at the door to the gymnasium. They hugged, and when Flora came, Dodie went in without a word to us. Beston walked into the gymnasium ahead of us and sat up in the bleachers with his friends. I had imagined a family sitting together for this one moment, for Dodie's sake. But that was impossible. I hesitated at the door. So many faces known to me from another time. They turned to us as we entered and I could feel the place go quiet. I had not imagined this, although I should have. Of course I should have. Crazy Doris Senter out and about in town after so many years. And her husband, a good farmer, but abandoning his wife and his remaining children to make a claim on a double life. Would the absence of Sonny be on anyone's mind?

Tup walked into the gym past the rows of chairs, looking straight ahead. I followed, and the heads turned with us as we passed. "Doris!" some people said. "Doris! How good to see you! Why don't you sit here with us?" and the women reached their hands to mine. No one looked at Tup or spoke his name. He found two seats on the aisle and stood waiting for me to step past him. Rita Shaw tapped my shoulder from behind and smiled hello. I held the gunwales of the rocking ship and waited to travel home. Tup sat next to me, stiff and silent.

I had not known that Dodie was named valedictorian for her class. When her name was called to give her speech, a terrible shame filled me. Beston whooped from the bleachers. I cannot recall the speech, only the image of our daughter calling her classmates, her old friends, to a good and large life. To the dreams we have. *Dum spiro, spero,* I remember her saying. *While I breathe, I hope.* Tup taught that to the children, a long time ago.

Dodie took her diploma with all the others. Tup stood up when he clapped for her, the only parent in the gymnasium to do so. Every person there saw him do that, his rising from the chair and clapping. Dodie did not turn to the audience. Was her father saying something to his daughter, or taunting his town? I do not know.

There was a great deal of milling around afterward. I headed straight out to the truck behind Tup. I saw Charlie and Esther Cummings hug their daughter, Susan, and hand her a wrapped gift. I had nothing for Dodie, and I do not believe Tup had anything for her. An oversight. I have forgotten how these things are meant to go. Beston chose to stay the night at Hovey's. Dodie chose to go to Marion's, along with Flora.

[178]

Tup and I climbed up into the truck, the empty space between. I felt a sudden crush of shyness, uncertainty. It unnerved me. The evening, mid-June, was open and bright. The trees arched over the familiar roads. How long has it been since Tup and I have been alone out in the world? It felt like a date, as if we had planned this time together without the children. But, of course, we had not. The children are growing up and away from us. Rushing, I am sure, to relief. What does a real mother feel on the night of her daughter's triumphant graduation? Not this. Not regret and shame so heavy I cannot elude it. And Tup? He is capable of such hope. Such faith. Did he watch his daughter as she addressed all the people she has ever known and fill with momentary pride? Momentary nostalgia for the closing of this time?

I turned to Tup Senter's profile. The formality of the suit, the tie. His legs bending, releasing as he changed gears. The truck unchanged. The windows open, my sleeve wavering in the wind. And then Tup was crying, silent, attentive to the driving. He reached for my hand, the weight between us suddenly shared. He pulled me close beside him. We drove through the tunnel of trees. When we pulled into the yard, Tup parked facing the sun setting low over the west pasture and fields. The air around us in the truck glowed golden, the light offering us an unburdening. Our shoulders, our arms, our hips and legs side by side. The vireo's song filled the early summer fields and woods. The cows wandered the south pasture, heads down, their ears and tails twitching. We sat side by side in silence.

The sun set and dusk came, and then the stars started to shine as the land darkened. Still, we sat. The house was empty of our children. I had never spent a night with all my children gone.

Tup finally kissed my hand and said, "Wait here." He went into the shed and then the lamp came on in the kitchen, and then the hallway and my bedroom. He came back to the truck and held the door open for me. "I could stay," he said.

I stood at the kitchen window looking out over the fences, their exactness, and listened to Tup drive away in the truck. It was a warm, still night, and I sat long on the shed steps. The rooms of the house spilled their emptiness into the yard around me.

Dodie

THE DAYS OF the week are the same now without school. I miss learning. I miss the opportunity to leave some of this behind. Beston squanders school. He goes because he has to, and probably, too, to be away from the complexities at home. I understand. Still, I would not mind another year of sitting each day in Latin and chemistry and world history.

I have considered carefully the question of college. My father has pressed me about it quite hard this past year, suggesting that I might regret not taking the opportunity. But I do not want to leave Beston alone, or take my father's money, and I want to be here at home. I wonder if I am compelled to stay because Sonny's blood binds me in obligation to this land, this house, these parents who can neither accommodate nor abandon their griefs.

MY FATHER AND Daniel slaughtered and scalded the pigs yesterday and this morning they butchered them. They work well together. Daniel has given himself over to the work of this farm. I worry how Beston sees this. I stood next to Daniel at the butcher shelf behind the workshop and wrapped each piece as he and my father handed it along. Daniel is quiet but very good-natured and offers my father the opportunity to elevate his own mood. I find that it saddens me to see my father release himself in this way, return to his own optimistic and cheerful self. A reminder of Tup Senter, my father. Daniel is unswerving in his belief in goodness and rightness, and with Daniel, my father, I believe, remembers that in himself. We stood at our cold, unpleasant work joking and laughing together, and my father told stories that Daniel likes to hear about growing up on the farm. He has no such stories, a very poor boy in a very small town. It is as if he borrows these stories and feels himself attach here. My father understands this, I know. They would appear to a stranger to be father and son. And to Beston? He loves Daniel. Perhaps he feels relieved of being son to this father.

We filled the freezer with meat and the men scrubbed down the cutting shelf with buckets of hot water. I could hear them laughing as I washed the mess off my hands and arms, and then they came in for midday dinner, which Mum had ready. Beston came in from the tractor shed where he is rebuilding the hydraulics on the harrow. He has somehow caught on to mechanics and my father allows him all those chores. He came in pleased with his work and scrubbed the grease off his hands, pretty hands that also play the piano, and sat with us for grace. We are a circle again now with Daniel on the long side of the table, Sonny's old place. Daniel takes our hands and we close our eyes and say thanks for the bounty of food. Sometimes I look up at Beston, his eyes open as he waits for us to finish our thanks. I told him one day that he doesn't need to believe in God to say a thank you out loud that we are so blessed with ample food.

He smiled, the way he does, and said, "I'll work that out myself, Dodie," and we have not spoken of it again.

I PULLED APART Sonny's room this week. Since my father left, it had grown so closed-in it smelled and the air felt dirty. My mother disapproved of my cleaning, I know. She followed me upstairs and stood in the hallway while I opened the windows and started to strip the bedclothes off. Without a sound she turned away and went back downstairs. I had hoped, I suppose, that she would decide to come in and would lean across the bed and help me lift off the musty blankets and linens my father used and throw them in the hallway to be washed and hung out in the sun, that she would open the closet and help me finally pull out Sonny's shirts and pants and Sunday jacket and pile them on the stripped bed and we would recognize these clothes we had both washed and ironed and mended so many times and we would nod to each other the acknowledgement that this was both hard and sweet, this touching again of Sonny. And she would open the dresser drawers and we would empty them and wipe them out with a damp rag and leave them open to air, we would lift the bedside rug and add it to the linens to be washed, we would sweep the floor and then, both of us on our hands and knees, wash the floor, changing the water until it came perfectly clean. She would take Sonny's books off his shelves above his desk, dusting them while I washed the shelves and we would line them up again, and we would clear his desk and its drawers, throwing away everything but his notebooks that held his thoughts and reflections and drawings and when we left the room, cleaned and stripped of everything that was Sonny's except for these few last mementos, we would leave the door open to the hallway and it would stay that way going forward.

But Mum could not stay. She turned away and went back downstairs and I heard the shed door open and close. I cleaned out my brother's room myself, ashamed that I had agreed to allow it to sit ignored for all this time, sad for my father that he had been consigned to this reliquary. There was no sign of my father's stay of several years in this room, his coming up the stairs each night and lying in this bed alone and climbing back down the stairs each morning to his work, nothing of him left here, as if he could not bear to make any claim on this place, as if the loneliness of lying in his dead child's bed, the loneliness of his wife across the hall behind a closed door, gutted him of himself and there was no mark to leave.

I washed all the linens and Sonny's clothes and hung them on the lines in the sun. The next day, I ironed the shirts and pants that might fit Best and showed them to him after supper. He was silent at first, staring at his brother's clothes, doing the arithmetic maybe, that Sonny had been fourteen when he died and here was

Best, fifteen but slight and so these shirts and pants would fit, and maybe sorting his way back in wonder that he remembered clothes he had not seen since he was eight years old and still so familiar, so fully part of his sense of this home and all of us in it. Then he nodded to me and smiled and carried them up to his own closet.

We have started to live with Beston in Sonny's clothes, and I thought that Mum might be distressed but she watches him come into the kitchen each morning and seems to accept this progression. My father's clothes remain in the closet next to my mother's in their room. Sonny's door has stayed open, and his windows to the spring air. When we pass his room, in daylight or moonlight, the shadows of the leaves on the elms sway across the bed and floor.

DANIEL AND I have never once spoken about that day in the front room. I do not know if it is me he blames.

Memory is both unequivocal and unaccountable. Like a play on a stage before me: the children in the warm room, the lamps on against the storm outside, the laughter and rough, happy movements, the sofa and Mum's chair, and the cataclysm of sound and silence, the sight each of us, and a mother and a father, will carry forever. Such clarity, every moment there before me. And yet also the obscurity, the irretrievable instant that I struggle toward. Was it I who reached in? I do not have the courage to ask Daniel.

The rhythms that have set in here will be permanent, I see that now. My father claims two lives. He believes he is justified. My mother has softened, but still she claims a separate orbit from her husband and children. We function. But there is a crippling. We limp and lurch and gain our balance and lurch again. We adjust. I am an adult now. This is my home. All this rises from that one moment.

But summer has arrived and our farm offers its balm. The hermit thrush sings his beautiful song, *oh, holy, holy, ah purity, purity, ay, sweetly, sweetly.* Great-grandmother's old shrub roses are coming into bloom, and the creek shimmers as it makes its way through the fields. The sun is hot on my back when I bend to my work in the garden. My mother works beside me for an hour or two each day, a help. I remind her of stories we used to like to retell. She listens as she works, her hands covered in our soil, her back to the same sun as mine. *Oh, holy, holy. Ah, purity, purity.*

Tup

THE YEAR CLOSED with a strong December nor'easter that left us with two feet of heavy snow. Then the wind came around northwest in the night and had cleared out the storm by the time I arrived home for the day. They got the roads open in time and school was held. Later, when I was done with my chores until evening milking, I gave myself over to the old pleasure of sitting at the kitchen table reading and watching Doris at her cookstove. The yard was plowed out. The cows and their calves were settled in the barn until some of the snow melted off. The woodbox was full. I don't mind this season, with its promise of rest from the work in the fields and woods, on the buildings and equipment, with the herd. The quiet waiting time, the barn tight and sheltering, the hay dry and plentiful, the snow covering every suggestion of the hard work coming in the spring.

Daniel brought Beston home from school, as he often does, and Beston egged the others on to sledding on the pine hill. I am not aware that Daniel has ever been to Sonny's grave, and I wondered if Beston was finding his way to arrange that. Daniel is a resilient and steadfast boy. They got the sleds from the shed cupboards and ran paraffin along the rusted runners.

Before they left the house, Daniel stopped Doris at her cooking and said, "Come out with us, Mrs. Senter. I bet it's been a while since you were on a sled."

She turned and stared at him, and then out the window where Best and Dodie were waiting.

She shook her head and Daniel said, "Then just walk out back with us," and he took her heavy coat from the hook and brought her boots and hat and the mittens she knit for herself long ago, blue with the extra-long cuffs she liked and Doris allowed Daniel to help her pull on her winter things and he held the door and she walked out before him and there was my wife walking between Dodie and Beston out the field road for the first time since before Sonny died. I wanted to join them, to join her, to be part of this pilgrimage.

I stood at the window looking across my fields into the afternoon light, my family and Daniel making their way toward the orchard and the pine hill, the snow deep around their legs, the old sleds hanging on Best's and Daniel's shoulders. For seven years I have asked Doris to accompany me to the grave of our son. On a quiet winter day like any other, Daniel had simply lifted the coat to her and spoken a few words and there she was trudging across the land with her children and this grown boy who has somehow entered our life here. I felt a flaring of anger at Daniel. I could see that Beston and Dodie were in high spirits, although Daniel seemed not to join them and Doris made her way through the deep snow with her head down, silent, I was sure.

I watched as they crossed the frozen creek and went among the apple trees, the branches and the four small figures dark against the low afternoon sun. The farm stretched as far as I could see, radiant white and sparkling in the light. The house felt confining and unreleasing. And then the four slowed and stopped at the far edge of the orchard as the land starts its rise to the pine hill. From here at such distance, from Doris's bedroom windows and the kitchen windows and the stoop, you cannot see the gravestones, not my father's or my grandfather's or my son's, but certainly Doris lifted her eyes to the hill as they approached for their sledding party and surely there was for her the familiar refusal and she turned suddenly and made her way toward home, calling back over her shoulder to her son and her daughter and their friend who seems, also, yoked to this land forever and she made her way back, her coat dragging heavy with snow, her head down and lifting occasionally as if to get her bearings. Her shadow stretched long in front of her as she came.

I pulled on my boots and crossed the yard and met her as she passed the buried garden and I said, "Come in, it's cold," and she allowed me to remove her coat and her hat and scarf and mittens and sit her on the chair in the shed and remove her boots packed with snow. I led her into the warm kitchen and turned on the lamp and told her to sit.

I brought dry socks to her, rubbing her feet between my hands before pulling them on. I poured hot coffee and returned to the shed and shook out and hung her heavy clothes. I stood at the kitchen window and looked out over the fields and said, "They are packing a good sled run," my voice easy to give the afternoon perspective and then I sat across from her at the table, our knees and feet touching. "One day we will go together," I said, and she did not contradict me.

I felt more charitable toward Daniel then, even grateful for the quiet way he has of pushing back against these rigid habits we have formed. The house was, as always, warm and bright. Doris allowed our feet to rest together, an intimacy.

Far away on the hill, young people bound to each other with memory played like children. Doris rose and stood at the window watching them and then returned and sat with me, her feet on top of mine.

"This farm has a lot of stories held in its land," I said to my wife. "When I was a boy," I said, "my sister and brothers and I carried our sleds across the fields to the hill and packed down a run and threw ourselves onto the sled, two or three of us piled together, and we barreled down that hill. It feels as if that is me out there."

Doris looked at me and nodded, an acknowledgement at last. I wanted to say everything else, to have her nod at every revelation, but I stayed quiet about it all.

When Best and Dodie and Daniel came in, their laughter and talk filled the shed and kitchen. Doris rose and silently helped them pull off their frozen, snowy clothes and she hung everything on the winter line in the shed and then she put together a good supper while I told stories of my childhood sledding on that hill.

The young people laughed with me and Doris nodded seriously. It came in very cold in the evening under a waxing moon, frosting the windows. It was too cold for Doris to sit outside. She stayed at the kitchen table after Dodie and Best and Daniel did up the dishes and moved to the front room. I chose to stay at the table with her. I read and she sat still. The room smelled of wet wool and leather, a clean and reminiscent smell. Best played the piano and sang, and sometimes Dodie and Daniel joined him with their imperfect but cheerful voices. The shadows in the house and outside had softened, assuaged. I reasoned that the river road would be unsafe. The cold of the valley freezes that road when all else is free. And so I stayed the night, trying the couch in the front room for the first time.

Daniel stayed, too, in the small spare bed in Best's room, his first time overnight in the house since Sonny's death. I understood— we all must certainly have understood—that he could not have done this easily and without thought. What does he find here? We all have been born into a story, each our own, that must, at whatever cost, play out to the end. If I could discern the course of my story, I would hasten it, would skip to its end, good or bad. Some days I am weighed down with dread. Yesterday was a day that offered a buoyancy, felt by everyone. I slept among our books, Best's piano music spread across the table, Dodie's sewing projects, the stars winking among the snow-laden branches of the great elms.

I started the fire in the kitchen range before dawn and when I headed out to milk, Daniel was there with me in the shed, pulling on his jacket and boots. We didn't speak. It remained clear and very cold. Stars still lit the sky.

The cows' warmth welcomed us as we entered the barn. They greeted us with their grumble and I told them to hush so they didn't wake the rooster. Daniel found that amusing and snorted and we got to our work, grain in the troughs and moving down the stanchions with the milking machine, relieving each cow of her heavy bag and on to the next. Daniel carried the milk cans to the milk room and dumped them into the separator for Dodie. We pushed the bales of hay aside that I keep packed around the water spigot and were pleased to find the pipes had not frozen in the night. Daniel went into the loft and threw down hay and filled the racks, and the cows were happy.

We went in and sat down to a big breakfast. Doris and Dodie and Best seemed happy to have Daniel there at the table in the fifth chair. After we ate, Dodie did up the dishes and packed a lunch for Beston. Daniel and I headed back to the barn to clean the side aisles and lay down fresh straw. Best surprised me by following us out and giving us a hand. The boys teased one another and the cows seemed to relax as the barn filled with their animation. I had not thought how silent the barn has become since Beston stopped sharing chores with me. Daniel took Beston to school before starting his milk route, and Dodie and Doris and I were left to the rest of the day's work.

That night I made my way back to Helen and Grace. Helen does not speak in anger, but I felt her wariness with me. I did not respond well and was short with her. I had done nothing wrong. I asked her if she meant that I should have risked the river road after such a storm and she turned away from me and spent the evening upstairs. The light in the living room felt dismal and the house cramped. The snow in town is dirty, packed into big piles to allow cars free movement. I found myself longing for the soft lamps of the kitchen and front room at home, and the clean wide sweeps of fresh snow across the open fields.

[1956]

Doris

THE SUN HAS gained strength and Tup's pastures have dried out enough to put the cows on them. There is an awakening. These cycles of time marked by seasons are a slow spin on the outer rim of a wheel.

Dodie has seeded the cole plants into the garden already, and the shed is filled with her seedling flats of the tender crops. I am trying to help out more than I have. In another few days Dodie will start setting the flats out in the yard to harden off. She keeps everything in good order here. After she did the spring cleanout of the henhouse, she whitewashed the inside and it looks very fresh. She also did the milk room. She has scrubbed and oiled all the floors inside and blacked the range. She asked me to air all the blankets and spreads and pillows, which I am doing, one room at a time. She also engaged me in sorting through the remaining canned goods to see what is left and what needs to be used up. Her garden will come in at just the right time.

Dodie has become the farm wife here. Tup asks a great deal of his daughter. She insists that she is willing. I hope that she will attend college. And do I hope that she will then return to this home, this farm? Yes. I often think about my mother and father buried in Colebrook. Those are lonely graves that I have not visited since Sonny. The fact is, I became a Senter. I became a Senter the day Tup and I got out of his old car in this yard and we stood under the big elms and looked at the decrepit house and the decrepit barn and milk room and the sagging fences and my young husband turned to me and said, "This is our farm now, Doris," and we felt such hope and potency. I remember walking across the dusty yard and the cows all turned to us from the north pasture across the road, their ears perked and their chewing stopped as if even they understood that this was the arrival of new life.

I was no longer a Canton. My mother and father must have known this, too, must have known that their daughter was not just leaving home into marriage but was entering a life apart from everything we had shared together in that unassuming little house and store. I was glad that Tup and I would have to rebuild every inch of the old farm. It was our turn on this land.

We crossed to the barn. The great doors were open and the swallows dipped and swooped in and out, pretty flashes tending their nests. All else was a mess, ropes and hay and rusted machinery, the grain bins chewed through by rats and the cow pens filled with wet, soiled bedding and light shining through holes here and there in the roof like stars high above us. Brooms and shovels lying anywhere in the chaff and dust. Tup kicked them aside without speaking. I knew he was ashamed, ashamed of his brothers and his father for allowing this and ashamed of himself for being away at college dreaming of another life altogether.

He led me to the loft ladder and came up behind me as we climbed to the upper loft and we stood in the dusty gold light coming through the broken windows.

"This is a very good barn," he said, and he looked happy.

He removed his jacket and laid it in the sweet clean hay that smelled still of sun and he pulled me down to him and kissed me and we touched each other in our barn.

"I won't always have time to do this in the middle of the day," he teased me afterward. "No," I said, "neither will I," and we lingered before the start of all our hard work, his hands warm on my back and his face close to mine so I felt his breath.

"Mrs. Senter," he said.

"Yes," I said. "Mrs. Tup Senter."

I regret now that I left behind my mother and my father. I am sure they did not ever imagine they would lose their only child so fully to her husband's world. The distance to Colebrook was not great and yet we seldom made our way there. I loved them. They knew that. But my taking on the Senter life dispossessed them of their child, and their grandchildren. I see that now. They wanted me to go to college. Perhaps they imagined me marrying a man who ran a business in town and maybe they even imagined I might stay working at the store, my children underfoot as I once was. That was what I had imagined, also, what I wanted. It is impossible for me now to recover those feelings. Who would I have become? What would the ballast of my life be without this farm?

I see that I am bringing myself to discomfort here: any slight difference in choices and I would not have had this life. I would not be Doris Senter, farm wife of the Senter place. I would not have this daughter and young son growing here into their own adult lives. I would not have the light of the moon lying white and untroubled across my bedroom floor. I would not have a cellar filled with food from this soil. I would not have the comfort of my kitchen, the table and the wood range with its steady warmth. I would not have the cows in the great, clean barn and their steaming milk coming off the separator and I would not have the owls sweeping the cut fields and filling the quiet of night with their hushed calls. I would not have the fireflies clinging to the screens of the summer porch, and I would have no memory of the children catching them in jars and releasing them in the darkened yard, watching them blink their signals into the night. I would have no memory of the voices of my children and my husband reading out loud on the couch in the front room. Of the warmth of my husband's body lying alongside mine, his breath in my hair, his hand on my leg. Of the quieting of the children as they slid into the tub in the shed on Sunday nights, the hot water sloshing, the stiff clean towels waiting, the rush to stand by the warm range in the light of the wall lamp.

But in any other life, I would not have a son lying on the hill under the pines, I would not hold this terrible guilt and sorrow, I would not travel in the outer orbits that have claimed me for so long. I would not have rooms unbearable to enter, I would not have a husband lying with another woman and caring for their child in a nearby town.

All of it. So much. Is this pain or rescue? I do not know.

What am I asking? I am asking if it has been worth being Doris Senter, here, this life, these memories and all the others. How is it possible this can even be a question after so much trouble? Would I choose a different life? Would I change all this? Would I rewrite this story with no Tup? No Sonny? The light in the day, in the night, across our land? How can it be possible that I might want this, with all its grief? Yes, I think I would claim this life, with all its sadness and all its grace. I am coming to know this now.

I know I am circling here around the conversations Dodie and Daniel are having about marriage. They want to stay on the farm. No college for Dodie. No going away, not even a going and a return. And so I am asking if this would be a life my daughter will someday regret.

Daniel is linked to this place and to this family forever. He is a very good boy, steady and devoted. He works hard and is willing to take on Tup's way of doing things. Is this a fulfillment of some sort of fate, a sacrifice by two harmed children to bring about an impossible restoration of order? Or is this simply a girl and a boy finding love and believing in it as Tup and I did? And in that case, should my daughter be warned, or should I celebrate for her?

Time. I have resisted the abatement, the soothing that time might offer. I do not deserve release. And yet it is true that the harsh edges seem to soften now. My eyes open at moments to the great and abundant beauty of this land. The stab of guilt and the stab of blessedness conjoin. Dodie loves this farm, even as her brother lies here in its soil. She and Daniel sit sometimes on the hill under the pines. But then they return to their chores, and to their quiet conversations over meals and on the porch, and to walks to the creek with Beston on the long afternoons. They trust that this land and this home and this barn full of cows is bounty enough to sustain their lives. I know that bounty.

If my daughter asked me, *Mum, shall I make my life here with this good man?* what should I say to her? I believe I would say yes. And if I say yes to her, I am also saying yes to myself. I am saying that this is a good life, offering more than we might deserve.

Dodie

I WONDER IF we are destined somehow to commit ourselves, the next generation, to an inescapable saga. I truly hope that is not the case. I believe that Daniel and I love each other. I believe that this farm offers all goodness, enough for us forever. I believe we are not bound to the past. My life and Daniel's life and Best's life spool ahead, mysterious and promising. I must believe that. And I believe in love. My mother and my father taught me that.

Daniel tells me that my father has not meant to abandon us. He says that Tup Senter is a man built with so much love that he has needed to protect himself from its withholding. And so I ask Daniel if the cause of all this is my mother.

He shakes his head and says, "No, Dodie, no. The cause of all this is grief."

If they did not love each other as fiercely as they do, my father would be sleeping each night in Sonny's old room and waking to the exactions of our lives on this farm.

MARION IS FINALLY home from the university for the summer. It has been several months since we have seen each other and I worried that we might have changed too much to pick up our friendship. Or perhaps that she would have changed and I have not.

She came out to the farm and stayed the night. It was stiff at first but we quickly remembered and gave ourselves to our old conversations. She is happy at college but finds the other students to be immature, not serious enough about their studies and insincere in their friendships. She seemed to be relieved to be home, and with her old friend, and so I was also relieved. I found myself envious when she spoke about her classes, but none of the rest of her new world tempted me. We talked late into the evening, and the months in between eased.

She wanted to collect the eggs after breakfast, our childhood pleasure, and then I took the morning off and we walked out to the creek. We lay in the sun and let the stream make its way through our fingers. This is still my favorite place on the farm. The pastures and corn and hayfields are just starting to green, the winter brown remaining just in the lowest and coldest parts. We were quiet and then Marion sat up and looked back along the creek to the house where Daniel was moving the heavy ladder.

"You should say yes," she said. "You are a lucky person to have Daniel."

"It's complicated," I said.

Marion snorted her laugh. "You think it would be less complicated with some other man? What do you think someone from outside would make of all this, Dodie Senter? Daniel understands your father. He has sympathy for your mother. He is kind to both of them. He cares about Beston and loves this farm. He is smart and good-tempered and most of all, he's crazy about you. You will consider yourself a fool someday if you don't grab this."

I did not know how to ask, *Am I seeking atonement from Daniel?* Still, I believe I know what love feels like.

We spent the morning telling our stories from the year apart, the sun warming the grass and lighting the gravel at the bottom of the stream. The arrival of spring, the return of my friend, the swallows' graceful and relentless hunt, the sun's sharp light and shadow—I felt a stilling, a comfort, a calming of the unease. We walked back through the fields and east pasture. The young leaves on the elms caught the light and threw lace shadows on the house and yard. The phoebes have returned and are freshening their nests under the porch eaves. The metal clink of Best's work echoed across the yard and the voices of my father and Daniel carried as they restacked the last of the winter's wood in the shed. Marion spent the day, helping me cut and plant the seed potatoes, our backs bent to the welcome sun, our hands deep in the still cold soil.

I said yes to Daniel. We were married by the garden when the peonies and larkspur were blooming. Mr. Shapleigh, the new minister at church, married us. My father gave me away. My mother stood by me, holding my hand until Daniel took my side. Afterward, Beston played the piano with the windows open so the yard filled with his music, songs he wrote himself about love and devotion. I am sure there are others, songs about love's loss, about loss of faith, about violent and unutterable endings, but he chose well for the day.

I am now Mrs. Daniel Marston. Daniel says I am Dodie Senter and always will be. He says he is Daniel Senter. Dodie and Daniel Senter. Mr. Shapleigh was shocked at the talk, but we were all amused.

Daniel shared my small bed for a week while we waited for a new double to be delivered.

It was big excitement when it came into the house, with all the new linens and pillows. Mum came up with me after Daniel and Daddy put it together and the mattresses on top, and together we shook the sheets over my bed and they floated down and we tucked them in and pulled the new blankets tight, and the spread. I think some days that my mother is moving closer to shore.

Daniel holds me in the night. He says, "You are a beautiful and strong woman. You can rest here with me." I have known this man since I was a child. He was my brother's best friend. We love each other. He is my husband, and he believes in me. We are bound to each other, and bound together to this farm, and maybe always have been.

Tup

DORIS MOVED TO Dodie's side as Daniel walked across the yard toward his bride and Doris reached for her daughter's hand and Dodie did not balk, which I would have understood but she did not, and they stood side by side, mother and daughter, holding hands until Daniel came beside her and then it was his hand she held and Doris moved to my side. I will remember the soft summer air and warm sun with its deep, palliative shadows, the cows at a distance in the west pasture on the heavy green grass and Dodie beautiful in her white dress. I will remember Daniel's fullness with happiness, and Dodie's, and Beston's music coming over the yard with its free and unbounded promise. Mostly I will remember my wife coming into the world, reaching for her daughter and spending love. Doris's hair has grayed but still, in the brightness of the summer sun, it shone golden down her back. We stood side by side and then I gave our daughter over into marriage.

Afterward we ate in the cool shade of the porch, Marion staying and Beston continuing with his music from the front room, the piano and his low, soft voice apart from us. Doris had risen to the occasion and made quite a feast of salads and breads and a big sheet of cake and she served each of us carefully, the table covered with the white cloth she used to bring out on holidays. Dodie had washed and ironed and rehemmed her mother's good blue dress, and she had pinned a white rose at her shoulder. Doris looked beautiful, the wear of these seven years gone on this day of ceremony. I have not seen my wife relieved of her grief in all this time. I felt the day of our own marriage powerfully, and moved through the afternoon belonging in both times, my wife and my daughter each on their wedding days, an alleviation of my own encumbrances.

After lunch, Dodie and Daniel walked to the creek, a sort of honeymoon afternoon. Doris and I sat together under the elms watching them move away and settle in the distance. "Do they remind you of us?" I asked her.

"Yes," she said.

"Our love endures, Doris," I said.

My wife was quiet. Then she moved her foot next to mine, pressing. The house and the barn and the fields were all in order. Our three children all here on this land, and now Daniel joining us. The great trees rose above us in all their power and protection. The garden at its peak, promising plenty. My wife's leg against mine. We stayed together for the afternoon, Doris accepting stories I wanted to tell, remembrances.

After supper we all sat on the porch, the table back against the wall and Dodie and Daniel sharing the old glider. We read, interrupting one another to share something of interest and sometimes laughing together. Doris sat with us on the porch, her knitting needles surprising us with the click of their old rhythm. Beston stepped outside for a cigarette and returned with a firefly glowing in his cupped hand, and, after he released it, he read to us some poems he likes by Langston Hughes, poems he says have music in them. Doris was attentive. Dodie and Daniel rose finally and we all said a very cheerful and teasing goodnight and they went upstairs. Later, Doris put aside her knitting and we all got up. I watched Doris follow Beston up the stairs, and she put out the light at the top, turning back to look at me for a moment as the dark fell.

I checked the barn, and the door to the coop in case Dodie had forgotten in her excitement to close up her hens. I stood uncertain, the new moon lighting the house and the yard and the silent fields and great white wall of the barn, and then I walked in the dark through the shed and then the kitchen and then the hall and then the front room where I settled for the night on the sofa, unready for the long dark drive along the river road.

DANIEL DROVE WITH me to the feedstore this morning. He is very good company. I risked suggesting to Beston that he come along but he shook his head and attended to his breakfast. I had thought perhaps that my presence through the night might soften Best to me, but it seems to have altered nothing. As Daniel and I drove out I could see that Best was under the manure spreader working on the beaters. He manages to avoid doing chores with me, but he is keeping the machinery in very good order, better than I am able with all my other responsibilities.

I resent the suggestion that Beston condemns me. He is not a man yet and cannot understand the adaptations we are forced to make. He believes he will be safe from his own children's judgment one day. I feel a great measure of compassion for my son, and sadness about our distance. But I trust that his judgments are going to relent as he matures and gains greater understandings.

Daniel's good nature leads him to find pleasure in every simple thing. I am not likely anymore to engage in conversation with the men at the feedstore. We have nothing to discuss. They ignore me and focus their talk on Daniel. He pays a price for his new family association, I am sure, but he seems not to need the approval of this town. He jokes with these neighbors, a surprising wit who keeps them at a distance with laughter.

This morning, the men congratulated Daniel, and me, to be fair, amidst a great deal of joking and clowning and then Luther Farley teased Daniel about when a child could be expected, and I saw Daniel tense. Everyone could see it, his open face and quick nimble body suddenly stopped still, wary, and there was an awkward moment among us.

Then Daniel smiled and said, "Luther, are you so lonesome you need to wonder about what goes on in another man's bed?" and there was release, movement again, and Luther laughed with the rest and it was over, whatever it was. It troubled me.

When we drew into the barnyard, Beston stood from his work and nodded to us. Later, apart from me, he and Daniel will be at ease together. Daniel and I carried the bags of grain into the barn, slit them open and dumped them into the bins, the sweetness rising around us in the humid air. With the corn that is ripening now, we will have plenty to carry the cows through winter, a great satisfaction. Daniel felt it, I am certain, topping off the bins and whistling as his wife does. She came into the barn just as we were folding the bags and told us Doris had noon dinner ready, an unnecessary invitation. There is a flirtation between my daughter and her husband, an awareness of one another, a reminder that somehow catches me with sadness, or a loneliness.

We washed at the kitchen sink and sat to eat Doris's meal. Dodie was high-spirited, teasing Daniel, and she was patient with her mother. Beston sat mostly quiet through the meal, smiling and nodding at whatever was said, and left the table as soon as he was done eating. Dodie sometimes slipped her arm over her brother's shoulder, leaning into him, their wordless connection. Daniel asked me his constant questions about the farm, about my boyhood on this land, and my family listened to my small, willing stories. There is vindication in their attention, an assertion of my place here.

May came for the afternoon to visit Doris. We see much less of her now that Dodie does the woman's work on this farm and Doris is helping a lot more in the house and garden. May and Doris wandered the yard admiring Dodie's garden and the flourishing flower and shrub beds, then they sat on the porch drinking the lemonade Doris keeps in the icebox, May chatting and Doris saying very little.

Later, I saw May walking out the field road through the pasture and orchard and up onto the pine hill. The day was calm. The barn swallows followed her, swooping low over the grass to catch insects she disturbed as she walked. It was a very pretty sight, the sun on the summer fields and pasture, my sister in her blue dress, the birds in their mastery. I looked several times across to the hill and saw that she sat without moving. The stones mark our family going back five generations. Our family. My son. I appreciated May visiting them. Doris has never, to my knowledge, sat beside her son. I will go myself tomorrow. Perhaps Beston or Dodie or Daniel would like to come along.

The farm will stay with Dodie and Daniel, and Beston should he choose. This is a gratifying realization, a good and comforting course of events. Dodie has made her decision. She is staying. Daniel belongs here, and perhaps always has. Beston shows little interest in his schooling and the prospect of college, so perhaps as he matures he will also choose this life that runs in our blood. With Dodie's marriage to Daniel, with their attachment to this life, I am able to recommit to the days' work. I drive home each morning before dawn toward the rising light in the east, its tenuous herald of a future.

[SPRING 1957]

Doris

BEST IS GONE. My second son is gone. This is a different absence, a renunciation. He is somewhere, alive in the fullness of his mind and his heart, but he is lost to me. This is a different loss, leaving no questions about fault. Beston has chosen to go. He is sixteen years old, my boy with his slender shoulders and frightened, earnest smile.

Tup says Best will return when he discovers the way the world works. I am sure he will not return, no matter the privations. Beston has quietly drifted outside our realm for a long time now. And we allowed him to drift, believing the wind would blow him back to us one day. I failed to shield him. I see clearly, at this moment, that I chose my own sufferings over those of my children. It did not feel like that, but how else can I understand it now?

But I stayed, at least that. I could have ended my own life. I could have made the choice Tup did and found another life. I did not. I stayed as best I could. But as if from afar, I have watched myself, and I understand the great shadow I cast on my children. And, yes, on my husband. Mine has been its own kind of leaving, I know that. The dread I have felt that I cannot prevent the unimaginable has overburdened our lurching little ship. Beston has been bravely swimming alongside, his hand on the gunwale since Sonny went, thinking at first, just a small boy, that his mother and father would steer us all to safety. And I? I sat looking over the stern, watching us move farther and farther from shore.

My son is sixteen years old, alone in Boston and surely very frightened, creating explanations to himself and to us about the future he is carving. The current carries him away.

And Dodie? She, too, has lost her boy. She echoes Tup. *Best needs to do this*, she says, arguing against her fear. *Best is smart and resourceful, Best is artistic and hungering, Best doesn't care about school, Best will be all right*, she says. *Best will come home.* Daniel has brought great happiness to my daughter. But I see the old constriction returning, the dark wariness that she carried after Sonny was gone, a little girl learning too much about sorrow. *Best just needs to try this*, she says, bravely, hopefully, but she, too, has lost her child. This has knocked me out of myself. I feel the change. I have allowed two children to be lost. Dodie cannot be the third.

I HAVE RETURNED to the work of the milk room. I had forgotten the comfort on a cool spring day of the warm milk, its heavy sweetness, the years of milk's sweetness in the boards of the floors and walls, the hum of the separator. I have lost the strength of my arms and am working to regain it as I balance the buckets against the rim and pour. We make wonderful milk on this farm, yellow with butter fat, free of straw and hair. The co-op favors us because of the milk we load on the co-op truck each morning. Daniel has taken over that chore since Beston left. I see that he feels pride in offering Senter milk to the co-op. I feel some of that old pride returning as I work at the separator. I have been absent from the work of this farm.

I try not to walk in the nighttime yard now. There can be no more inattention.

Best played the piano every evening, and so the quiet is strong. Daniel does little reading, but he likes to make things, to carve animals and create new handles for tools. Dodie's sewing machine whirs. I have returned to my knitting and mending. My hands remember it all. There are shirts and trousers in my basket that

Best gave to Dodie to mend before he left. I am fixing them and Dodie washes and irons them. They hang in Best's closet in his room, waiting.

Tup reads. He is alone on the sofa now, a sight that saddens me, as if it is the culmination of all history. At times he seems knocked quiet by Beston's going. Other days, he reassures us all and goes forward with the work at hand. Sometimes Tup looks up from his book and says, "Listen to this." We are happy to look up from our work and be bound together in the lamplight by Tup's voice. Sometimes I feel him watching me as I sew, and I look up and we are looking at each other across a room that holds all our stories. He might smile, and although I cannot smile, I also do not turn away. He returns to his reading, and I to my sewing. Dodie sometimes catches these exchanges and watches us carefully.

On those nights, when Tup drives away in his truck, Dodie takes my hand and we walk upstairs together, past Sonny's open door and Beston's.

"Night, Mum," my daughter says, and she smiles at me.

"Night, Dodie," I say.

My daughter is a brave and loyal person. Daniel tends the stoves and then comes up the stairs. They close their door behind them, and from my quiet room I can hear their voices, and sometimes their laughter, and once, just once, after Beston left, Dodie's crying.

There is a lot of absence in these upstairs rooms, Sonny and Beston and Tup. But there is also Dodie and her husband and all the life they breathe into this farm. I lie in the dark, recalling. My father told me once that he lived in his memory more than in the real days, that this is how it is when we get older. He said that he remembered lying on the cool soil under the giant rhubarb leaves on a hot summer day, the sun filtering through, and he watched the shimmering shadow of his mother as she worked in her garden. "It can make me cry," my father said. With my daughter and her husband sleeping down the hall, I lie in my bed, remembering.

I used to believe in happiness. I did not understand that we never fully arrive in that universe. We visit for miraculous moments, and then travel all the other universes, and if we have any kind of wisdom, we refuse bitterness or regret when the happiness subsides. I have been slow to that wisdom. I imagined lives of happiness for my children, lives with no forethought of grief. Did I promise that to them? I hope not. They knew happiness when they were small children, real happiness. Joy, daily joy. Did they misunderstand and think that joy would carry through their lives? I want to say to Dodie and to Beston, *I am sorry if I allowed you to believe in the grace we created for you here. It does not last.*

But that is not what I really need to say to my children.

My father also told me that we gather regrets as we age. Yes. Regrets gather, and gather. Then Dodie turns to me in the kitchen, from within her own sorrows, and holds me with her eyes, and she says, "Let's go out and move the seedling flats into the sun, Mum," and the swallows lift and float into the light over the fields.

Dodie

I FOUND THIS in Sonny's notebooks when I cleaned out his room last spring: "*Desideratum*: hope, dream, wish, the heart's desire." Beston understands this heart's desire. He says all he wants is to make music, that nothing else matters. I hope that is true. If it is true, I believe my brother will return to us when he has had his fill. If not, if instead it is this family itself he needs to escape, he is truly gone. These rooms I love have constrained Best. The barn has become our father's and Daniel's, if it ever felt like his own. Maybe it has always been my father's and Sonny's, with no room for Beston.

The trigger for this—trigger, is there always a trigger?—was a slight tension between Daddy and Best. Nothing more than that, although I wished even at the moment that my father had been more alert to his son's discomfort, his obvious flinching from us over midday dinner. This recoil is not unfamiliar, and each time I want to pull Best to me and absorb some of whatever the hurt is that he endures. Our everyday table talk has eased, due mostly to Daniel's presence, I am certain. Daddy enjoys periods of inclusion now, an easing we all must have desired and fell into gratefully. Daniel's goodness precludes the daily expression of whatever our judgments are. There is no room at our table for condemnation, Daniel makes that very clear. In Best, though, I can see that he will smile, that he will nod toward his father, but still he brings his judgments, and feels those of his father, whether well-interpreted or not. Daddy was saying that he knows he should appreciate the slower pace of work while we wait for the fields to dry out, but that he gets bored and feels lazy. He said he couldn't wait to start hauling manure out onto the fields, and it was a joke because no farmer really loves that job, no matter how critical and gainful the work is. But he looked to Daniel as he spoke, leaving Best outside.

We all laughed, all except Beston, whose face clouded under his smile, and the kitchen went quiet for a moment. We watched him to see if he could share the family joke, if he could alleviate this silent tension, and we took his smile as permission to believe our family is bound and enduring. I knew his smile said nothing like that, and still I allowed myself release.

Best finished eating and rose first and carried his plate to the sink and when he passed behind my chair on the way to the front room he placed his hand on my shoulder and leaned to me and kissed the top of my head firmly, slowly, pressing his face into my hair. An urgent sense rose in me, a crushing understanding that I will return to that gesture again and again all my life, that it was the end of something and the start of something new, something unnamable and perilous. I understood that my brother's kiss will hover for the rest of my life, an inscrutable key to all that went wrong for this boy, to all that was insufficient in my love for him. Dread filled me, and fills me now.

ONCE, WHEN BESTON was just five years old, Sonny asked Best and me if we wanted to climb the ledges across the road in the north pasture. Mum didn't like us going over there but there was no rule and even as children we knew it was one of the prettiest places on the farm. We climbed through the fence and followed Sonny across the pasture. It was a cool day late in spring. The leaves were just coming and the air felt green the way it does at that time. We had to walk slowly for Best to keep up through the thickening grass. Crows cawed from the trees at the edge of the pasture. They lifted their heads and squalled and then watched us pass by. Their feathers gleamed purple in the sun. Farmers don't like crows and shoot them but my father says they are intelligent and resourceful animals and have a right to these fields just as we do. He had put the cows to graze on the west pasture beyond the creek that morning so we had the pasture to ourselves. The ledges spread high and wide, imposing themselves on the land. Our grandfather and his father once cut granite from this stone and we could see the old rough drill marks still, and the pieces not suitable that were left tumbled on the ground. Dad says the granite at our doorsteps and on the skirt of the barn ramp came from these ledges. Like a puzzle, as if every part of this farm and its families fits somehow.

I could tell that Sonny had no mission. Just a walk with a good destination. He pulled first me and then Best up the steep parts of the ledge. I had only been to the top a couple of times. I would not tell Sonny that I felt afraid of the edge, and I held Beston back. But Sonny walked forward and lay down at the rim. We followed, creeping forward on our knees, and lying next to our older brother we were able to look down across the green brilliance of the pasture, over the fence line and the road, a lazy brown ribbon, and across to our house, a miniature of itself now, far off in the distance, and the shining white barn. The cows in the far pasture seemed to stand still in the shimmering June sun, a photograph of a moment caught forever. The crowns of the crow trees swayed at eye level as if swept by the flow of a quiet river, the new leaves turning light, dark, light, dark in the breeze. I could see that my window, now so small, was open, and the white curtains my mother sewed drifted in the same soft sweep. I knew that I was a girl named Dodie who lived a full and smart and interesting life in that room and in that house with my parents and my brothers.

But from this height, so far from that room across the wide field, I felt a decoupling, an estrangement from that girl and her safe place inside that house. Far adrift, as if I, too, were slipping away in the current, fear caught at me, the height and the detachment and the void where love and safety had been, and panic rose. I searched my memories of curtains at a window, great elm trees at a door, a house, a barn, cows in a faraway field. I lunged for a lifeline, and in the great weight of stillness I turned to my little brother, too young to rescue me, and he turned from the sun and the grass and the faraway house and barn and the tiny cows and he smiled with joy, with such astonished gratitude and wonder I was startled back to the beauty that holds us on this farm, and the curtains at my window billowed inward toward my bed and my quilt and my bureau and my top drawer holding my socks and my underwear and my little box of old pennies and nickels my father finds in the fields, and Beston leaned to me and laid his head against my shoulder and his joy spread through me as if it were my own.

Sonny rolled onto his back and we copied him and watched the crows cut their arrows across the sky, our arms shielding our eyes from the sun that was too much to look at, our lashes iridescent and fluttering. Beston held my hand and the afternoon slid over us.

BESTON WRITES VERY sad songs. My father teased him about them, but gently, allowing a boy his lament. Daniel and I have started to attend church again, and last winter there was a Saturday night talent show on New Year's Eve. Daniel prodded Best to play the piano, and at first Best refused, saying that no one in Alstead, Maine, wants to hear his kind of songs.

But Daniel said, "Try them," and Beston finally agreed.

My father suggested to my mother that they might go to hear him, but my mother shook her head and said no and my father did not ask again. Beston dressed up in one of Sonny's shirts and Sonny's wool dress jacket. I polished his shoes and he washed his hair at the sink and combed it back. His blue eyes are startling with his dark hair and the girls at school think he is a prize, but Best keeps to himself. I had asked him a few days before the show if his friends knew that he was going to perform.

He smiled and said, "Dodie, I don't have any friends like that."

"What kind of friends?" I asked him.

"Friends who want to give up a night to hear me play the piano and sing a few songs," he said.

I protested, asking about Hovey and Ben Crotty and Jackie McKenny.

"No, I am not going to ask them," he said and that ended it.

Later, sitting next to Daniel, I realized that I have missed something that should have worried me. There was a time, when Best was just a boy, that he preferred his friends to being here at home. But that was a long time ago. My little brother has moved inside himself and stays apart. How did I miss this? I have been too caught up in my own troubles, and lately in my own happiness. He must be very lonely. He must have been very lonely for a long time now. Watching him climb the stage steps in the Grange Hall and sit at the old upright piano, I saw a fragility beyond the fine, handsome face. His hands shook as he opened his sheets of music. He looked just once out into the audience before he played, and there was his beautiful shy smile like a great gift to all of us, a bestowal of his innocence and his hope.

He played three songs. The first was "Love Me Tender." Best transformed. He played a little introduction and then he closed his eyes and his generous low voice carried across the hall. I have only heard his music in the front room. Hearing it in the big hall, with him on a stage and one hundred people listening, I suddenly understood that this is what Beston is. That God has given this boy a great talent. I wanted Mum and Dad to be here, to watch their young son slide beyond us and into a place that has no room for us. Beston is an artist. He is and always has been different. I wanted to cry, for him and the power of his gift, and for us, who will not be able to travel with him.

The town listened to my brother, and then they clapped and cheered and whistled. Beston looked out over his audience and then quickly changed the music sheets and started to play his own tender songs, "Winter Dream" and "Count on Me." When he rose to leave the stage, the audience stood, his friends and schoolmates and our neighbors, and they clapped loudly and long. Beston stopped and looked out over us all, and bent in a shy and perplexed bow.

I told him that no one in town will ever forget his performance.

He said, "Of course they will, Dodie. Every single person in that room has something much larger to remember than my little songs." He was sharp with me but then undid the uneasiness with his smile and a nudge of his shoulder as if we had both been joking.

Daniel was quiet for a while and then said, "All I know, Best, is that something awfully big seems to go on with your music and I don't think you can ignore that."

Beston was quiet, looking out the truck window at the familiar woods and fields as we headed home.

Dad had stayed late to hear how it all went. I made too much of it, trying to allow our mother and father my new understanding, and Beston stood awkwardly at the kitchen table. He refused a cup of hot tea offered by my mother, who was obviously proud and excited as she hovered around her son. He remained standing and finally we said our goodnights and my father left, his headlights hard and piercing as they swept out of the yard and into the cold spring night.

Beston stayed downstairs, and later I heard him at the piano, playing so softly I could barely hear. The notes were slow and uneasy. Beston climbed the stairs finally and closed his door, and the house went dark. The half-moon shone brightly over the Senter fields. In the night an owl called, and another responded, an invitation or a warning, I couldn't tell. The grace and the unease.

Tup

B ESTON PUT HIS note on the kitchen table for us to find after he left sometime last night:

DON'T ANY OF you worry. I just need to try this music out. You can be certain I will get along okay. I will be in Boston, where I hear boys are making a lot of music. Mostly, don't any of you worry that I have not been happy here at home. I know that will be your thought. But it is wrong. This is a good home, and good and loving people have cared for me. I am grateful for that. A large part of me regrets having to leave, especially thinking of spring arriving and the hay making up and the corn coming and the calves on the pasture with their mothers. That is a good time of year on this farm.

I HOPE YOU will wish me well. I do, each of you. Beston.

DODIE WAILED AND ran from the house. Daniel followed her, with whatever thoughts he had about the troubles that follow the Senters. Doris sat at the table next to me, holding the letter and staring beyond me. I moved through every word, every gesture of last night, wondering what set this off. I find nothing large enough to carry a boy out the door from home. Instead, a kind of sickness settled and has stayed with me. Beston, the most innocent of us. I pray that music is what has called him from us.

Beston has been working in the lee of the barn, rebuilding the head of the corn picker. He has been hard at the job, after school and after supper until the light goes. He completed the work yesterday and pulled the picker through the mud back into the equipment shed under the barn, lining it up carefully and lifting the tongue onto a block to keep it out of the dirt. I thanked him generously at supper and he nodded seriously.

Beston is not Sonny. I pray that I never tried to make him so. How could this boy ever forget his father lying through the night holding him all those months and even years until he could make it through on his own?

There are days when I truly do not want any of this anymore. Not Doris, especially not Helen and Grace, not these cows and these fields of hay and corn, not the dawn light in the kitchen calling us to the next day. But there is nowhere to go, and so we each stay in our daily efforts. We are diminished here. Silenced.

We will regain our fortitude. Our tenacity. Beston has fortitude, his own sort. I disallow myself from imagining him alone somewhere. I would have given him money. He must have known that, and so it means he needs to do this on his own.

The day's work waited. Daniel came back in and said, "Let's get milking," and we put on our heavy barn coats and hats and moved among the cows in the early gray light. I busied myself sweeping the aisles, the radio turned up and the thin spring sun filling the barn from the lofts to my feet. This is all I know to do. I feel restless for real spring to come, wishing I could mow the orchard, or haul some of last year's manure to Dodie's garden. I long to see her bent to her work along the rows, Doris beside her. The swallows would flash and swoop over the fields. The creek would spark silver as it makes its way.

Doris stayed close to her daughter all day, working in the henhouse and organizing the root cellar. I heard their voices across the yard, woman talk, without laughter but still there was the tenderness, their devotion. Daniel left them to themselves. We attended our chores, a reduced little family.

I MADE MY way in the evening to Helen's without any of the usual hope for consolation. The dark river held hard against the long road. I left a tableau of lamplight and quiet, and arrived at a tableau of lamplight and quiet. But there was no comfort now.

Helen greeted me in her robe, ignorant of the events of the day. She woke her child and offered her to me. Grace laid her head on my shoulder and allowed herself to release into me. Her smell was sweet and heavy with sleep. I felt my familiar resistance, without excuse, and handed her back to her mother. Helen carried the child upstairs, and returned to make a sandwich for me. We sat together at the table, the details of her day at the mill and her evening with Grace spilling between us. I have never been unkind to this earnest and diligent woman. I listened and nodded, which she accepted as acknowledgement enough. We ask very little of each other, and receive what we most need. This is our arrangement. There is an acceptance between us, still. I tried to quiet my longing for home, for my family, for the sense of us sleeping near each other in the sheltering house. I tried to quiet my apprehension that I should never have come here, no matter how remote and unforgiving my wife. My wife, who knows such grief.

In the night, I felt Beston standing behind me on the tractor, leaning into my back for balance, and together we made our way back and forth in the long straight rows, toward home and away, toward home and away, our presence on the land clear and benevolent, our work together a covenant.

[AUTUMN 1957]

Doris

DODIE FORGIVES HER mother and father too readily, blaming herself for Sonny and then Beston. Had I understood that, I might have seen this coming, or if not this, which is not imaginable, then at least I would have marked her refusal to speak about having children.

Had I understood that, I would have prepared myself for the blood, my daughter's blood in the outhouse. In the outhouse, of all unsanctified places for my daughter's lonely termination of a child and her blood running down her legs to pools widening on the floor, her look of terror and a sudden sense of squandering as she looked from me to her bloodied hands and back to me. From my bed I had heard her from far off.

"Mum!" she kept screaming. "Mum! Mum!"

"I'm here, Dodie," I said and I reached for her and drew her to me, her body shaking with fear and already regret, shaking with all the years of embodied grief.

My young daughter leaned into me and still she screamed, "Mum! Mum!"

The blood was black red, slippery, familiar to a mother as it never should be, and I held my daughter and my son in the same moment, ten years between, the stories fusing and I sat her down on the bench and said, "Stay," and ran to the kitchen yelling for Daniel and when I returned to the outhouse Dodie raised her face and looked at me, her bare feet and mine in her blood, her eyes wild, and she cried, "What have I done? What have I done?"

"Dodie!" I heard myself call across the river to her. "Dodie!" And I held myself here in this time and not in the front room in another time, this is my daughter and she has harmed herself but she will stay with us, we are not losing her. I will not let go. I drew myself into the moment and took my daughter's blooded hands and hushed her, hushed her, and then Daniel was beside us seeing his wife in her blood and he understood.

"Dodie," he moaned, and he drew her to him. "Oh God, Dodie."

"Daniel!" I said. "Drive to find Tup and bring him home! Do you know where he is? Bring him home! Call for Dr. Addison and tell him to come."

And Daniel stared for only one moment and then spoke to his wife and he was gone. I half-dragged my daughter to the tub in the shed and pulled her nightgown off and stood her in the tub and poured over her pans of warm water from the stove. The blood slowed and I washed her with a cloth and folded a towel between her legs and wrapped her in towels and we walked together up the long dark stairs to her bed. Her body shook hard and she cried, "What have I done? I didn't mean for it to be like this! I am sorry, Mum! I am sorry! My God, forgive me!" and I laid her in the bed, still warm with Daniel's sleep, and I laid on an extra blanket and I sat by the bed kissing her face and hands and still Dodie cried and shook. I climbed into the bed and lay against my daughter, holding her to me, my warmth, and my hushing that sounded low and wild, I could hear, and I held my daughter close against me, her heart beating against my ribs, the towel catching all that ran from her. Remembering.

The night shadows wandered the room. "Daniel and Daddy are coming," I told her. "You are all right," I said. "I am sorry, Dodie, I am sorry. I am sorry," I said. "This will be all right." I held my daughter and whispered, her body curled against mine, my arms around her, desperate to deliver her.

Tup came with Daniel and they knelt by the bed stroking Dodie's face and hands and I held her against me, feeling her sobs in my body.

My daughter cried, "I am so sorry. I didn't know this would happen." And she cried, "I can't be responsible for harming any more children! There can be no more children in this house I might harm!"

Tup said, "Shhh, Dodie, shhh. Mum and I have never thought once that you were responsible for Sonny dying. Or Beston going. Not once. You never did a thing but bring kindness to your brothers. Your mother and I carry that fault, not you. You have to know that."

Still she cried, and Daniel took her face in his hands and wiped her tears and said in a low, tight voice I had never heard before, "Dodie. I was there. We were just playing. You never did anything! It wasn't you. It wasn't Best. It wasn't even me. No one, Dodie. Just Sonny. We had an old gun. It was a toy." Daniel's voice rose and he said, "Tup played with that gun when he was a boy. Didn't you, Tup! It was a toy!"

And Daniel said to us, his voice pitched low and thick, "All of you. Call this what it is. For God's sake. Call it grief, not guilt! A tragedy. Call it what it is and leave it behind. You have to leave this behind," and Daniel looked at each of us, one after the other, the room silent, his face strained and reddened, and he knelt again beside his wife.

Tup helped me from the bed, my nightgown still bloodied and my feet, and later the doctor went upstairs. When he came down to the kitchen, he said that Dodie was going to be all right, he gave her medicine to help her sleep, she will heal. Daniel quietly went up the stairs to his wife, and Tup stood silently in the doorway to the shed and then he knelt by the tub and started to wash it down, inside and out and the floor and I rose and carried a bucket to the outhouse and we worked in the low morning light without speaking, pouring the stained water down the tub drain and scrubbing the outhouse floor and bench, and then Tup put the bucket and rags away and drew me to the tub and he lifted my nightgown over my head and I let him, let him help me step in and I stood while he slowly poured pans of warm water over me, my shoulders and my legs and then I sat and he filled the tub and I lay back and he knelt beside me and sloshed the water over my body and then he laid his head on his arms at the edge and closed his eyes and I reached for his face. We cried together for the same reason, finally, our exhausted acceptance that losing our son could devastate our faithful little family through so many years. That we once believed we were unassailable, fierce, unchangeable. Our failure—not mine alone, not his alone—has cost these children terribly, and now our daughter's child. I rested my hand against my husband's face. He opened his eyes and looked at me in silence. There is no blame. We seek forgiveness. I lay in front of my husband, each of us naked to the other.

Dodie

Mum lay in my bed and held me.

There are things I don't know how to say to her. That I should never be a mother. That I cannot be trusted to keep any child safe.

Daniel hushed me, "Shhh, Dodie," he said, "there is no one more able to love than you."

My mother lay against me, her arms around me, my head on her shoulder, her softness so long forgotten.

Daniel spoke to us, very upset, saying I am not to blame. Saying none of us are to blame.

My father found my hand beneath the covers and brought it to his lips.

Sonny led Beston and me to the orchard and helped us into the branches and we lay back in the crooks and he said to us, *Close your eyes*, and I tried to pretend I did but the wind blew the branches and I was afraid. Sonny said, *It will be all right, you won't fall*, and I closed my eyes. It was autumn, a soft cloudy day, and I could hear my father splitting wood behind the house far away, the hard crack just a muffled *thunk*. Beston said, *I am not going to close my eyes*, and Sonny said, *That's okay*. The dying leaves clicked against each other in the wind, and sometimes one of the last apples dropped, a very small and close *thunk*, the branches swayed softly, and all my world felt bound and complete. My brothers allowed the quiet. Sometimes I opened my eyes and the tree reached above me to the gray unclouded sky. The bark pricked my legs and shoulders through my clothes, and I liked the slight hurt amidst so much peace.

When I get better I am going to return to the orchard and sit in the branches. I have forgotten to do that.

My mother stroked my shoulder, my hair. The long night was dark. No moon or stars shone in the window.

"Forgive me, Dodie," my father said.

I HAVE FRIGHTENED Daniel, and he cried as the morning came when we were alone. "Oh, Dodie," my husband said. "I am so sorry you believed this was necessary."

He said, "What happened in this family, Sonny and Beston, has never been from a fault in you. Not even your good mother or father has been able to protect this family from harm. Hush. Hush."

He held me to him, and I let myself cry with him. What have I done?

I HEARD MY mother's voice downstairs, and then my father's, drifting dreams from my childhood.

Beston is playing the piano. Sonny stands among the calves in the barn, the sun in splashes on their backs as they lean against him. Sonny and Beston and I lie in the wet grass, the water striders pulsing across the creek, the tiny shadows from their feet on the surface roaming the bottom. Daddy and Best and I sit on the pine hill as if we are visiting with Sonny. Marion lifts the basket of eggs high and smiles at me. I ride with Best on the bus and he holds my hand. Flickering photographs. I push the door to the front room open after Sonny is gone, and step inside. Daddy reads out loud to us on the porch and Mum holds her sewing closer to the lamp. Shadows from the elms float across my walls in the night, and I hear a barred owl call across the fields. Another calls back from a great distance. Beston and Sonny sit on the well cover and let me pour cold buckets of water over them. Beston suddenly runs away yelling and comes back for more. His wet footprints in the dust loop and return.

DANIEL RISES FROM our bed and says, "I will be back. Sleep now."

He has opened the window. Voices of my mother and my father rise from the yard, the sun is high. I feel the great flow of water in this river, continuous, moving in its course, bearing us safely if we are willing. My husband asks my father a question, he answers yes. My mother calls after them, "I will be in the garden," and they move into the day.

Tup

W HAT DOES THIS mean?
Doris and I have believed in our own suffering. We have believed in our own limits. Our children have been depleted. We have asked too much. Beston did not leave home at sixteen years old to make his music. He left, a child exhausted. Dodie has denied her own child, disbelieving her capacities for love and devotion.

These reckonings are anguish. I see now that this is what lies ahead to my end, regret and bafflement that my unbounded love has been so inadequate. It has caused such harm. I feel an incredulity.

THE MAIL COMES each day before noon dinner. My hopes are always present that Best will have sent a note. I am convinced that he is safe. I would like to hear that from him. There is deep longing to hear from him.

DORIS HAD DODIE settled and so we all went back to our work. Daniel left for his milk deliveries. The late corn is nearly ready, and the second cut of hay, so I spent much of the morning clearing the upper loft for the new cutting and bringing out the corn picker to ready it. It would be nice to have Beston here to see the machinery he tended so well go out into the fields. I saw that Doris was in the garden already, her baskets filling. This is the first time in many years that the garden was hers alone to tend. She was bent to her work, her hair pulled back, the sun on her shoulders. I watched her from the barn door, and then crossed the yard and stood at the edge of the garden. Doris stood to greet me, the abundance of the growing plants rising around her, and she waited for my question.

"Doris," I said to her.

And my wife said, "She'll be all right."

We watched each other.

"Are you all right?" I asked.

There was a pause, and then Doris said, "Yes, Tup. I believe everything will be all right."

The soft wind swept across the great fields and the pond, bringing the warmth of the September sun. The cows lifted their heads at a sound I did not hear, their ears tense, and then they returned to their mindless and contented grazing. Doris's white blouse billowed in the wind and lay loose again. She nodded to me and bent back to her work. I felt released, at least for the moment, and returned to the barn and the long coils of new water hose I was setting up. The radio was on, "Autumn Leaves," and I remembered Sonny humming in this barn and later Beston singing along, all the words familiar. I sang as I worked in my barn, my voice rising into the immense roof, my confidence struggling to become manifest.

[1958]

Doris

THERE HAS BEEN a letter finally from Beston, providing such immense relief after so many long, silent months. We had come to speak less and less of him as the fear grew in each of us that he was gone from us forever. His letter provides few details, but he assures us all that he is doing well. He has found two friends and they are sharing a place in an area of Boston he calls Back Bay. He is playing his music in a club, and works for a printer. His letter is smudged with ink from that work. There is a sense here of loosening. We have not had other news from him, but Best invited us to send letters in return, which we each have been doing every week.

Dodie suggested that he need not hear anything about last fall's problems, so the news we send is, I believe, cheering and encouraging. The season's corn and hay, the garden, the cows, milk prices, Daniel's hard efforts at learning what Best seems to know instinctively about farm mechanics. Tup tells his son that he imagines the city is interesting and to pay it his full attention. Dodie speaks about her household chores and the hens and her sewing, always with the pleasure she finds in keeping order here. She reminds him sometimes of some small adventure only the children knew.

We read our letters to each other every Sunday night before putting them in the mailbox for pickup. I believe we each have come to anticipate and appreciate these readings, the storytelling about our lives, but perhaps also because we reveal ourselves so fully. It is as if we offer to each other a window to the better part of ourselves that we all may have forgotten.

Somehow, reading to each other from the pages of our letters, we are a family again, Beston, too. Our stories and thoughts are meant to make home a place Best might like to return to when he is ready. We sit on the sofa, the lamps lit in the winter evening, and one by one we read, inviting Beston to sit with us as we once were. There is great comfort on these evenings, a sense that this turbulent river is calming and eases us home.

Most important to me is that Beston understand that I have returned to this family and its labors. I do not know the language for this idea. As I struggle to say what it means to be here again, I am forced to make clear, at least to myself, what I am returning from. Where have I been? I have not voiced any answers yet. They all condemn this mother. I lost a child. I know his blood and his torn flesh. And yet I cannot come up with an explanation that excuses me from not remaining here, mother to my other children. Wife to my husband. I always believed myself to be strong, enduring. How did I allow that absence, then? That abdication? The words are about travel—I went away, I went into myself, I disappeared, I was lost. Such small and insufficient words to tell the story of my long journey. A mother does not explain to her children her abandonment with any such language. And what if there is never a more adequate explanation?

I want to write this letter to Beston, this accounting. I want to read it aloud to Tup and to Dodie, to have all of them hear me say that I should never have allowed myself this going away. That I recognize now the costs to all of them. That I feel shame. But there seem to be no words. Forsaken. I was forsaken. I forsook. I hope to reach a fuller understanding. I hope to find forgiveness.

WHEN BESTON WAS about three years old, Sonny and Dodie asked if they could go to the creek and I said yes, but not with Beston.

He was too young for them to watch by the water. Best cried when I held him back and so I interrupted my afternoon work and took his hand and went with him to the barn. It was early summer and there were a few newborn calves and their mothers still in the nursery pens. I remember that the day was heavy and hot, but the barn was shadowed and cool as it always is with the big doors open to the east and west. I carried Beston into one of the pens, asking if he would like to say hello to the new calf. He was a very cheerful boy, as sweet as any child I have ever known, and he nodded earnestly and so we sat in the hay near the resting calf and Beston watched silently. He was very patient, taking his time in sizing up the calf and her enormous, hovering mother. I stayed quiet.

Finally Best slid off my lap and sat closer to the calf, and he started to sing the little songs that Dodie liked to teach him. When he ran out he quietly leaned into the sleeping calf and lay his head on her shoulder. We sat in the stillness of the barn, unmoving, until Best started to sing again, a lullaby to the newborn. And then he was quiet again, far away in his own thoughts and imaginings. The barn was hushed. Beston's face was still, inward, radiant. We stayed like that until the calf suddenly lurched to her feet to nurse, and Beston climbed back into my lap. We watched as the contented mother licked and nudged and reassured her calf. When Best was ready, we returned to the routines of the afternoon, and the other children came home from the creek, full of chatter and excitement, I am sure, but I will remember always that tender hour with my son, the privilege I felt to be allowed to sit with him in his thoughts. I feel still the rising rush of love, so powerful it sometimes scares me.

I will write this story in a letter for Beston, and I will share it Sunday night with Tup and Dodie and Daniel, who have never heard it. A small story, an afternoon a long time ago. Tup and Dodie will write their letters and we will sit together, stitching Beston, far away and creating another life, back to us.

Dodie

B ESTON WROTE A letter and my spirits have lifted considerably. Daniel says I am a new woman. I believe now that he will, someday, return to us. Probably not to this farm, but to this family. Beston signed his letter, *My great and unwavering love to each of you.* He has released me. My little brother. I feel a mother's love for him. Best and I moved in our own desperate world, apart from our parents, for a long time. He was a frightened and injured boy. How could I protect him? I tried. Daniel says I was just a child myself, as frightened and injured as Beston. I understand that now. But I cannot escape the feeling that my love for Beston failed him. His letter unbridles me from some of this burden.

The days are short and dark comes early. After our Sunday supper, Dad stays for a while now and we sit together in the front room and read aloud from our letters. It is as if we move into a conversation we cannot have with each other. We say to one another, *This is what I think and feel. This is what I remember. This is what my happiness has been.* We do not say, *This is what has been lost.* We do not speak about griefs. Best can imagine those.

And so I wrote this week:

Dear Best,

I like to imagine you at your work with the man who runs the printing shop. I see you in a big bright room, and the machines clatter and thump around you. I think it must be very good work. I know your boss understands how smart and capable you are. Does he ask you to take care of the machinery? Does he know yet those talents? Sometimes I wonder what it would be like to work off the farm, to measure and cut cloth at Hanson's or teach school in Sheldon, Latin maybe, or to keep books for Mr. McAvoy at the insurance office. It must make you proud to be earning real cash for your labors.

It is slow on the farm, as you can imagine with winter here. I have always liked this slowing time of year—no garden, no putting up food, no fresh paint to get on. The days start easy and then it is evening, like now, when I can settle for a few hours, not too exhausted to enjoy my sewing and reading. We have already started to choose seed for next year's garden. Mum and I are thinking of trying two new tomatoes and an earlier strain of peas. Looking through the catalogue listings is fun when I am curled up in my chair on a January night and know I won't be in the garden planting and weeding tomorrow morning. But you know I am not complaining. I am happiest when I am at my chores.

Daniel and I went to church this morning, as we do most Sundays now. I think you might have found the sermon interesting, about our efforts to maintain faith in the face of man's cruelty. Mr. Shapleigh spoke about the atrocities of war and what happened to the Jews, and he asked us, "How do we explain the capacity of mankind to create such evil?" I don't think he delivered a real answer, but he spoke at length about God's love for us and the grace that comes if we allow that love to guide us. He said that we are created imperfect by God, but I also have heard him say that God created us in his own image, that each of us embodies the perfect goodness of God. How can both be true? I have many questions about this, but there seems to be no place or time to ask them. I wish you could have heard the talk and we would sit together afterward and make our way through these ideas. If we are created imperfect, destined to fail, then can't everything be forgiven? If we are embodiments of God, then isn't every bad thing we do a reprehensible and unatonable failure? These seem to be vital questions.

The sermon was challenging, but I am glad to sit again in our pretty little church. Do you remember Sunday School in the meeting room in the old basement, singing "Jesus Loves Me" and "This Little Light of Mine"? And eating Mrs. Taber's peanut butter crackers we never got at home?

We feel your absence every day, Beston. Daniel asks that I send along his best regards.

With love from your sister, Dodie

WE READ OUR letters tonight, and I was glad that my father entered a conversation with me about the questions I raised in my letter. There are no answers. Still, I asked my father, "Do we seek forgiveness from God or from the people we love?"

It stopped him, and then he said, "God tells us he forgives everything if we love him truly. Maybe that is true for the people we harm, also, that if we love them fully they will forgive us whatever harm we bring to them."

But it was a question, not an assured response.

OTHER NIGHTS, MY father sometimes stays through the evening. We sit together in the front room and he reads aloud to us while Mum knits and Daniel lays newspaper on the table and tinkers with a carburetor or alternator and I sew. This is not a return, a circling back, I know that. But I know enough to be grateful.

Tup

W E HAVE HAD two blizzards back-to-back this week. Snow is piled high under the windows of the house and barn and has drifted in great sweeps along the fence lines. A distinct calm has come to us with these fierce storms, as if we have been suddenly unbound from an exhausted sense of preordination and allowed finally a return to our own free will. The winds shook our sturdy old house, rattled the sashes in their frames, sucked the heat from the rooms. Daniel and I brought in extra wood and kindling and piled it against the walls in the kitchen and front room, and we have kept the stoves burning hard. Doris and Dodie closed off the bedrooms and prepared the candles and lanterns in case the electric went out. It did, and I made the decision as the storms came in not to try to make the drive to Helen's. I have spent six nights here, the longest stretch at home in several years. I was not able to get word to Helen but assume she will understand the decision.

We sat together day and evening while the storms blew, moving from the kitchen to the front room and back to the kitchen. There was no agitation. We seemed to welcome the tumult, each of us strangely ready, each willing and receptive. We sat as if we had been waiting for a longed-for guest, a bearer of revelation, and when he arrived in fury and roar, we were glad. And by the second day we moved to talking quietly of small things, memories and stories and plans for the coming growing season, and then in the next days we heard ourselves laugh sometimes, laugh together, and Dodie or Doris brought food and we ate on our laps by the fire, a respite, a joy really, feeling a joy as the house shook and groaned and the land laid itself beneath the silent and forgetting snows. The rooms around and above us were cleansed by the wind and cold. Dodie has regained her color and her fortitude. Doris said she would. It has been five months. It has been nine months since Beston left.

It has been ten years.

The storms offered a threshold, an opening. The dark and wild beauty of the storms, pressing at us for days, held promise, and I believe we were hungry, finally, to be grateful. As we quietly set about our chores to prepare for the blizzards we recognized the time. Recognized the grace of the wind and the dark and the snow and the radiant quietude that followed. Each dawn we gathered at the shed door and took measure of the snow and its enfolding of the land.

"All this beauty," Dodie said.

And I said, "We are blessed with the gift of loving this beauty. God gives us beauty, and then the gift of loving beauty."

We turned back to breakfast, to the plenty offered to us by this land, and then we pulled on thick, warm clothes and made our way into the wind to tend our patient and generous animals, the cold in our lungs and against our muffled faces hard and wondrous. The dark storms roared across our land, the fields and the pastures and the orchard and the hill with its enduring stones under the old pines. Later, joined again by the fire, by the beneficence, our voices rose and the familiar stories extended and the remembering was wide and thankful. Why this moment? Days of tempest bringing us finally to an edge, a genesis? I do not believe that I imagined any of this. It rode among us each day and each night, unspeaking and hopeful.

The nights I stayed I decided to warm Best's bed, a communion of sorts with my son. It was not uncomfortable to be back among the long shelves of objects he and Sonny found and loved. The shadows and night sounds in this room are known to me even now.

The storms had come in, both from the northeast with their tremendous loads of snow. There was not time between for the skies to clear. And then they passed. The sharp, cold air of February was here, the light brilliant and reassuring, the fields and pastures and woods at rest. I crossed the snowbound yard and shoveled away the snow that had drifted on the wind in the night against the big doors. From the barn I could hear Dodie in the coop sweet-talking her hens. Everything else, all across the land, was silence. Long morning shadows from the house and the barn slanted in sharp blue blocks over the snow. The storms blasted the earth and the sky clean, and here in their wake was all possibility.

We ride this little planet with all its sorrow and all its love and all its beauty and all its hard mysteries. There is not time to waste. Learning love is, I think, why we have this inexplicable chance, these few years on this earth. I am grateful for this offering, this beckoning toward all that we can make here.

Still, in the midst of this purified calm, I carry deep longings. I would like to find my way clear of the sense that I have failed. That I have disappointed Doris, and my children. I would like to feel forgiven.

FINALLY, THERE WAS no reason any longer to stay, and on the seventh night I made the long dark drive through the river valley, filled with snow, to Helen and the child. She challenged me when I entered as she never has. I was not surprised, as if this conversation with Helen was also part of the purification of the storms. Finally, an accounting of this double life I have tried to sustain, my true family and its complexity of love and grief, and this unrequiring family that has silently offered quiescence but receives so little of me. Now, at last, I am answerable.

"You have been away for six nights!" Helen yelled at me as I removed my jacket. "Why do this so-called sister and her children earn so much of your devotion and you leave us here unremembered?"

"You are not unremembered," I protested, but I found the confrontation so uncomfortable I walked away and into the living room.

Helen followed with the frightened child on her hip. I was moved to reach for Grace, to try to comfort her, or shield myself, but Helen went on up the stairs without another word to put the child to sleep for the night. When she returned she was no less angry and she sat on the hassock facing me.

"You have come here into my home," she said fiercely, "and you have made a child with me and still you choose every day to keep yourself apart. You do not marry me or give your child your name."

I watched her as she spoke, feeling shame, but for actions or nonactions that felt untied to the true course of my life. It was as if another man, not Tup Senter, were facing this woman, a kindly but intangible woman, an illusory creature making charges of actions Tup Senter could never have committed.

I sat without speaking, reaching for Helen's hands, but she pulled away from me.

"You have never called this home," she said angrily. "If I have not created home enough for you, what is it you imagine you have coming to you?"

I stood and said helplessly, "But I do not ask for anything from you."

She rose abruptly, her face close to mine and said, "You ask for nothing, Tup Senter? For nothing?" And she took my arm and pressed it angrily against my chest. "Nothing? I am an unmarried woman with a five-year-old child who carries my name. I am an unmarried woman who is visited each night by a man from somewhere away who has never spent an hour of daylight with me or his child. Do you think I don't know where you go every day?" Her voice was pitched high and accusing. "Do you think I don't hear all the talk about you in this town? Nothing?" she cried and she pushed me away. "I am a woman whose bed you share, whose food you eat, whose warm and clean and wholesome home you claim every night. Your daughter sleeps in her bed upstairs. Do you think I don't know who you are? What you are? You ask for nothing?"

I pulled away from her, too ashamed to speak.

"You promised me your loyalty and protection," she said.

"I do not believe I ever promised you anything like that."

She cried at me, "Then what? What do you think you offered me?"

I stood before this woman and said, "I needed a place to rest and you needed someone to need that."

Helen stepped back from me and still I said, "I needed to be allowed to be a stranger. I believed you accepted what we made here together."

She said, crying, "And at what cost to me and to Grace? Do you know what people say about me? About your daughter? About you?"

I could not find an answer for her.

"I did not intend to do harm here, Helen," I said gently, trying to hold her.

She roared at me, "What do you think you brought here? A married man coming here and making a child."

I said, "So you have known." I stepped back from her. "I thought you got what you wanted, Helen. We have been comfort to one another, and you received a child you never imagined would come, a child you love."

She yelled at me, "But you do not. You do not love this child. You have never allowed room to love this child."

And I was quiet and she stared at me and then turned and ran up the stairs and I heard the door to the room we have shared for five years close hard and I was left in a room that held nothing for me, as if I had found myself dropped from the sky into an alien land far from home. I sat down in the chair, my books stacked on the floor and the lamp adjusted to my nightly reading but still a stranger's room and I listened to a car and then another come past up the hill, the lights sweeping the walls, and then the quiet in this house and in this street.

Helen wanted a husband. I understand that now, although I had convinced myself otherwise. What woman would want what

I brought to her, a child and a lot of rumors and an absence of devoted love? I am already a husband. I have always been Doris Senter's husband. I am already a father. I have always been Sonny and Dodie and Beston Senter's father. I have no right to be here.

I walked up the stairs and stood by the door and then I knocked and walked into the familiar room. I could not sense Helen in the dark.

"I am truly sorry, Helen," I said into the night. There was no answer. "I was a gutted-out man," I said. "I believed you offered this freely and knowingly. I believed we had an arrangement." There was no movement, no response. "You are telling me that you have known all along who I am. It seems to me that I was right, then. We both made this arrangement."

Helen said nothing.

I felt the effect of my words, the weight between us settling down hard.

"I see now that this has been an unequal taking," I said.

And then she said, "You made a child with no intention of loving her. Or me."

And I answered into the dark, "You are wrong, Helen. To the degree that I am able, I have come to love you." There was silence. "And the child." And we waited, with neither speaking. "I truly did not mean to harm you or Grace," I said. "I hope you will someday know that. I hope someday she will know that."

And then I went down the stairs, the railing smooth and polished in the darkened house, and I picked up my books and my jacket and I closed the door quietly and started the truck and made my way down along the river, riding with the current, the snow piled high on both bankings.

When I climbed the stairs at home, Doris stood in the low-lit hall in her white nightgown and watched me come without speaking. I stood before her and she reached and touched my hand and then she went into her room and I went into Sonny's room and undressed and lay in the bed. There is no undoing what I have made. There is no possible understanding for what I have done. I felt Helen unmoored, alone in her house far up the river. I felt her child, my daughter, innocent still of this forsaking. I have done great harm. I did not mean to. All I have ever known is this impossible true-heartedness to my wife and my three children. This love and its hungering. At last, I draw my family back to our unity, and I am finally closer to happiness again. In turn, I plunge a decent woman and her child—my child—into despair. Did God know I am capable of such blind harm?

The night was deep. I felt myself cross a threshold. I was home. My wife slept in our old bed, aware of me here. My daughter and her good husband slept, and would wake to me. An owl called again and again across our snow-filled fields, and the answer came from the woods beyond the ledges. I planned out my work for the coming morning, and finally sleep came to me.

PART FOUR

....

HERE

There is another world,
but it is in this one.

Paul Éluard

[1962]

Doris

Early yesterday morning Thomas climbed in between Tup and me and told his grandfather that he wanted one of the enormous icicles he could see hanging off the eaves. Tup said he believed that was possible but not until the light of day came, and Thomas settled in with us to await the December dawn. He laid his head on his grandfather's shoulder and we were quiet for a long while in the morning dark.

Finally he whispered, "Grandy, what is that sound?"

"That is your icicle dripping as it wakes up," Tup whispered back.

Later Thomas asked where the water came from to make the icicle and Tup said, "The snow and sleet make the ice and the sun frees the water from it. Do you remember when you held the icicle from the milk room roof and it melted in your warm mouth and on your hands?"

Thomas nodded his remembering and we were quiet in our room as the light came.

When finally Tup told Thomas, "All right, let's go find the biggest one. Get your sweater," and Thomas ran from the room, Tup came around to my side of our bed and sat again. He lay his hand on my chest gently, his fingers spread, and nodded to me. I laid my hand on his. The rising sun shone in its big blocks across the floor. Some mornings, with Thomas between us, our room unchanged in all these years, I allow myself to slip back to the time it was Sonny climbing into our bed to wait for dawn, the child

[251]

starting the day with his questions, Tup and me tired but smart enough to be grateful. This is not a sad feeling, Thomas instead of Sonny. The memories are softened with the presence of this little boy.

Thomas returned with his sweater over his pajamas and socks in his hand. He and Grandy opened the window and Tup broke the long, dripping icicle high and handed it in to Thomas, who carried it with two hands out of the room, so pleased he could not speak. Tup allowed him the silence and followed him down to the kitchen. I rose and dressed and made up the bed. The cows had started their callings to be milked, and the snowy woods beyond the pastures to the west rimmed the land with the gold dawn. I could hear Dodie and Daniel in their bedroom and the day had started.

Dodie dressed Thomas on the chair in the warm kitchen and after breakfast the child followed his father and his Grandy out to the barn. Dodie and I washed up the dishes and I put beans to soak for supper and then we went down cellar to organize the canning shelves and root cellar to account for what is available until the garden starts to produce this spring. There is always an abundance, never a concern, and so it is a chore we both enjoy. Later I went out to the milk room to put up the milk for Daniel to load on the co-op truck when it pulled in. Thomas stood on the stool beside me, waiting patiently to flick the separator switch on and then off, on and then off when I told him. His hair is fine, brown, and his eyes are dark like his father's. But he is Dodie's child, alive and watchful, a curious and busy boy. Everything we do here on the farm seems to circle him like a golden sun.

Dodie and I have never spoken of that terrible fall night when she doubted her capacities to love and protect. As soon as she sensed Thomas's life starting inside her belly, she relinquished her fears and allowed the child to come to the world already loved. Thomas has known nothing but his mother's protection. And her good humor. Her busy and smart child erupts with pleasure as he tumbles to her jokes. Tup is a gentle tease, and Thomas is quick to tease his Grandy back. We all laugh and Thomas is clearly filled with delight that he has caused us pleasure. The sound of that laughter fills the rooms of our home, and it has been released. Our small patterns seem large enough again. There is purpose.

TUP ASKED ME on Christmas afternoon to walk up to the pine hill with him. I said no, and I could see he was distressed, wanting to mark the day together. Instead, I told my family after supper that evening that I wanted to take a walk in the snow to the hill. Dodie brightened at the idea and said, "I'll come!" But I said no, and I could see the concern, the discomfort reaching back to those years of my nighttime wandering in the yard, but I told them I just wanted some time alone with my son, and they did not argue with me.

I dressed for the cold and made my way along the field road, through the east pasture and then the orchard. It was a bright night with a coming moon and the enormous sky stretched above, silver with stars. The fields and woods were filled with snow and cold rose from the land. The fence lines were half-buried, the top wire holding its own fine line of soft snow. Everything was still. I have always loved the night on this land.

The great pines stood guard over the Senter stones. I stopped where Tup's mother and father are buried, and his grandparents, then made my way slowly in the unbroken snow up the hill among the headstones, in and out of night shadow, the sentry trees towering into the boundless winter sky. I touched the hard stone, shining in the light of the moon, and brushed the snow from it. "Sonny." *Thomas Edward Senter. Beloved Son of Thomas Arlen and Doris Canton Senter. Born January 12, 1934. Died March 26, 1948, aged 14 years. We thank our God upon every remembrance of you.* The stab was sharp. I sat and laid my face against my son's marker and looked out across the silent and gentle land. My son. My young son who had come to rest among his ancestors, men and women who had the chance to live out their lives. The hair on my son's arms was fair and soft, a child's. The old indiscriminate rage rose in me.

He would be twenty-eight years old. He would be a man, perhaps with a wife and a child, perhaps here on the farm with his father and mother, perhaps in a life I cannot imagine for him. I cried quiet tears that froze on my cheeks. My child's voice, a little boy, *Mumma?* I lift him from the tub into a towel and hold him to me. His shoulders and hips are bony, angles. I bury my face in his neck and draw in his sweetness. My son turns to me in the yard and says, *Will you come with me?* and his hand is in mine and we make our way to the barn or the well cover or the workshop where his father is measuring and cutting new boards. My son looks up from his book at the big table in the front room and says, *Did you know that ravens mate for life?* The stories that hold.

The orchard stood below me in its ordered rows in the luminous snow light. The creek is frozen, a ribbon of silver through the white fields and pasture to the pond. I understood this beauty. And it came to me that I was not remembering that terrible day, the terrible sights that live now inside each of us in this family. Instead, Sonny was alive in this place. I rested back against his stone and watched the nighttime land. A visit.

When I had been gone too long I made my way back along my tracks in the snow, a trail cutting through the darkened orchard and the field and across the yard. The kitchen light fell softly on the pure white snow, a river running to me from my home. I stomped my boots noisily on the doorstep and hung my coat and hat. My family was in the front room, Thomas upstairs in bed, the lamps on and everyone watching me carefully as I entered.

"It is a beautiful night," I said, and the room released its discomfort.

"Has the wind come up yet?" Tup asked.

I replied, "No, everything is still."

Tup said, "Maybe I will go out with you tomorrow evening."

"Yes, let's do that," I said, and my family eased and returned to their evening tasks, Dodie and Daniel and Tup, and I sat to my knitting, a sweater for Thomas.

Later, Tup held me in our bed and he said, "You have visited with our son, Doris." And I told him it was very hard, and he said, "Yes, it is very hard, all of it. No one can know how hard it is."

Thomas was asleep in Sonny's old room. We make a safe place for him here, as safe as we know to make. There can be no rewriting of these stories, no matter how desperate the longing.

Tup put my fingers to his lips and kissed them. I make the decision each time Tup touches me to commit to this love, to believe in it as he does. As he always has. I know that.

Is what is required forgiveness? Tup should not need my forgiveness. We built this life together, with all its failures, his and mine both. Acceptance, not forgiveness, is what I work toward. He comes to me a husband seeking forgiveness. I come to him a wife seeking forgiveness. We pray for this from each other. From our children. From God. But forgiveness presumes a maker of harm and a victim. I do not believe either of us ever felt that sort of authority. We allowed ourselves to drift, out of control, beyond accountability. We have much to accept in each other, and much to atone for. And Dodie and Beston. How do they accommodate that drifting? It is there that we most seek forgiveness. We do not speak of that time, either mine or his. Maybe we should.

Tup drew the blankets over our shoulders. Senter Farm lay in the moon's light, quiet and sheltering. In the morning, Thomas will come into our warm bed and wait with us for the new day. We live in blessedness again, undeserved, ephemeral. Tup laid his face beside mine in our dark room, his breath in and out also mine.

Dodie

R AIN DRIPPED FROM the eaves all night, sounding like the creek running in spring, a sound so sweet and kind it makes me ache. The house is at peace this summer.

Thomas brings joy. He is a happy child. He feels safe and fully loved. I know that I am a strong woman, a capable woman. I believe I am a good woman. I face off against my fear that something will harm my son, that I will fail to keep him from harm. But I have learned we have a great gift of recovery, of time's quieting.

The good rain drenches the corn and the hayfields and greens the pastures for the cows. Daddy and Daniel are pleased with the summer, and far more so because Thomas is among us, our next generation. Mum tells me that I have brought a gift to the world. "Another gift among the many you have always offered," she says. My son has come to me his own gift. In the dark of the night with the rain making its creek song and my child sleeping at ease in his bed and my good husband's hand on my belly and the farm accepting the grace of the rainfall, my mother and my father lying together in their bed, my fears slip off and I rest in this goodness.

Yesterday, while Mum and I picked the summer squash and string beans, Thomas asked for a bucket of water and played in the mud he made by the well cover. Finally, he came into the garden and Mum gave him a small pail and told him to help pick the beans. He walked along the rows, reaching up the beanpoles as far as he could and tugging hard, then examining each string bean and adding it to his pail. Mum has taught him to use both hands so he doesn't pull the vines down, and he tries hard at his work. I watch my mother, with her patience and kindness and good humor, and understand that I am watching the mother who raised Sonny and Beston and me. She affirms my memory. Doris Senter was a very good mother.

[257]

The past is with us here. We have returned to that life. But all of the past, not just the benevolence, is with us here. The front room and Beston's empty bedroom and Sonny's room, now my son's, the objects Sonny brought home and labeled in his small, careful handwriting, baby rats in the lofts that may be waiting for their mother's return, the stone on the hill standing over the farm. Like a cloud shadow moving over the beautiful land, this past, too, is here with us.

EACH EVENING BEFORE bed, Daddy takes Thomas into his lap on the porch glider and reads the books he once read to Sonny and Beston and me. Tonight, Daniel and Mum and I bent to our evening tasks but we listened, too, and the familiar stories and the child's interruptions settled us together at the end of the busy day. My father stroked his grandson's leg as he read and I remembered the comfort of that gesture. Thomas leaned into his Grandy's chest, tired and contented.

"And what did Reddy Fox say to Grandfather Frog?" my father asked.

Thomas answered in his high voice, "Where do you think you are headed?"

And his Grandy said, "Yes, that's right, and then what did he do?"

My mother's knitting needles clicked. My father's voice has not changed in all these years, and we rode on it out into the great sea. We are voyagers, brave and devoted voyagers.

Later, Daniel carried Thomas to bed and they said prayers and when Daniel returned, we all settled into our own familiar conversations about the day and the cows and the garden and milk prices and the funny or clever things Thomas did during his busy day.

My mother and father have aged. Their faces are lined from sun and sorrow and smiling. When they rise from their chairs they stretch before they can easily move around. My mother sometimes kneels in the garden rows if her back is stiff instead of bending over all morning as she used to. Some days Daddy leans on his axe for a quick rest as he splits the winter wood. Beyond those small accommodations, they are strong and vigorous still.

Beston sometimes writes a song for Thomas, the words to tunes we know, and we sing these songs to Thomas and he smiles a far-away smile of pleasure.

"Your Uncle Beston wrote that for you," we tell him, and so this boy talks about his uncle as someone who is among us. We do not tell him about his Uncle Sonny, his namesake, Thomas Senter, not yet, but someday Sonny will be part of my child's stories of the life that has been lived on this farm.

The quiet thoughts on a rainy night. Daniel sleeps. Thomas sleeps, and my mother and my father, in their bed together. I am happy. I recognize that I am happy.

Tup

THERE HAS BEEN much to do this last week with the hay coming in. The work is hard but deeply satisfying, especially with Daniel's help. We have managed without Beston's care to have the mower and rake and tedder in good working order. In my letter to my son several weeks ago I suggested that he ask for time to come home to participate in the haying but he responded this week with a kind refusal. I will explain to him in my next letter that he is badly missed here but I understand that the course he has chosen for himself is good and worthwhile. Perhaps I should say to my son that he is making a terrible mistake, that he should be on this land, his root source. Perhaps this is another way in which I fail my son, by not saying what I believe. But our connection is tenuous, and so I simply tell him I am proud of him, which I believe he knows.

When I mowed the field across the road early in the morning yesterday, I sensed movement in the grass but could not locate any creature. The sun was already high at midmorning and a good breeze swept the field. The grass swayed in great drifts with the wind. Swallows darted and rose on the currents, flickers of blue and black. The woods are filled with birdsong when we rise each morning. I like to think of them singing, whether I can hear them or not over the rumble of the tractor. Whether we are present or not for the beauty and bounty, it is here, not for us but in its own right. This thinking allows me to rest. I am part of this mystery, but only part. My children grew up within this order, whether they understood that or not.

Across the road, I could see Dodie and Doris at their work in the garden, Thomas making his play near the women. Daniel had not returned from his milk run and so I had the rhythms of the back and forth to myself, the light and shadow at the woods' edge, the steady whir of the sickle bar. I allowed myself memory of Sonny and later Beston standing behind my shoulder at this job, their narrow and naked and sweaty chests pressed against my own sweaty skin, and for long passages up and back I was accompanied by my sons. I invited a certain peace, a longing kind of peace, to ride along with me, tolerable, I know, because there is another boy now who is waiting to be big enough to mow with his Grandy and Daddy. Thomas has brought great easing to this family and to this farm. Doris and I understand this chance.

I caught the movement in the tall grass again and was watchful. There has been a fox and her kits on this field this summer. Mowing is slow work and I believed that she would, if she were still here, lead her young into the safety of the woods ahead of me. But then there she was, a leap toward me in her fear and I felt the knock of the sickle. I threw the take-off out of gear and ran to the rear of the mower. Two kits appeared close to their mother and to me, scared and reckless. I found her in among the long cut grass, alive, a good portion of her hind haunch and entire leg gone. She cried a high squall, not cat or dog, a wild animal wounded, her kits sniffing and darting away, returning to find comfort and backing away. I watched myself hovering over her, the hot June sun on my back and on hers. I tried to shade her with my body, but that is not what she needed and I knew it.

I drew aside the sweet grass and found myself concerned with finding the severed leg, a powerful desire to bring the leg into proximity, to lay it beside her, her bloodied and mangled leg. The wind lifted her shining, silver fur where she had not been ripped open by the mower. The crows danced in the trees, already cawing their anticipation. She turned her black eye to me and the cry rose again and again. I knew what I had to do and could not move. The kits touched her nose and fled back into the uncut hay, watching me, trotting back and forth in their terrible agitation. Finally I stood and pulled the jack pipe from the tractor and returned to her, lying cradled in the tall, thick grass. She watched me raise the pipe above her head, and we were joined in the slow, inescapable minute. The blow stilled her, and the crows in the trees beyond. Her kits fled onto the ledges. The birds came in on the scent and I knew they would clean away the body, but I could not bear to walk away from her and so I turned off the tractor and lifted the fox to my chest and then her disjoined leg and carried her out of the field to the woods. She was all fur, a tiny little thing, her head hanging and her eyes open. Her blood dripped down my arm and across my belly and down my pant leg, a slick, and in the heat it dried sticky.

I pushed through the cut grass tangling at my knees and finally into the cool woods and I knelt by an old oak and laid her among the roots, trying to place her haunch and leg as it might have been, and then I sat against the tree and found that I was crying, an old man suddenly, a man too old to accommodate this kind of necessity without response. I was glad that Sonny and Beston were not still riding with me in that dream we had occupied just a few minutes before. I was glad that Thomas is not yet old enough to ride along in these fields with his old Grandy. I laid my head against my knees and let the crying come.

We have brought ourselves back to calm here on this farm, and within this family, yet sadness is always ready if we are not on guard. Doris is quick to laugh, especially with Thomas but also with me and with Dodie and Daniel, but sometimes our eyes meet and I see there her careful work. We study acceptance. We study gratitude. My beautiful wife, her shining hair drawn up and clipped for her work, her body moving easily, still, beneath her cotton dresses, her legs and arms strong. I do not pretend that Doris loves me now without reserve. My life away from this family cannot be erased, a woman in a town up the river harmed, and, a truth I cannot explain even to myself, a child deserted. I have abandoned a child and turned back toward my waiting family. But Doris loves me. Doris understands that she made her own long journey away from me and her children, and then back. And so here we are. The enduring sadness is ever present, the past so insistent every day. It is inevitable that I will find cause at times to cry, an aging man and his reckonings. I do not see my wife cry, but I know she does. We love and trust each other, but we hold these moments of submission close and private.

I returned to the tractor ready to resume the mowing. Daniel would be coming along soon to relieve me until noon dinner. Then I remembered the kits on the ledge, orphaned by my dutiful work, and made my way to find them. I sat, hoping they would appear if I were quiet. When Daniel came striding across the field, I gave up looking. Maybe they will prove old enough and resilient enough to make it on their own. Daniel took over the mowing.

I returned to the well in the yard and pumped cold water to pour over my hot back and chest and arms, the dried blood washing red onto the soil. Doris watched me from the garden, then went into the shed and came to me with a clean towel and laid it over my shoulders.

"You're not hurt. What happened?" she asked.

"A fox got under the sickle," I said. "She was with kits."

"I'm sorry," she said.

"Yes," I said, "it saddened me greatly. I don't want the responsibility."

"Will you find the kits?" she asked.

"No, they don't want to be found. They will make it or not."

And my wife said kindly, "I believe they will be all right. It is high summer and there is plenty of food." She pulled me to sit beside her on the well cover.

The cows wandered the far edge of the east pasture along the shade line of the woods. The tractor droned toward us and away in the distance across the road. The breeze dried my skin and the reddened mud I had made. We sat together in the noontime quiet until Thomas discovered us and climbed between us and started his questions. He wanted to know about a large garter snake he had found by the workshop. Doris told him about the big milk snake the children once found under the shed steps, and so Thomas moved to the steps to watch for the snake, alive more than fifteen years ago. The boy squatted in the dust and peered into the dark under the steps, ready for every miracle.

The crows came in as I expected. The hay is very good this year, ripening all at once, and the weather has held hot so it is going into the lofts dry. Daniel and I worked side by side for several days, with satisfaction. Doris and Dodie offered plentiful food each day to feed the work, and Thomas ended the long days on the porch in his Grandy's lap for his book.

Doris, as she does now, lay on her side of the bed until I pulled her to me. She stretched against me and we lay in the summer wind coming through the open windows. The nights have been clear and bright, haying-time nights. Thomas slept across the hall, unaware of everything but immutable goodness and hope.

I held my wife to me. Late in the night, I woke and she had moved back to her side of the bed, but her hand lay across my hip. There is a quiet loneliness in these nights that accompanies the great comfort. Love and its costs.

[1965]

Doris

B ESTON'S YEARLY VISIT was deeply satisfying, a gift I once never dared hope for. The day after he arrived home, I watched from the kitchen window as Thomas shadowed Best from place to place, from the barn to the shed to the garden where Dodie was planting the onion sets she grew in flats, from the workshop where Tup was sharpening the field tools to the shed steps where finally Beston sat down and allowed his nephew to claim his full attention. I could hear their voices but not what they each said, just the pleased tone of both. It is evident that Best has developed a deep feeling for his sister's child. He sends a long letter to Thomas every week with details about his work at the printing shop and about the music he writes and with questions for Thomas to answer when he sends his own letters off. I believe that Best is a lonely young man, and these visits home allow some calming of that aloneness, especially because Thomas is so attached to him. Their talk and laughter carried from the steps into the house. My work was sweet with the sounds of my son and grandson rising and falling.

Beston likes to return to the work of the farm when he is home and so Tup involved him in the jobs he knows he most likes. He asked Best to replace several tines on the tedder and pack the wheel bearings of the harrow, and they worked all one day moving along the fence lines splicing and tightening sagging or broken wire. On a clear, windy day, they ran new water lines in the barn and scrubbed down the aisles and the floors and the half-walls to the pens. Tup asked Beston to load the tractor wagon with last year's rotted manure and haul it to the garden for Dodie and me. Best whistled as he made his trips back and forth and teased his sister each time he dumped another load. He is not a boy anymore. We lost all those years. But this farm and its work have their hold on him, I see that, and this family does, too. I trust that. He comes home.

Daniel is a thoughtful and kind man. When Beston made his first visit home three years ago, Daniel took a chair beside Dodie and left Beston to sit in Sonny's old place, which he did without speaking. Every meal brings good conversation about the work of the day and the next day coming and about Beston's life in the city, and a good share of laughter. Thomas slides his chair next to his uncle's and interrupts to add his opinions and ideas. Now there are six of us at this table. Thomas carries us all forward to a future, a blessedness, none of us could bear to imagine not long ago.

ONE CLEAR WINTER day a long time ago, I watched Tup walk from the barn and greet the three children as they got off the bus. He seldom interrupted his work and so the children clung to his arms, laughing and talking. I could see all this but from inside the house it was a wonderful silent movie, and then the shed door opened and their happiness entered the kitchen with them, noisy and unguarded as it still was then.

Sonny threw his arms around my hips. "Daddy says we are going to drive to Newfields and watch the sun set on the beach! He wants us to pack a picnic and we'll make a fire on the beach!"

And so I packed up the soup and bread I had made for our supper and leftover pie and we all changed into our warmest clothes. This was Tup's magic, stirring us all to happiness and excitement and freedom, asserting the bonds that sustain us. We are the Senters, he announced ardently at these times, the Senters from Senter Farm in Alstead, Maine. He concocted unrestrained outings and off we went, his purpose really to be able to turn back at the end of the day, renewing our claim to each other and to this land, the coming home.

We listened to songs from *Carmen* on the truck radio, the "Toreador Song" and "Habanera." We all sang along, especially Tup, who has always loved this music, and we drove slowly on the snowy roads through the quiet farmlands to Newfields and then down the long dirt road through the rugosa scrub to the winter beach. The children tumbled out, shrieking their pleasure. It was low tide and they ran away across the vast wet sand. Tup took my hand and carried the picnic until we found a drift log below the high tide line where there was no snow.

"You stay here and watch the children play," he said, brushing the snow off the log and laying the folded truck blanket we used for our outings.

The air smelled of iodine and salt. Small stick-legged birds I could not identify darted along the edge of the small waves lapping the shore. Tup gathered wood and made a good fire while Sonny and Dodie and Beston raced on the hard sand, dragging long fronds of slippery kelp. The fire whooshed up and snapped green and blue with salt.

"Watch us," the children cried and we did, sitting side by side on the log, the heat of the fire building against our shins and the sun slowly sinking behind us, the wet sand shining silver. I leaned against my husband's strong shoulder and he brushed my hair from my face and held my hand. Our children ran to the end of the beach and turned, trying to slap each other with the heavy wet fronds, and dusk came and the tide rose and still they played their games, their voices small and joyful and distant. As the light left, they became silhouettes against the purple and silver water, shadows shaped like our children, as if they had slipped away from us and left behind their ghosts. It was a beautiful sight in the closing day, but it made me uneasy, a parting from my children.

The cold came with sunset and drove the children to the fire.

Slowly, as they came nearer, they transformed from distant dancing silhouettes to brightly clothed children to my children, Sonny
and Dodie and Beston, and they arrived with all their laughter
and vigor, falling into their father and mother in the circle of light.
They laid the shells and sea glass they had found on the end of
our log and we ate our hot supper as the land and water around us
disappeared fully into the dark, and all that remained was there in
the tight circle of us, in the heat and the light of the fire.

The chatter quieted and Tup allowed Beston to lay branches
onto the fire as it burned down. The momentary rush of sparks
rose into the night and then just the crackle and snap broke the
dark quiet. Tup asked the children if he had ever told them about
traveling to see his mother's sister and her family in Nova Scotia,
and we dipped into that world, their small farm and the tidiness of
the old house and barn and the sheds and the kindness of his aunt
and uncle. The fields ran down to a tidal beach and Tup and his
cousins went each day to look among the rocks for periwinkles and
lobsters, the food of shore people with not enough to eat.

"There were parts of broken-up boats and lobster traps in the
drifts of seaweed," he said, "and one day we found a man's rubber
boot. My cousins were untroubled, but it struck me quite hard.
Whose boot was this? How had it come to be separate from the
man who owned it, who wore it at his work each day? My cousins
were amused by my concern and so I laughed it off with them, but
I could not forget that boot lying tangled in the seaweed.

"I came to understand that any story might have led to it being
on that beach, and I could never know which story was true. And
so I made the decision that the owner had caught and dried sufficient fish that year and he had made a very good crop of hay and
corn and he had cut and sold many cords of wood in the winter,
and so he had been able to buy cloth and buttons and coffee and
sugar and school tablets for his wife and children and a new pair of
boots for himself. One day he walked down to his fish house and
he heaved the old worn boots into the water and watched them

float away on the tide. He felt happy and optimistic, a man proud of his work. I became glad that I found his boot that day so I could know him in this way. I have somehow always loved him."

The children leaned against our legs, the waves of the incoming tide rolling the beach rocks in a rumble and hiss in the dark quiet. Beston fell asleep and I lifted him into my lap and wrapped my coat around him. Sonny and Dodie gathered up their shells and laid them in the empty picnic basket and we made our way along the peaceful nighttime beach to the truck, Tup carrying Dodie and me Beston. All three children slept on the way home and Tup drove with his hand on my leg, the radio low, and we returned along the roads that had brought us to our day away, the head-lights sweeping the wide snowy fields and the edge of the woods. We made our way back home, the return of our family to its shelter and nurturance. We had left the yard light on to welcome us. The cows greeted Tup with their low grateful conversations when he entered the barn to check on them.

This was all before Sonny died, of course. The time when our own story was not yet known to us. This story, the ways in which we have come to this moment, here, together.

LAST NIGHT, WHEN we rose from the table, Best said, "Let Thomas and me wash the dishes," which the boy does enthusiastically, and the rest of us stayed at the table while they washed and dried and put away the dishes Tup had eaten his own suppers on when he was just a boy. Then we moved to the porch and put the lamps on and Tup read aloud to Thomas while we listened. Beston went into the front room and opened the window to the porch. He sat at the piano, quietly picking out a melody. The music was soft and slow, a song about a man wandering back roads alone as the sun goes down.

"The trees stood in line along the road, sentinels watching over me," he sang.

I was glad that Beston feels some sort of protection. Thomas leaned against his Grandy, listening.

Later, Beston came out to the porch and said quietly, "That old piano needs tuning, but it is still my favorite one to play." He sat on the glider with his father and nephew and folded his fine hands and listened while Grandy returned to Thomas's story.

We climbed the stairs and put out the lights. Tup and I lay together in our dark bed, his hand in my hair, his breath on my shoulder. The spring night was cool and damp.

"Listen," Tup whispered. "There is so much."

Partridge drummed from the edge of the woods, and the spring peeper chorus rose from the pond and overflowing creek.

"We have lain together in this bed for most of thirty-two years, listening to spring rising on this land," my husband said quietly in the dark.

The cows slept with their calves in the safety of the barn. The night offered all its promise. Tup and I moved to each other, our heat and our weight and our devotion. We slept without guard. There is never a going back. What we say and what we do stays, always. The great price of love and attachment is loss, with us every day. But here, too, each day, are their great easings.

THOMAS WAS NOT happy to see Beston pack his luggage in the trunk of his car this morning.

Thomas is six years old, but he cried quietly and allowed Best to hold him while we looked on. Each of us felt like crying, I am sure.

Best spoke softly to his nephew, "I'll be back soon," but Thomas shook his head and said, "Next spring is not soon!"

Beston was quiet, and then he said, "Well, maybe I'll come back at Christmas time. Would that be good?"

And Thomas pushed his head into Best's chest and nodded silently.

Now we have a winter visit coming, too. Beston hugged me and his father and his sister and Daniel, and told us he loves us, and we told him, and we all waved as he pulled out of the driveway.

There are low drifts of old snow still along the fence lines and the base of the ledges across the road. But spring is here. Beston drove away slowly, looking out over the Senter fields and pastures, across the creek to the orchard and the pine hill where his brother lies. The land is greening quickly under the warm April sun, and Tup and Best had let the cows out on the south pasture this morning for the first time. They moved quickly through the grass, heads down, eager for the early spring shoots. Their calves felt the contentment of their mothers and leaped off to play together. It must have been a reassuring sight for Beston, his home mostly unchanged, the farm in good shape.

His father said to him at breakfast, "There is a place for you here if you ever desire that."

Beston said seriously, "I know that, but thank you for saying it."

Of course Thomas jumped into the conversation, not understanding the privacy and weight of the moment, and begged his uncle to move home.

Beston laughed and said, "Thomas, if I came home you'd never get a piece of Grammy's blueberry cake. I'd eat it all before you ever got to the table," and Thomas grinned and argued with Beston that Grammy would just make more for him.

The fear I once felt that Beston was gone for good has given way. Now that he has driven away, I will think of him as I work, the pleasure of ironing his shirts again and overhearing him and his sister laughing in the yard and watching him bent under the hood of the tractor, back at the work he is very good at, work that is appreciated here. He will return this winter. He is here among us. I will not ever again make the mistake of inattention.

Dodie

THOMAS ASKED TO accompany his Gram and Grandy on their walks to the pine hill, and finally we said yes, and so he has slipped into knowing that once there was a boy named Sonny. Uncle Sonny is a fact for him as much as the cows and the hens and the milk funneling through the separator. Part of this farm. He understands that he sleeps in Uncle Sonny's room. He says to his grandmother and Grandy, "It makes me sad that Uncle Sonny died."

"Yes. It was very sad, Thomas," they say.

"He was your little boy like I am Daddy's and Mum's little boy."

"Yes," my mother and father say kindly. "He was."

"But we can go up on the hill and remember him."

"Yes," they say, "we can sit and remember him. We like to do that."

Then Thomas moves to something else on his mind, and we do, too.

The story of what happened has calmed. It was a long time ago. A wild and powerful river swept us far from shore, and then the current stilled and allowed us to make our way home. Thomas reminds us of this story again and again, and so it has become a story we finally are able to speak aloud and understand. *This is what happened*, we can say. *Once, a long time ago, on a sleeting day here in this house*, we can say. *This is the shape of the journey we each have taken*, we say. Thomas recites this story, free of dread. We rebound in his light.

This kind of happiness requires courage. It requires a willingness to love. A willingness to forgive. A willingness to believe in some sort of goodness. It requires that we each accept what has been lost and offer ourselves to what we have now.

WE WENT TO the Harvest Bazaar at church on Saturday. Daniel and I promised Thomas we would stay for the dance that night. He begged his grandmother and Grandy to go with us, and both said no, but then that morning, he asked again and my mother said, "Well, if Grandy says yes, I will come."

My father was clearly pleased and so we all rode together, me on Daniel's lap and Thomas on his grandmother's, and already it felt festive and special. My mother does not attend church, but she spent the summer knitting mittens and scarves and hats for all the children who might need them and she carried them in her large cotton bag to be left in the vestry for Mr. Shapleigh to distribute. For the church bazaar tables, Daniel donated several of the knives he found in the old farm dump in the woods across the road. He had cleaned and sharpened and fitted them with new handles he carved.

My father made wooden spoons with Thomas, burning *TS* on the back of each one, Tup Senter and Thomas Senter, both. Thomas asked to keep one for our own kitchen, and it lies now beside the one Sonny made a long time ago. And I gave three matching nightgown sets I sewed, each set for a mother and a little girl. At the end of the day, everything we made had sold. We will settle through the winter evenings in the warm front room and the making will start all over again for another year.

We had plenty of rain over the summer, so all the farms are having a good harvest and the mood at our little church fair was optimistic. My father and Daniel are again the top producers of milk in the county, and our neighbors greeted them with back slaps and congratulations. The afternoon allowed my father and my husband to wander among the men they know and respect, as they talked milk prices and almanac predictions for the winter and offered to help butcher pigs on each other's farms.

Time has eased this town's judgments. If these men ever condemned the life Tup Senter chose after his son died, if they condemned him for whatever wreckage he left at home in Alstead or in Grafton, there is no longer any sign of scorn or judgment. It has taken many years, but they seem to have come to believe that Tup Senter sought comfort from his suffering, a sympathy, and never meant to create harm.

My mother was less at ease, but perhaps she always has been. Time has worked its change among the women, too. They circled close in their pleasure at seeing her in town. She held her arm around Thomas's shoulder, perhaps suggesting to these neighbors another boy long ago. They drew my mother to a cluster of chairs behind the bazaar tables. Thomas ran off with his Sunday school friends, and my mother settled among the women. They seemed to want to convey their kindliness, their welcoming, as if to say to my mother they know every kind of story and make no blame. These neighbors were witness to a very private suffering, my mother's and my father's. The men and women in my church, in my town, from the farms nearby, seemed to believe that my mother's and my father's misfortunes were great, and that those misfortunes and their responses to them could be anyone's, perhaps even their own. Still, I know that my mother and my father, both, carry a deep shame, an old and intimate shame held between them, beyond the reach of our neighbors' efforts to understand and accept.

Late in the afternoon, the men served bean-hole beans and frankfurters out on the lawn, and then, as the dark and the cold closed in, we made our way into the warm church basement, which had been decorated with pumpkins and cornstalks and straw on the floor. Jim Malek and Nathan Calder played the piano and sang and we had a real fall dance. Thomas and the other children ran loops around the edge of the big room, but Daniel and I danced, and my mother and my father danced. My father held his wife in close, their hands clasped tight, her head on his shoulder. My mother's hair is turning gray now and their bodies have stiffened with work, but still there is something binding them, evident even in that public place, something they claim in each other that is beyond the rest of us, private and potent. Sometimes my mother said something, a flirting smile and cock of her head, and my father grinned and teased her back. I felt grateful to them, for lasting, and for showing their steadfastness to the people of our town.

"Ready to go home?" my father asked Thomas when we piled into the truck. Thomas nodded, played out and satisfied.

"Ready to go home?" my father asked my mother. Holding her tired grandson on her lap, my mother said, "Yes. That was a good day."

Daniel put his arms around me, our hands together in my lap.

The golden leaves swirled in the headlights on the familiar roads, the cars ahead turning off one by one to their own homes. When we came around the long corner, the yard light shone and the bare trees swayed in the fall wind. The moon was crisp and bright, the harvest moon, and the fields and woods and fences and creek and orchard and barn waited in the crystalline light with all their offerings for our return. My mother had left the kitchen light on and a fire laid up in the front room stove. My father and Daniel went to the barn to check on the cows, and I carried Thomas upstairs to his bed.

We sat in the front room without conversation, contented after our day with our neighbors and contented to be home again. Later, I could hear my mother and father talking quietly in the darkened house, and a laugh. Daniel held me. Foxes yipped back and forth beyond the creek. Our son slept through the night with no reason not to trust. We ride the quieted sea.

Tup

O NE DAY THIS fall, I came into the kitchen from the yard and Dodie was washing all our wool socks at the sink. Without turning, she said, "Your other daughter is twelve years old, I think."

At first I was greatly startled, as if I were being drawn from our kitchen to an obscured place and time. I did not know how to answer, or perhaps did not want to, and so I stood by the table, wanting to move back outside to my familiar chores.

Dodie turned to me, her hands wrapped in a towel, and said slowly, "Her name is Grace."

What are my obligations, I wondered? Is this a conversation I must have with my daughter?

"Yes," I said. "Her name is Grace. I cannot think of her as my daughter. You are my daughter."

Dodie watched me, and then said, judgment, or great tiredness, or sadness, in her voice, "I don't think you should abandon her."

"She has no memory of me," I said. "I am sure of that, Dodie. I did not abandon her. I left her unburdened of the complexities I brought to her and her mother."

Dodie studied me, and was quiet.

Then I said, ashamed of that evasion, "I made a decision, and then another, and then another. I am left with each of them every day."

"But you are not the only one left with them," Dodie said.

The cookstove hissed and snapped its heat. I looked out the window to the pasture and the orchard beyond.

"I know that. I regret that very much. I carry the weight of what I have done to all of you every moment of every day. I hope you will always know that."

Dodie turned back to the sink.

We stood in the late morning kitchen, a disquiet between us. I left the kitchen and went upstairs to the top drawer of my dresser. I came back down to the kitchen. Dodie was wringing out the socks in old towels and hanging them on the rack. I handed her a folded letter. She opened it slowly, sat down, and read:

Dear Grace. I am your father. I live with my family on a farm not far from Grafton. I would like to try someday to tell you the story of how this came to be. It will not be an easy story to tell, or to hear. If there is ever a time you decide you might like to know your father, there is room waiting for you. I don't know what that might mean, and you cannot possibly know either. But we could try to make some sort of understanding between us. I hope you will someday be willing to try that.

Respectfully,
Tup Senter

DODIE SAT QUIETLY studying the paper, and then looked up at me. "Does Mum know you wrote this?"

I nodded. "Yes. She knows."

"And she knows you might send it someday?"

"Yes, Dodie," I said. "Your mother promised me she would send it if anything ever happened to me before I decided it was time."

Dodie rose and moved closer to me. "And when will that be?"

I felt a dark dread that had not come to me for a long time. "I am thinking when she is twelve years old. That is not long from now. But I can't do it if it will cause more harm for you and Best." I could hear the beseeching in my voice.

Dodie was quiet.

"Your mother says she wants me to send it," I said.

After a long silence, she said, "I do, too." And then, "This is a great relief to me, Daddy. Beston will think so, too." My daughter turned again to her work and said, her back to me, "This is what is right. We will all figure this out. Grace cannot be the only one of us left behind."

The past is a pressing mystery. I circle obsessively every act, every thought. Memory is an obligation, and becomes less and less explicable. How is it possible that I, Tup Senter, have created this life? I believed in myself. I did not ever imagine the harm I would make.

In the silence, I said to my daughter, "I have made terrible mistakes, Dodie. I had no right to enter that life. To create a child who would have no father. I know that leaving her may be unforgivable. But I also know just as surely that I would do it again to regain your mother and you and Beston."

Dodie turned again to me and held my eyes. "I know that," she said. And then, in a tight voice, "I am ashamed that I want to hear that."

The kitchen was silent except for the cookstove's steady *shush*. I said, "I need to believe that I am a good man."

Dodie finally said, her voice softened, "I know that. I know that you were left forsaken here. I believe you are a good man."

And that was all. My daughter loves me. No child should ever have to accommodate such a father. She returned to her work, and I went back to the barn to mine.

The constant churning I do has eased, but I know it is with me for the rest of my life. This is regret. I look back with wonder and shame. The effort of my life now is atonement, a private and silent penance.

ON BEST'S LAST day home this spring, when I went out early in the morning to feed and milk, I found him sweeping the center aisle. He had turned the cows out and cleaned the pen aisles and filled the grain troughs and water buckets. He was singing quietly with the radio, an old country tune we both knew from when he was a boy in this barn. He was not surprised to see me. He turned as I entered and leaned on the broom handle, smiling at me the most wonderful welcome.

"It is very good to find you here, Beston," I said.

He nodded and said, "It smells really good in here. I miss it." And then he returned to his sweeping and to the song and I called the cows in to their stanchions and we started the morning's milking.

The sun was still very low on the horizon and its light had not yet found the inside of the barn. We worked in the peace of the half-light, the calves milling around their mothers. The barn swallows had made their welcome spring return, swooping through the great doors and up into the invisible lofts above us, their twitterings filling the high reaches of the barn over the radio and Best's quiet accompaniment.

Later, I saw Doris come out with her arms full of the winter's heavy blankets. She laid them up over the laundry lines to freshen before she put them away for the summer, and then she turned a slow circle, taking in the house and the gardens and the coop and work shed and the barn, the ledges across the road and the fields and the cows moving in their innocent grazing. The breeze ran in wide swift rivers through the spring grass. The orchard was in white bloom. The hens shimmered iridescence as they pecked in the yard, and the swallows flashed blue-black over the pond. Doris fixed her blown hair into her clip and made her way back toward the house. I caught her eye and she smiled, startled, and maybe glad, to have been watched.

"It is a very nice spring day, Mrs. Senter," I called to her.

"Maybe," she called back, her face pleased with her flirtation, "but I am too busy to notice." She passed into the shadows of the shed.

As I returned to my work on the paddock gate, I saw that Dodie and Beston had each stood from their chores and watched us. The heavy old blankets rippled in the wind.

There are times when I would like my father to return for a few moments. I would like him to say to me, *I am proud of you. You have made a lasting stronghold here.*

[282]

We will ourselves to live this day grateful and unguarded. We decide. We make ourselves ready to participate in beneficence and goodness. There is no peace outside that.

DANIEL AND I have just finished putting up the second cut of hay. The lofts are full, a security for the coming winter. It was a good hay year, with plenty of rain early in the season and then sun into September. After six days of making hay, I felt like an old man and was very happy to have Doris run warm water into the tub for me and, when I was dressed, place a heaping plate of food in front of me. She teased me about my tired and sore body, and Thomas picked up the teasing until we settled onto the sofa.

The screen porch is too chilly in the evening now and we have made the move into the front room, our usual cycle. Thomas leaned against me, as he still does at six years old, and I read. We are halfway through *Oliver Twist*, which has Thomas indignant and sympathetic, a good response to these poor characters.

"Why does Fagin make Oliver do bad things, Grandy?" he asked.

"But he doesn't," I said. "He tries, but Oliver can't find it in himself to steal from people."

Thomas wept as I continued to read, and Dodie asked if he would like to change books. "No!" he said. "Someone is going to find Oliver and take care of him."

And so I read on. Doris worked at her knitting, a hat for Thomas, but she watched and listened as I read.

I went up the stairs to bed when Thomas did, the teasing of the old man picking up again. Nothing feels more wonderful than Doris's stiff, clean sheets in our orderly room after the strain and satisfaction of a hard day of work. I lay awake as the moon rose low over the orchard hill and let its white light spill onto the floor and bed. I heard Thomas come across the hall and he stood next to my bed. I reached for him and drew him in under the covers.

"Are you doing all right?" I asked.

"I wish we could bring Oliver here," he said.

"Yes, I think he would be very happy here," I said. "But remember that this is just a story."

"I know," Thomas said, curled in against me. "No one will ever be mean to me like that."

"No, Son," I said, "it is safe here. You are safe here among the people who love you."

"And among the cows and hens," he said.

"Yes, and the beautiful wild coyotes and the deer and the foxes and the raccoons who are free in the woods and the fields tonight."

"And the salamanders who are digging down into the mud for the winter."

"Yes, you are safe among the salamanders," I said, and we drifted together in the story we were making.

Later, I carried my grandson, loose and trustful, back to his room.

When I returned to bed, Doris stood by the window, drawing her dress over her head. I lifted it and laid it over the chair, and her slip, and she let her hair loose and I stood behind her, my hands on her hips. The silver light flowed across our fields to us.

I pulled back the covers to our bed and drew her to me. "We are here," I said, and I put my face into her hair.

We entered the flow of the river together, its deep, dark current known to us, and its assurance, and we gave ourselves to ablution. The light shifted across our room. And then Doris lay against me, her hand in mine on my chest, our breathing quieted.

"We are not perfect," my wife said in the night.

"No," I said. "We are not at all perfect. We are just us."

In the night, with my wife beside me, geese honked as they flew high over our fields on their long, hard flight south. The wind moved through the great pines on the hill and across the wide fields of ripe corn, gathering and stilling by turn in the yard. We slept, each of us in this house carrying all that has happened and restoring ourselves for the day ahead.

[284]

We dwell in a complex and uncertain grace. I am Tup Senter. This is my wife, Doris Senter. This is our family. This is our farm. A creek moves through the land, binding memory and whatever is about to be.

Acknowledgements

In gratitude to my brilliant editor, Joshua Bodwell, for his care and dedication; to the team at Godine—Beth Blachman, Celia Johnson and David Allender; and to Jennifer Muller for her cover design.

And every day, for every reason, to my family.

A Note on the Type

Beneficence has been set in Fairfield Medium and Medium Italic. Originally designed for Mergenthaler Linotype by Czech-born wood engraver, and illustrator Rudolph Ruzicka in 1940, the Medium weight being cut and released in 1949. While Ruzicka designed several other faces for Linotype, Fairfield is one of only two to see commercial release.

1970~2020

David R. Godine
❧ Publisher ❧
FIFTY YEARS